BRICK DRACULA AND FRANKENSTEIN

TWO CLASSIC HORROR TALES TOLD IN A WHOLE NEW WAY

AMANDA BRACK, MONICA SWEENEY,
AND BECKY THOMAS

Skyhorse Publishing

Contents

INTRODUCTION BY THE AUTHORS

Bram Stoker's *Dracula* and Mary Shelley's *Frankenstein* are among the best-known horror stories of all time, spawning hundreds of derivative works and inspiring the dark imaginations of storytellers all over the world. As works of gothic fiction in the late Victorian era, these stories share many similarities, as each tell the tale of a fantastic monster and the people who try to defeat him. In both cases, the villain is depicted as not only physically but also spiritually dangerous. In *Dracula*, the vampires' victims have both their souls and their lives at stake, while, in Frankenstein, the title character risks spiraling into madness as he is confronted with the ramifications of trying to play god. These stories highlight our terrified fascination with the consequences of interfering with things beyond our understanding.

While this pair of infamous tales has been retold countless times on stage, in film, on television, in works of art, and through secondary literature, they have never before been told with LEGO bricks. Through artfully crafted scenes and inventive construction, these plastic bricks bring you the humor and horror of *Dracula* and *Frankenstein* in one volume. Each novel has been carefully abridged, maintaining the dramatic arcs and most memorable dialogue of both stories. For lifelong LEGO builders, horror-story aficionados, and young readers new to Transylvanian castles and the first mad scientist, we hope you enjoy these harrowing horrors in incredible LEGO form.

Dracula

CONTENTS

Humans have always told stories about monsters: undead walkers, super-strong brutes, insidious fairies, and demonic beings. But among these, the vampire has always been different. They look human; they are created from humans; and to stay alive, they must consume humans. They have the power to beguile and trick you, and they also have a strange power of seduction. As modern vampire stories have shown, these monsters somehow seem more attractive than the rest. For that you can thank Bram Stoker's Dracula.

Dracula was written in 1897 by Irish author Bram Stoker. It is an epistolary novel, written as a series of letters, diaries, newspaper clippings, and other written exchanges. Stoker did not invent the vampire: the name itself and the monster it described were discussed across Europe during the 1800s, while bloodsucking demons have existed in human mythologies as early as the Mesopotamians. But Stoker's vampire is classier than earlier versions, which had often been depicted as walking rotting corpses. Count Dracula uses charm and manners along with his more otherworldly powers to manipulate the people around him as he carries out his plans. He presents himself as a member of the nobility, speaks intelligent but accented English, lives in an ancient and forbidding castle in Transylvania. He is also known to turn into a bat. Thus Stoker's Count Dracula became the most recognizable version of the myth, parodied in cereal commercials and children's shows alike. Stoker's formidable Count is met by the equally formidable Professor Van Helsing, a character who has also become part of the vampire myth and is often reimagined as a vampire expert with kung fu skills.

While the story of *Dracula* has been adapted and readapted on stage, on screen, and on the page, the original is still fresh and delightful as ever. The text thrills and excites readers with its big cast of gallant characters, quaint dialogue, quick pacing, and truly classic story. Once you enjoy it in brick, you might just have to go read the whole thing!

Chapter I – Jonathan Harker's Journal
(*kept in shorthand*)

3 May. Bistritz. [. . .] All day long we seemed to dawdle through a country which was full of beauty of every kind. [. . .] It was on the dark side of twilight when we got to Bistritz, which is a very interesting old place. Being practically on the frontier—for the Borgo Pass leads from it into Bukovina—it has had a very stormy existence, and it certainly shows marks of it. [. . .]

Count Dracula had directed me to go to the Golden Krone Hotel, which I found, to my great delight, to be thoroughly old-fashioned, for of course I wanted to see all I could of the ways of the country. I was evidently expected, for when I got near the door I faced a cheery-looking woman in the usual peasant dress . . .

When I came close she bowed and said, "The Herr Englishman?" "Yes," I said, "Jonathan Harker." [She] immediately returned with a letter.—"My Friend.—Welcome to the Carpathians. I am anxiously expecting you. Sleep well to-night. At three to-morrow the diligence will start for Bukovina; a place on it is kept for you. At the Borgo Pass my carriage will await you and will bring you to me. I trust that your journey from London has been a happy one, and that you will enjoy your stay in my beautiful land. Your friend, DRACULA." [. . .]

4 May . . . Just before I was leaving, the old lady came up to [me] and said in a very hysterical way: "Must you go? Oh! young Herr, must you go?" She was in such an excited state that she seemed to have lost her grip of what German she knew, and mixed it all up with some other language which I did not know at all. [. . .]

She then rose and dried her eyes, and taking a crucifix from her neck offered it to me. [. . .] She saw, I suppose, the doubt in my face, for she put the rosary round my neck, and said, "For your mother's sake." [. . .]

5 May. The Castle . . . When I got on the coach the driver had not taken his seat, and I saw him talking with the landlady. They were evidently talking of me, for every now and then they looked at me, and some of the people who were sitting on the bench outside the door—which they call by a name meaning "word-bearer"—came and listened, and then looked at me, most of them pityingly. I could hear a lot of words often repeated, queer words, for there were many nationalities in the crowd; so I quietly got my polyglot dictionary from my bag and looked them out. I must say they were not cheering to me, for amongst them were "Ordog"—Satan, "pokol"—hell, "stregoica"—witch, "vrolok" and "vlkoslak"—both of which mean the same thing, one being Slovak and the other Servian for something that is either were-wolf or vampire. [. . .]

Then our driver, whose wide linen drawers covered the whole front of the box-seat—"gotza" they call them—cracked his big whip over his four small horses, which ran abreast, and we set off on our journey. [. . .]

As we wound on our endless way, and the sun sank lower and lower behind us, the shadows of the evening began to creep round us. This was emphasized by the fact that the snowy mountain-top still held the sunset, and seemed to glow out with a delicate cool pink. [. . .]

When it grew dark there seemed to be some excitement amongst the passengers, and they kept speaking to him, one after the other, as though urging him to further speed. He lashed the horses unmercifully with his long whip, and with wild cries of encouragement urged them on to further exertions. Then through the darkness I could see a sort of patch of grey light ahead of us, as though there were a cleft in the hills. The excitement of the passengers grew greater; the crazy coach rocked on its great leather springs, and swayed like a boat tossed on a stormy sea. I had to hold on.

Whilst [the driver] was speaking the horses began to neigh and snort and plunge wildly, so that the driver had to hold them up. Then, amongst a chorus of screams from the peasants and a universal crossing of themselves, a calèche, with four horses, drove up behind us, overtook us, and drew up beside the coach.

I could see from the flash of our lamps, as the rays fell on them, that the horses were coal-black and splendid animals. They were driven by a tall man, with a long brown beard and a great black hat, which seemed to hide his face from us. I could only see the gleam of a pair of very bright eyes, which seemed red in the lamplight, as he turned to us.

He said to the driver:—"You are early to-night, my friend." [. . .] One of my companions whispered to another the line from Burger's "Lenore":—"Denn die Todten reiten schnell"—("For the dead travel fast.") The strange driver evidently heard the words, for he looked up with a gleaming smile. [. . .]

Then I descended from the side of the coach, as the calèche was close alongside, the driver helping me with a hand which caught my arm in a grip of steel; his strength must have been prodigious.

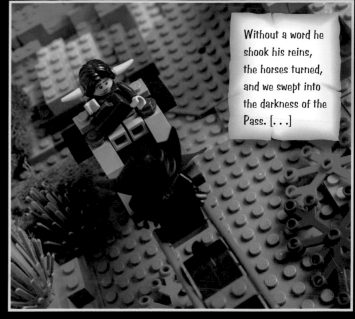

Without a word he shook his reins, the horses turned, and we swept into the darkness of the Pass. [. . .]

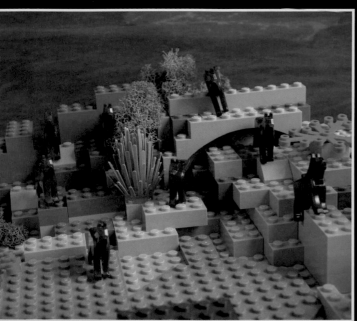

Then a dog began to howl somewhere in a farmhouse far down the road—a long, agonized wailing, as if from fear. The sound was taken up by another dog, and then another and another, till, borne on the wind which now sighed softly through the Pass, a wild howling began, which seemed to come from all over the country, as far as the imagination could grasp it through the gloom of the night. [. . .] Then, far off in the distance, from the mountains on each side of us began a louder and a sharper howling—that of wolves—which affected both the horses and myself in the same way—for I was minded to jump from the calèche and run, whilst they reared again and plunged madly, so that the driver had to use all his great strength to keep them from bolting. [. . .]

Suddenly, away on our left, I saw a faint flickering blue flame. The driver saw it at the same moment; he at once checked the horses, and, jumping to the ground, disappeared into the darkness. [. . .]

[B]ut just then the moon, sailing through the black clouds, appeared behind the jagged crest of a beetling, pine-clad rock, and by its light I saw around us a ring of wolves, with white teeth and lolling red tongues, with long, sinewy limbs and shaggy hair. They were a hundred times more terrible in the grim silence which held them than even when they howled. [. . .]

I called to the coachman to come, for it seemed to me that our only chance was to try to break out through the ring and to aid his approach. I shouted and beat the side of the calèche, hoping by the noise to scare the wolves from that side, so as to give him a chance of reaching the trap. How he came there, I know not, but I heard his voice raised in a tone of imperious command, and looking towards the sound, saw him stand in the roadway.

As he swept his long arms, as though brushing aside some impalpable obstacle, the wolves fell back and back further still. Just then a heavy cloud passed across the face of the moon, so that we were again in darkness. When I could see again the driver was climbing into the calèche, and the wolves had disappeared. This was all so strange and uncanny that a dreadful fear came upon me, and I was afraid to speak or move. [. . .]

We kept on ascending, with occasional periods of quick descent, but in the main always ascending. Suddenly, I became conscious of the fact that the driver was in the act of pulling up the horses in the courtyard of a vast ruined castle, from whose tall black windows came no ray of light, and whose broken battlements showed a jagged line against the moonlit sky.

Chapter II — Jonathan Harker's Journal (continued)

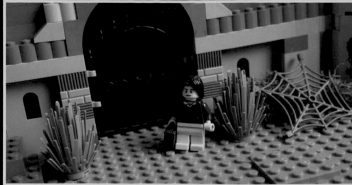

5 May . . . When the calèche stopped, the driver jumped down and held out his hand to assist me to alight. Again I could not but notice his prodigious strength. His hand actually seemed like a steel vice that could have crushed mine if he had chosen. [. . .]

The time I waited seemed endless, and I felt doubts and fears crowding upon me. What sort of place had I come to, and among what kind of people? What sort of grim adventure was it on which I had embarked? Was this a customary incident in the life of a solicitor's clerk sent out to explain the purchase of a London estate to a foreigner?

Then there was the sound of rattling chains and the clanking of massive bolts drawn back. A key was turned with the loud grating noise of long disuse, and the great door swung back. Within, stood a tall old man, clean shaven save for a long white moustache, and clad in black from head to foot, without a single speck of color about him anywhere. [. . .] The old man motioned me in with his right hand with a courtly gesture, saying in excellent English, but with a strange intonation:— "Welcome to my house! Enter freely and of your own will!" He made no motion of stepping to meet me, but stood like a statue, as though his gesture of welcome had fixed him into stone.

The instant, however, that I had stepped over the threshold, he moved impulsively forward, and holding out his hand grasped mine with a strength which made me wince, an effect which was not lessened by the fact that it seemed as cold as ice—more like the hand of a dead than a living man. [. . .]

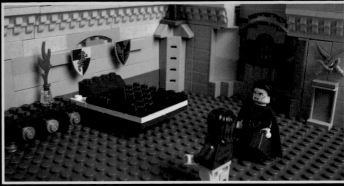

The strength of the handshake was so much akin to that which I had noticed in the driver, whose face I had not seen, that for a moment I doubted if it were not the same person to whom I was speaking; so to make sure, I said interrogatively:—"Count Dracula?" He bowed in a courtly way as he replied:—"I am Dracula; and I bid you welcome, Mr. Harker, to my house." [. . .]

[H]e opened another door, and motioned me to enter. It was a welcome sight; for here was a great bedroom well lighted and warmed with another log fire,—also added to but lately, for the top logs were fresh—which sent a hollow roar up the wide chimney. The Count himself left my luggage inside and withdrew, saying, before he closed the door:—"You will need, after your journey, to refresh yourself by making your toilet. I trust you will find all you wish. When you are ready, come into the other room, where you will find your supper prepared." [. . .]

I found supper already laid out. My host, who stood on one side of the great fireplace, leaning against the stonework, made a graceful wave of his hand to the table, and said:—

"I pray you, be seated and sup how you please. You will, I trust, excuse me that I do not join you; but I have dined already, and I do not sup."

"I handed to him the sealed letter which Mr. Hawkins had entrusted to me. He opened it and read it gravely; then, with a charming smile, he handed it to me to read. One passage of it, at least, gave me a thrill of pleasure. "I must regret that an attack of gout, from which malady I am a constant sufferer, forbids absolutely any travelling on my part for some time to come; but I am happy to say I can send a sufficient substitute, one in whom I have every possible confidence. He is a young man, full of energy and talent in his own way, and of a very faithful disposition. He is discreet and silent, and has grown into manhood in my service. He shall be ready to attend on you when you will during his stay, and shall take your instructions in all matters." [. . .]

We were both silent for a while; and as I looked towards the window I saw the first dim streak of the coming dawn. There seemed a strange stillness over everything; but as I listened I heard as if from down below in the valley the howling of many wolves. The Count's eyes gleamed, and he said:—"Listen to them—the children of the night. What music they make!" [. . .]

Then he rose and said:—"But you must be tired. Your bedroom is all ready, and to-morrow you shall sleep as late as you will. I have to be away till the afternoon; so sleep well and dream well!" With a courteous bow, he opened for me himself the door to the octagonal room, and I entered my bedroom. [. . .] I am all in a sea of wonders. I doubt; I fear; I think strange things, which I dare not confess to my own soul. God keep me, if only for the sake of those dear to me!

7 May . . . I slept till late in the day, and awoke of my own accord. [. . .] There are certainly odd deficiencies in the house, considering the extraordinary evidences of wealth which are round me. [. . .] But still in none of the rooms is there a mirror. There is not even a toilet glass on my table, and I had to get the little shaving glass from my bag before I could either shave or brush my hair. I have not yet seen a servant anywhere, or heard a sound near the castle except the howling of wolves. [. . .]

In the library I found, to my great delight, a vast number of English books, whole shelves full of them, and bound volumes of magazines and newspapers. [. . .]

The books were of the most varied kind—history, geography, politics, political economy, botany, geology, law—all relating to England and English life and customs and manners. [. . .]

Whilst I was looking at the books, the door opened, and the Count entered. He saluted me in a hearty way, and hoped that I had had a good night's rest. Then he went on:—"I am glad you found your way in here, for I am sure there is much that will interest you. These companions"—and he laid his hand on some of the books—"have been good friends to me, and for some years past, ever since I had the idea of going to London, have given me many, many hours of pleasure. [. . .]

"But alas! as yet I only know your tongue through books. To you, my friend, I look that I know it to speak." "But, Count," I said, "you know and speak English thoroughly!" He bowed gravely. "I thank you, my friend, for your all too-flattering estimate, but yet I fear that I am but a little way on the road I would travel. [. . .] You shall, I trust, rest here with me awhile, so that by our talking I may learn the English intonation; and I would that you tell me when I make error, even of the smallest, in my speaking." [. . .]

I asked him of some of the strange things of the preceding night, as, for instance, why the coachman went to the places where he had seen the blue flames. He then explained to me that it was commonly believed that on a certain night of the year—last night, in fact, when all evil spirits are supposed to have unchecked sway—a blue flame is seen over any place where treasure has been concealed. [. . .]

Then we drifted into other matters. "Come," he said at last, "tell me of London and of the house which you have procured for me." [. . .] I read to him the notes which I had made at the time, and which I inscribe here . . . "The estate is called Carfax, no doubt a corruption of the old *Quatre Face*, as the house is four-sided, agreeing with the cardinal points of the compass. It contains in all some twenty acres, quite surrounded by the solid stone wall above mentioned. There are many trees on it, which make it in places gloomy, and there is a deep, dark-looking pond or small lake, evidently fed by some springs, as the water is clear and flows away in a fair-sized stream."

When I had finished, he said:—"I am glad that it is old and big. I myself am of an old family, and to live in a new house would kill me. A house cannot be made habitable in a day; and, after all, how few days go to make up a century. I rejoice also that there is a chapel of old times. We Transylvanian nobles love not to think that our bones may lie amongst the common dead. . . ."

[T]he Count stayed with me, chatting and asking questions on every conceivable subject, hour after hour. [. . .] All at once we heard the crow of a cock coming up with preternatural shrillness through the clear morning air; Count Dracula, jumping to his feet, said:—"Why, there is the morning again! How remiss I am to let you stay up so long. You must make your conversation regarding my dear new country of England less interesting, so that I may not forget how time flies by us," and, with a courtly bow, he quickly left me. [. . .]

8 May.—I began to fear as I wrote in this book that I was getting too diffuse; but now I am glad that I went into detail from the first, for there is something so strange about this place and all in it that I cannot but feel uneasy. I wish I were safe out of it, or that I had never come. It may be that this strange night-existence is telling on me; but would that that were all! If there were any one to talk to I could bear it, but there is no one. I have only the Count to speak with, and he!—I fear I am myself the only living soul within the place. [. . .]

I only slept a few hours when I went to bed, and feeling that I could not sleep any more, got up. I had hung my shaving glass by the window, and was just beginning to shave.

Suddenly I felt a hand on my shoulder, and heard the Count's voice saying to me, "Good morning." I started, for it amazed me that I had not seen him, since the reflection of the glass covered the whole room behind me. In starting, I had cut myself slightly, but did not notice it at the moment.

Having answered the Count's salutation, I turned to the glass again to see how I had been mistaken. This time there could be no error, for the man was close to me, and I could see him over my shoulder. But there was no reflection of him in the mirror! The whole room behind me was displayed; but there was no sign of a man in it, except myself.

This was startling, and, coming on the top of so many strange things, was beginning to increase that vague feeling of uneasiness which I always had when the Count is near; but at the instant I saw that the cut had bled a little, and the blood was trickling over my chin. I had laid down the razor, turning as I did so half round to look for some sticking plaster. When the count saw my face, his eyes blazed with a sort of demonic fury, and he suddenly made a grab at my throat.

I drew away, and his hand touched the string of beads which held the crucifix. It made an instant change in him, for the fury passed so quickly that I could hardly believe that it was ever there.

"Take care," he said, "take care how you cut yourself. It is more dangerous than you think in this country." Then seizing the shaving glass, he went on: "And this is the wretched thing that has done the mischief. It is a foul bauble of man's vanity. Away with it!" and opening the heavy window with one wrench of his terrible hand, he flung out the glass, which was shattered into a thousand pieces on the stones of the courtyard far below. [. . .]

When I went into the dining-room, breakfast was prepared; but I could not find the Count anywhere. So I breakfasted alone. It is strange that as yet I have not seen the Count eat or drink. He must be a very peculiar man!

After breakfast I did a little exploring in the castle. [. . .] [D]oors, doors, doors everywhere, and all locked and bolted.

In no place save from the windows in the castle walls is there an available exit.

The castle is a veritable prison, and I am a prisoner!

Chapter III – Jonathan Harker's Journal (continued)

When I found that I was a prisoner a sort of wild feeling came over me. [. . .] Of one thing only am I certain; that it is no use making my ideas known to the Count. He knows well that I am imprisoned; and as he has done it himself, and has doubtless his own motives for it, he would only deceive me if I trusted him fully with the facts. So far as I can see, my only plan will be to keep my knowledge and my fears to myself, and my eyes open. [. . .]

I had hardly come to this conclusion when I heard the great door below shut, and knew that the Count had returned. He did not come at once into the library, so I went cautiously to my own room and found him making the bed. This was odd, but only confirmed what I had all along thought—that there were no servants in the house. [. . .]

This gave me a fright, for if there is no one else in the castle, it must have been the Count himself who was the driver of the coach that brought me here. This is a terrible thought; for if so, what does it mean that he could control the wolves, as he did, by only holding up his hand in silence. How was it that all the people at Bistritz and on the coach had some terrible fear for me? [. . .] To-night he may talk of himself, if I turn the conversation that way. I must be very careful, however, not to awake his suspicion.

Midnight.—I have had a long talk with the Count. I asked him a few questions on Transylvania history, and he warmed up to the subject wonderfully. In his speaking of things and people, and especially of battles, he spoke as if he had been present at them all. This he afterwards explained by saying that to a boyar the pride of his house and name is his own pride, that their glory is his glory, that their fate is his fate. Whenever he spoke of his house he always said "we," and spoke almost in the plural, like a king speaking. [. . .]

It was by this time close on morning, and we went to bed. (*Mem.,* this diary seems horribly like the beginning of the "Arabian Nights," for everything has to break off at cockcrow—or like the ghost of Hamlet's father.)

12 May . . . Last evening when the Count came from his room he began by asking me questions on legal matters and on the doing of certain kinds of business. [. . .] When he had satisfied himself on these points of which he had spoken, and I had verified all as well as I could by the books available, he suddenly stood up and said:— "Have you written since your first letter to our friend Mr. Peter Hawkins, or to any other?"

It was with some bitterness in my heart that I answered that I had not, that as yet I had not seen any opportunity of sending letters to anybody. "Then write now, my young friend," he said, laying a heavy hand on my shoulder: "write to our friend and to any other; and say, if it will please you, that you shall stay with me until a month from now."

"Do you wish me to stay so long?" I asked, for my heart grew cold at the thought.

"I desire it much; nay, I will take no refusal. When your master, employer, what you will, engaged that someone should come on his behalf, it was understood that my needs only were to be consulted. I have not stinted. Is it not so?"

What could I do but bow acceptance? [. . .] I understood as well as if he had spoken that I should be careful what I wrote, for he would be able to read it. So I determined to write only formal notes now, but to write fully to Mr. Hawkins in secret, and also to Mina, for to her I could write in shorthand, which would puzzle the Count, if he did see it.

Later . . . When he left me I went to my room. [. . .] I have placed the crucifix over the head of my bed—I imagine that my rest is thus freer from dreams; and there it shall remain. [. . .]

After a little while, not hearing any sound, I came out and went up the stone stair to where I could look out towards the South. [. . .] As I leaned from the window my eye was caught by something moving a story below me, and somewhat to my left, where I imagined, from the order of the rooms, that the windows of the Count's own room would look out. [. . .] I drew back behind the stonework, and looked carefully out.

What I saw was the Count's head coming out from the window. [. . .] At first I could not believe my eyes. I thought it was some trick of the moonlight, some weird effect of shadow; but I kept looking, and it could be no delusion. I saw the fingers and toes grasp the corners of the stones, worn clear of the mortar by the stress of years, and by thus using every projection and inequality move downwards with considerable speed, just as a lizard moves along a wall.

What manner of man is this, or what manner of creature is it in the semblance of man? I feel the dread of this horrible place overpowering me; I am in fear—in awful fear—and there is no escape for me; I am encompassed about with terrors that I dare not think of. . . ."

I knew he had left the castle now, and thought to use the opportunity to explore more than I had dared to do as yet. I went back to the room, and taking a lamp, tried all the doors. [. . .] At last, however, I found one door at the top of the stairway which, though it seemed to be locked, gave a little under pressure. [. . .]

This was evidently the portion of the castle occupied by the ladies in bygone days, for the furniture had more air of comfort than any I had seen. [. . .]

I determined not to return to-night to the gloom-haunted rooms, but to sleep here . . . I drew a great couch out of its place near the corner, so that as I lay, I could look at the lovely view to east and south, and unthinking of and uncaring for the dust, composed myself for sleep.

I suppose I must have fallen asleep; I hope so, but I fear, for all that followed was startlingly real . . . In the moonlight opposite me were three young women, ladies by their dress and manner. I thought at the time I must be dreaming, for, though the moonlight was behind them, they threw no shadow on the floor.

They came close to me, and looked at me for some time, and then whispered together. Two were dark, and had high aquiline noses, like the Count, and great dark, piercing eyes, that seemed to be almost red when contrasted with the pale yellow moon. The other was fair, as fair as can be, with great wavy masses of golden hair and eyes like pale sapphires. [. . .] All three had brilliant white teeth that shone like pearls against the ruby of their voluptuous lips.

There was something about them that made me uneasy, some longing and at the same time some deadly fear. I felt in my heart a wicked, burning desire that they would kiss me with those lips. [. . .] The fair girl shook her head coquettishly, and the other two urged her on. One said:—"Go on! You are first, and we shall follow; yours is the right to begin." The other added:—

"He is young and strong; there are kisses for us all." I lay quiet, looking out under my eyelashes in an agony of delightful anticipation. The fair girl advanced and bent over me till I could feel the movement of her breath upon me. Sweet it was in one sense, honey-sweet, and sent the same tingling through the nerves as her voice, but with a bitter underlying the sweet, a bitter offensiveness, as one smells in blood. [. . .]

But at that instant, another sensation swept through me as quick as lightening. I was conscious of the presence of the Count, and of his being as if lapped in a storm of fury. As my eyes opened involuntarily I saw his strong hand grasp the slender neck of the fair woman and with giant's power draw it back, the blue eyes transformed with fury, the white teeth champing with rage, and the fair cheeks blazing with passion. [. . .]

In a voice which, though low and almost in a whisper seemed to cut through the air and then ring round the room he said:—"How dare you touch him, any of you? How dare you cast eyes on him when I had forbidden it? Back, I tell you all! [. . .] I promise you that when I am done with him you shall kiss him at your will. . . ."

"Are we to have nothing tonight?" said one of them, with a low laugh, as she pointed to the bag which he had thrown upon the floor, and which moved as though there were some living thing within it.

For answer he nodded his head. One of the women jumped forward and opened it. If my ears did not deceive me there was gasp and a low wail, as of a half-smothered child. The women closed round, whilst I was aghast with horror; but as I looked they disappeared, and with them the dreadful bag. [. . .]

They simply seemed to fade into the rays of the moonlight and pass out through the window, for I could see outside the dim, shadowy forms for a moment before they entirely faded away. Then the horror overcame me, and I sank down unconscious.

Chapter IV – Jonathan Harker's Journal
(*continued*)

I awoke in my own bed. If it be that I had not dreamt, the Count must have carried me here. [. . .]

18 May.—I have been down to look at that room again in daylight, for I *must* know the truth. When I got to the doorway at the top of the stairs I found it closed. It had been so forcibly driven against the jamb that part of the woodwork was splintered. I could see that the bolt of the lock had not been shot, but the door is fastened from the inside. I fear it was no dream, and must act on this surmise.

19 May.—I am surely in the toils. Last night the Count asked me in the suavest tones to write three letters, one saying that my work here was nearly done, and that I should start for home within a few days, another that I was starting on the next morning from the time of the letter, and the third that I had left the castle and arrived at Bistritz.

I would fain have rebelled, but felt that in the present state of things it would be madness to quarrel openly with the Count whilst I am so absolutely in his power; and to refuse would be to excite his suspicion and to arouse his anger. He knows that I know too much, and that I must not live, lest I be dangerous to him; my only chance is to prolong my opportunities. Something may occur which will give me a chance to escape. [. . .]

28 May.—There is a chance of escape, or at any rate of being able to send word home. A band of Szgany have come to the castle, and are encamped in the courtyard. These Szgany are gipsies; I have notes of them in my book. [...] I shall write some letters home, and shall try to get them to have them posted.

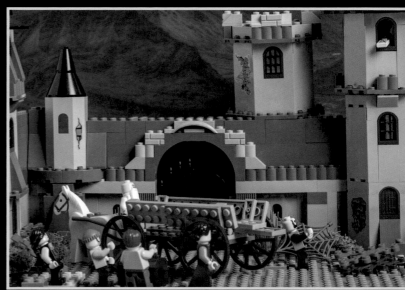

I have already spoken to them through my window to begin acquaintanceship. They took their hats off and made obeisance and many signs, which, however, I could not understand any more than I could their spoken language. [...]

I have given the letters; I threw them through the bars of my window with a gold piece, and made what signs I could to have them posted.

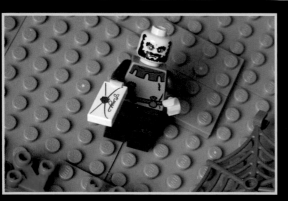

The man who took them pressed them to his heart and bowed, and then put them in his cap. I could do no more. I stole back to the study, and began to read. [...]

The Count has come. He sat down beside me, and said in his smoothest voice as he opened two letters:—

"The Szgany has given me these, of which, though I know not whence they came, I shall, of course, take care. See!"

And he calmly held letter and envelope in the flame of the lamp till they were consumed. [. . .] When he went out of the room I could hear the key turn softly. A minute later I went over and tried it, and the door was locked.

31 May.—This morning when I woke I thought I would provide myself with some paper and envelopes from my bag and keep them in my pocket, so that I might write in case I should get an opportunity, but again a surprise, again a shock! Every scrap of paper was gone, and with it all my notes, my memoranda, relating to railways and travel, my letter of credit, in fact all that might be useful to me were I once outside the castle. [. . .] The suit in which I had travelled was gone, and also my overcoat and rug; I could find no trace of them anywhere.

24 June, before morning . . . [T]he Count left me early, and locked himself into his own room. As soon as I dared I ran up the winding stair, and looked out of the window, which opened south. [. . .] I had been at the window somewhat less than half an hour, when I saw something coming out of the Count's window. I drew back and watched carefully, and saw the whole man emerge. It was a new shock to me to find that he had on the suit of clothes which I had worn whilst travelling here . . .

There could be no doubt as to his quest, and in my garb, too! This, then, is his new scheme of evil: that he will allow others to see me, as they think, so that he may both leave evidence that I have been seen in the towns or villages posting my own letters, and that any wickedness which he may do shall by the local people be attributed to me. [. . .]

As I sat I heard a sound in the courtyard without—the agonized cry of a woman. I rushed to the window, and throwing it up, peered out between the bars. There, indeed, was a woman with disheveled hair, holding her hands over her heart as one distressed with running. She was leaning against a corner of the gateway. When she saw my face at the window she threw herself forward, and shouted in a voice laden with menace:—"Monster, give me my child!" [. . .]

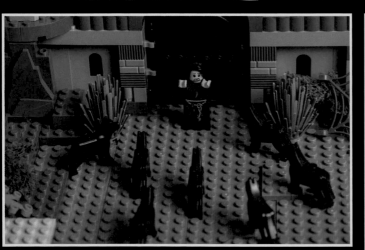

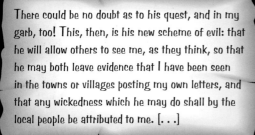

Somewhere high overhead, probably on the tower, I heard the voice of the Count calling in his harsh, metallic whisper. His call seemed to be answered from far and wide by the howling of wolves. Before many minutes had passed a pack of them poured, like a pent-up dam when liberated, through the wide entrance into the courtyard. There was no cry from the woman, and the howling of the wolves was but short. Before long they streamed away singly, licking their lips. [. . .]

25 June, morning . . . I have not yet seen the Count in the daylight. Can it be that he sleeps when others wake, that he may be awake whilst they sleep? If I could only get into his room! [. . .] Where his body has gone why may not another body go? I have seen him myself crawl from his window. Why should not I imitate him, and go in by his window? The chances are desperate, but my need is more desperate still. I shall risk it.

Same day, later . . . I did not feel dizzy—I suppose I was too excited—and the time seemed ridiculously short till I found myself standing on the window-sill and trying to raise up the sash. I was filled with agitation, however, when I bent down and slid feet foremost in through the window. Then I looked around for the Count, but, with surprise and gladness, made a discovery. The room was empty! [. . .] The only thing I found was a great heap of gold in one corner—gold of all kinds, Roman, and British, and Austrian, and Hungarian, and Greek and Turkish money, covered with a film of dust, as though it had lain long in the ground. [. . .]

At one corner of the room was a heavy door. [. . .] It was open, and led through a stone passage to a circular stairway, which went steeply down. I descended, minding carefully where I went, for the stairs were dark, being only lit by loopholes in the heavy masonry. At the bottom there was a dark, tunnel-like passage, through which came a deathly, sickly odor, the odor of old earth newly turned.

At last I pulled open a heavy door which stood ajar, and found myself in an old, ruined chapel, which had evidently been used as a graveyard. [. . .] The roof was broken, and in two places were steps leading to vaults, but the ground had recently been dug over, and the earth placed in great wooden boxes . . .

There was nobody about, and I made search for any further outlet, but there was none. Then I went over every inch of the ground, so as not to lose a chance. I went down even into the vaults, where the dim light struggled, although to do so was a dread to my very soul. Into two of these I went, but saw nothing except fragments of old coffins and piles of dust; in the third, however, I made a discovery.

There, in one of the great boxes, of which there were fifty in all, on a pile of newly dug earth, lay the Count! He was either dead or asleep, I could not say which—for the eyes were open and stony, but without the glassiness of death—and the cheeks had the warmth of life through all their pallor; the lips were as red as ever. But there was no sign of movement, no pulse, no breath, no beating of the heart. [. . .]

I thought he might have the keys on him, but when I went to search I saw the dead eyes, and in them, dead though they were, such a look of hate, though unconscious of me or my presence, that I fled from the place, and leaving the Count's room by the window, crawled again up the castle wall. [. . .]

29 June . . . I was awakened by the Count, who looked at me as grimly as a man can look as he said:—"To-morrow, my friend, we must part. You return to your beautiful England, I to some work which may have such an end that we may never meet. Your letter home has been dispatched; to-morrow I shall not be here, but all shall be ready for your journey. [. . .] But I am in hopes that I shall see more of you at Castle Dracula." [. . .]

[I] asked him point-blank:—"Why may I not go to-night?" "Because, dear sir, my coachman and horses are away on a mission." "But I would walk with pleasure. I want to get away at once." He smiled, such a soft, smooth, diabolical smile that I knew there was some trick behind his smoothness. He said:—"And your baggage?" "I do not care about it. I can send for it some other time."

The Count stood up, and said, with a sweet courtesy which made me rub my eyes, it seemed so real:—"You English have a saying which is close to my heart, for its spirit is that which rules our *boyars*: 'Welcome the coming; speed the parting guest.' Come with me, my dear young friend. Not an hour shall you wait in my house against your will, though sad am I at your going, and that you so suddenly desire it. Come!" [. . .]

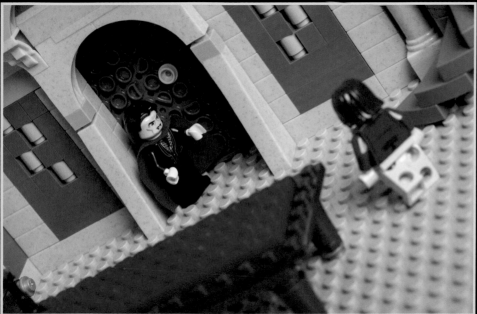

Suddenly he stopped. "Hark!" Close at hand came the howling of many wolves. It was almost as if the sound sprang up at the rising of his hand, just as the music of a great orchestra seems to leap under the baton of the conductor. After a pause of a moment, he proceeded, in his stately way, to the door, drew back the ponderous bolts, unhooked the heavy chains, and began to draw it open. To my intense astonishment I saw that it was unlocked. Suspiciously, I looked all round, but could see no key of any kind.

As the door began to open, the howling of the wolves without grew louder and angrier; their red jaws, with champing teeth, and their blunt-clawed feet as they leaped, came in through the opening door. I knew then that to struggle at the moment against the Count was useless. With such allies as these at his command, I could do nothing. But still the door continued slowly to open, and only the Count's body stood in the gap. Suddenly it struck me that this might be the moment and means of my doom; I was to be given to the wolves, and at my own instigation. There was a diabolical wickedness in the idea great enough for the Count, and as a last chance I cried out:—

"Shut the door; I shall wait till morning!" and covered my face with my hands to hide my tears of bitter disappointment. With one sweep of his powerful arm, the Count threw the door shut, and the great bolts clanged and echoed through the hall as they shot back into their places. [. . .]

[Later that night,] I thought I heard a whispering [in the library]. I went to it softly and listened. Unless my ears deceived me, I heard the voice of the Count:—"Back, back, to your own place! Your time is not yet come. Wait! Have patience! To-night is mine. To-morrow night is yours!"

There was a low, sweet ripple of laughter, and in a rage I [peered around the corner], and saw without the three terrible women licking their lips. As I appeared they all joined in a horrible laugh, and ran away. [. . .]

It is then so near the end? To-morrow! to-morrow! Lord, help me, and those to whom I am dear!

30 June, morning . . . I slept till just before the dawn. [. . .] Then came the welcome cock-crow, and I felt that I was safe. With a glad heart, I opened my door and ran down to the hall. I had seen that the door was unlocked, and now escape was before me. With hands that trembled with eagerness, I unhooked the chains and drew back the massive bolts. But the door would not move. Despair seized me. I pulled, and pulled, at the door, and shook it till, massive as it was, it rattled in its casement. I could see the bolt shot. It had been locked after I left the Count.

Then a wild desire took me to obtain that key at any risk, and I determined then and there to scale the wall again and gain the Count's room. He might kill me, but death now seemed the happier choice of evils. Without a pause I rushed up to the east window, and scrambled down the wall, as before, into the Count's room. [. . .]

The great box was in the same place, close against the wall, but the lid was laid on it, not fastened down, but with the nails ready in their places to be hammered home. I knew I must reach the body for the key, so I raised the lid, and laid it back against the wall; and then I saw something which filled my very soul with horror.

There lay the Count, but looking as if his youth had been half renewed, for the white hair and moustache were changed to dark iron-grey; the cheeks were fuller, and the white skin seemed ruby-red underneath; the mouth was redder than ever, for on the lips were gouts of fresh blood, which trickled from the corners of the mouth and ran over the chin and neck. [. . .] There was a mocking smile on the bloated face which seemed to drive me mad. This was the being I was helping to transfer to London, where, perhaps, for centuries to come he might, amongst its teeming millions, satiate his lust for blood, and create a new and ever-widening circle of semi-demons to batten on the helpless. [. . .]

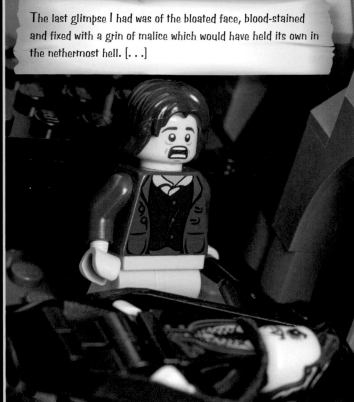

A terrible desire came upon me to rid the world of such a monster. There was no lethal weapon at hand, but I seized a shovel which the workmen had been using to fill the cases, and lifting it high, struck, with the edge downward, at the hateful face. But as I did so the head turned, and the eyes fell full upon me, with all their blaze of basilisk horror. The sight seemed to paralyze me, and the shovel turned in my hand and glanced from the face, merely making a deep gash above the forehead. [. . .]

I shall try to scale the castle wall farther than I have yet attempted. I shall take some of the gold with me, lest I want it later. I may find a way from this dreadful place.

And then away for home! away to the quickest and nearest train! away from this cursed spot, from this cursed land, where the devil and his children still walk with earthly feet! At least God's mercy is better than that of these monsters, and the precipice is steep and high. At its foot a man may sleep—as a man. Good-bye, all! Mina!

Chapter V – Letters—Lucy and Mina

Letter from Miss Mina Murray to Miss Lucy Westenra.

"*9 May.* My dearest Lucy,— Forgive my long delay in writing, but I have been simply overwhelmed with work. The life of an assistant schoolmistress is sometimes trying. I am longing to be with you, and by the sea, where we can talk together freely and build our castles in the air. I have been working very hard lately, because I want to keep up with Jonathan's studies, and I have been practicing shorthand very assiduously.

"When we are married I shall be able to be useful to Jonathan, and if I can stenograph well enough I can take down what he wants to say in this way and write it out for him on the typewriter, at which also I am practicing very hard. [. . .] I have just had a few hurried lines from Jonathan from Transylvania. He is well, and will be returning in about a week. I am longing to hear all his news. It must be so nice to see strange countries. I wonder if we—I mean Jonathan and I— shall ever see them together. [. . .]

"Your loving
"MINA."

Letter, Lucy Westenra to Mina Murray.

"*24 May* . . . My dear, it never rains but it pours. How true the old proverbs are. Here am I, who shall be twenty in September, and yet I never had a proposal till to-day, not a real proposal, and to-day I have had three. Just fancy! THREE proposals in one day! Isn't it awful! I feel sorry, really and truly sorry, for two of the poor fellows. Oh, Mina, I am so happy that I don't know what to do with myself. And three proposals . . . !

"Well, my dear, number One came just before lunch. I told you of him, Dr. John Seward, the lunatic-asylum man, with the strong jaw and the good forehead. He was very cool outwardly, but was nervous all the same. He had evidently been schooling himself as to all sorts of little things, and remembered them; but he almost managed to sit down on his silk hat, which men don't generally do when they are cool, and then when he wanted to appear at ease he kept playing with a lancet in a way that made me nearly scream. [. . .]

"[N]umber Two came after lunch. He is such a nice fellow, an American from Texas, and he looks so young and so fresh that it seems almost impossible that he has been to so many places and has had such adventures. [. . .] Well, Mr. Morris sat down beside me and looked as happy and jolly as he could, but I could see all the same that he was very nervous. He took my hand in his, and said ever so sweetly:—'Miss Lucy, I know I ain't good enough to regulate the fixin's of your little shoes, but I guess if you wait till you find a man that is you will go join them seven young women with the lamps when you quit. Won't you just hitch up alongside of me and let us go down the long road together, driving in double harness?' Well, he did look so good-humored and so jolly that it didn't seem half so hard to refuse him as it did poor Dr. Seward. [. . .]

"P.S.—Oh, about number Three—I needn't tell you of [dear Arthur], need I?

"Besides, it was all so confused; it seemed only a moment from his coming into the room till both his arms were round me, and he was kissing me. I am very, very happy, and I don't know what I have done to deserve it. I must only try in the future to show that I am not ungrateful to God for all His goodness to me in sending to me such a lover, such a husband, and such a friend. Good-bye."

Dr. Seward's Diary (Kept in phonograph).

25 May.—Ebb tide in appetite to-day. Cannot eat, cannot rest, so diary instead. Since my rebuff of yesterday I have a sort of empty feeling; nothing in the world seems of sufficient importance to be worth the doing. [. . .] As I knew that the only cure for this sort of thing was work, I went down amongst the patients.

I picked out one who has afforded me a study of much interest. He is so quaint that I am determined to understand him as well as I can. To-day I seemed to get nearer than ever before to the heart of his mystery. [. . .] R. M. Renfield, ætat 59.—Sanguine temperament; great physical strength; morbidly excitable; periods of gloom, ending in some fixed idea which I cannot make out. [. . .]

Chapter VI — Mina Murray's Journal

24 July. Whitby.—Lucy met me at the station, looking sweeter and lovelier than ever, and we drove up to the house at the Crescent in which they have rooms. This is a lovely place. [. . .]

Right over the town is the ruin of Whitby Abbey . . . It is a most noble ruin, of immense size, and full of beautiful and romantic bits; there is a legend that a white lady is seen in one of the windows. [. . .] Outside the harbor on this side there rises for about half a mile a great reef, the sharp edge of which runs straight out from behind the south lighthouse. At the end of it is a buoy with a bell, which swings in bad weather, and sends in a mournful sound on the wind. They have a legend here that when a ship is lost bells are heard out at sea. I must ask the old man about this; he is coming this way. [. . .]

1 August . . . I got him on the subject of the legends, and he went off at once into a sort of sermon. I must try to remember it and put it down:—"It be all fool-talk, lock, stock, and barrel; that's what it be, an' nowt else. These bans an' wafts an' boh-ghosts an' barguests an' bogles an' all anent them is only fit to set bairns an' dizzy women a-belderin'. [. . .]

"Look here all around you in what airt ye will; all them steans, holdin' up their heads as well as they can out of their pride, is acant—simply tumblin' down with the weight o' the lies wrote on them, 'Here lies the body' or 'Sacred to the memory' wrote on all of them, an' yet in nigh half of them there bean't no bodies at all; an' the memories of them bean't cared a pinch of snuff about, much less sacred. . . ."

Lucy and I sat awhile, and it was all so beautiful before us that we took hands as we sat; and she told me all over again about Arthur and their coming marriage.

Dr. Seward's Diary.

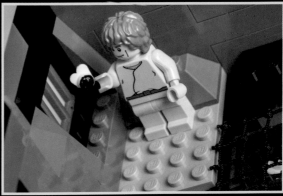

That made me just a little heart-sick, for I haven't heard from Jonathan for a whole month.

5 June.—The case of Renfield grows more interesting the more I get to understand the man. He has certain qualities very largely developed; selfishness, secrecy, and purpose. I wish I could get at what is the object of the latter. He seems to have some settled scheme of his own, but what it is I do not yet know. His redeeming quality is a love of animals, though, indeed, he has such curious turns in it that I sometimes imagine he is only abnormally cruel. His pets are of odd sorts. Just now his hobby is catching flies. [. . .]

18 June.—He has turned his mind now to spiders, and has got several very big fellows in a box. He keeps feeding them with his flies, and the number of the latter is becoming sensibly diminished, although he has used half his food in attracting more flies from outside to his room. [. . .]

8 July . . . Things remain as they were except that he has parted with some of his pets and got a new one. He has managed to get a sparrow, and has already partially tamed it. His means of taming is simple, for already the spiders have diminished. Those that do remain, however, are well fed, for he still brings in the flies by tempting them with his food.

19 July.—We are progressing. My friend has now a whole colony of sparrows, and his flies and spiders are almost obliterated.

When I came in he ran to me and said he wanted to ask me a great favor—a very, very great favor; and as he spoke he fawned on me like a dog. I asked him what it was, and he said, with a sort of rapture in his voice and bearing:—

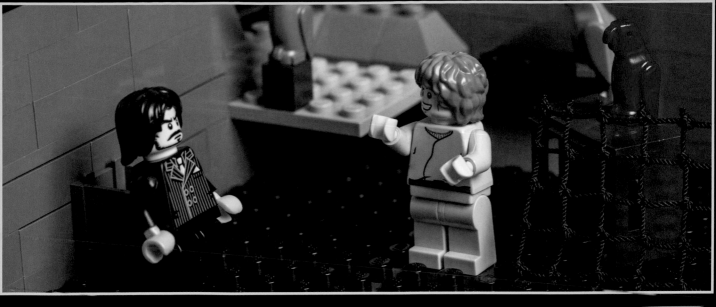

"A kitten, a nice little, sleek playful kitten, that I can play with, and teach, and feed—and feed—and feed!" I was not unprepared for this request, for I had noticed how his pets went on increasing in size and vivacity, but I did not care that his pretty family of tame sparrows should be wiped out in the same manner as the flies and the spiders; so I said I would see about it, and asked him if he would not rather have a cat than a kitten. His eagerness betrayed him as he answered:—"Oh, yes, I would like a cat! I only asked for a kitten lest you should refuse me a cat. No one would refuse me a kitten, would they?"

I shook my head, and said that at present I feared it would not be possible, but that I would see about it. His face fell, and I could see a warning of danger in it, for there was a sudden fierce, sidelong look which meant killing. The man is an undeveloped homicidal maniac. I shall test him with his present craving and see how it will work out; then I shall know more.

20 July.—Visited Renfield very early, before the attendant went his rounds. Found him up and humming a tune. He was spreading out his sugar, which he had saved, in the window, and was manifestly beginning his fly-catching again; and beginning it cheerfully and with a good grace. I looked around for his birds, and not seeing them, asked him where they were. He replied, without turning round, that they had all flown away. There were a few feathers about the room and on his pillow a drop of blood. [. . .] *11 a. m.*—The attendant has just been to me to say that Renfield has been very sick and has disgorged a whole lot of feathers. "My belief is, doctor," he said, "that he has eaten his birds, and that he just took and ate them raw!" [. . .]

My homicidal maniac is of a peculiar kind. I shall have to invent a new classification for him, and call him a zoophagous (life-eating) maniac; what he desires is to absorb as many lives as he can, and he has laid himself out to achieve it in a cumulative way. He gave many flies to one spider and many spiders to one bird, and then wanted a cat to eat the many birds. What would have been his later steps? It would almost be worth while to complete the experiment. [. . .]

Mina Murray's Journal.

26 July.—I am anxious, and it soothes me to express myself here . . . I had not heard from Jonathan for some time, and was very concerned; but yesterday dear Mr. Hawkins, who is always so kind, sent me a letter from him. I had written asking him if he had heard, and he said the enclosed had just been received. It is only a line dated from Castle Dracula, and says that he is just starting for home. That is not like Jonathan; I do not understand it, and it makes me uneasy.

Then, too, Lucy, although she is so well, has lately taken to her old habit of walking in her sleep. Her mother has spoken to me about it, and we have decided that I am to lock the door of our room every night. [. . .]

27 July.—No news from Jonathan. I am getting quite uneasy about him, though why I should I do not know; but I do wish that he would write, if it were only a single line. Lucy walks more than ever, and each night I am awakened by her moving about the room. Fortunately, the weather is so hot that she cannot get cold; but still the anxiety and the perpetually being wakened is beginning to tell on me, and I am getting nervous and wakeful myself. [. . .]

6 August . . . no news. This suspense is getting dreadful. If I only knew where to write to or where to go to, I should feel easier; but no one has heard a word of Jonathan since that last letter. [. . .]

Here comes old Mr. Swales. He is making straight for me, and I can see, by the way he lifts his hat, that he wants to talk. [. . .] I have been quite touched by the change in the poor old man. When he sat down beside me, he said in a very gentle way . . . "I'm afraid, my deary, that I must have shocked you by all the wicked things I've been sayin' about the dead, and such like, for weeks past; but I didn't mean them, and I want ye to remember that when I'm gone. [. . .] There's something in that wind and in the hoast beyont that sounds, and looks, and tastes, and smells like death. It's in the air; I feel it comin'. Lord, make me answer cheerful when my call comes!" [. . .]

I was glad when the coastguard came along, with his spy-glass under his arm. He stopped to talk with me, as he always does, but all the time kept looking at a strange ship. "I can't make her out," he said; "she's a Russian, by the look of her; but she's knocking about in the queerest way. . . ."

Chapter VII — Cutting from "The Dailygraph,"
8 August (*Pasted in Mina Murray's Journal.*)

From a Correspondent. *Whitby.* One of the greatest and suddenest storms on record has just been experienced here, with results both strange and unique. [. . .] A little after midnight came a strange sound from over the sea, and high overhead the air began to carry a strange, faint, hollow booming. Then without warning the tempest broke. With a rapidity which, at the time, seemed incredible, and even afterwards is impossible to realize, the whole aspect of nature at once became convulsed. The waves rose in growing fury, each overtopping its fellow, till in a very few minutes the lately glassy sea was like a roaring and devouring monster. [. . .]

Before long the searchlight discovered some distance away a schooner with all sails set, apparently the same vessel which had been noticed earlier in the evening. The wind had by this time backed to the east, and there was a shudder amongst the watchers on the cliff as they realized the terrible danger in which she now was. [. . .]

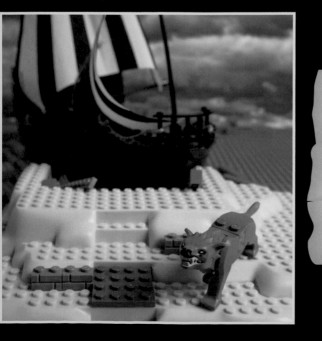

There was of course a considerable concussion as the vessel drove up on the sand heap. Every spar, rope, and stay was strained, and some of the "top-hammer" came crashing down. But, strangest of all, the very instant the shore was touched, an immense dog sprang up on deck from below, as if shot up by the concussion, and running forward, jumped from the bow on the sand. Making straight for the steep cliff, where the churchyard hangs over the laneway to the East Pier so steeply that some of the flat tombstones—"thruff-steans" or "through-stones," as they call them in the Whitby vernacular—actually project over where the sustaining cliff has fallen away, it disappeared in the darkness, which seemed intensified just beyond the focus of the searchlight. [. . .]

The coastguard ran aft, and when he came beside the wheel, bent over to examine it, and recoiled at once as though under some sudden emotion. [. . .] By the courtesy of the chief boatman, I was, as your correspondent, permitted to climb on deck, and was one of a small group who saw the dead seaman whilst actually lashed to the wheel. It was no wonder that the coastguard was surprised, or even awed, for not often can such a sight have been seen. The man was simply fastened by his hands, tied one over the other, to a spoke of the wheel. Between the inner hand and the wood was a crucifix, the set of beads on which it was fastened being around both wrists and wheel, and all kept fast by the binding cords. [. . .] In his pocket was a bottle, carefully corked, empty save for a little roll of paper, which proved to be the addendum to the log.

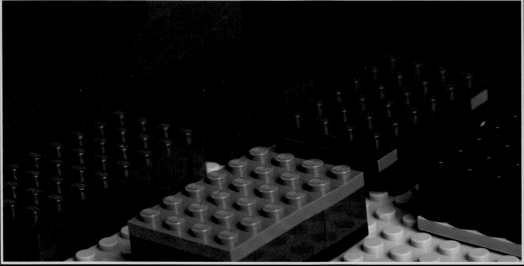

9 August.—The sequel to the strange arrival of the derelict in the storm last night is almost more startling than the thing itself. It turns out that the schooner is a Russian from Varna, and is called the *Demeter*. She is almost entirely in ballast of silver sand, with only a small amount of cargo—a number of great wooden boxes filled with mould.

Log of the "Demeter."

Varna to Whitby. Written 18 July, things so strange happening, that I shall keep accurate note henceforth till we land. [. . .]

On 14 July was somewhat anxious about crew. Men all steady fellows, who sailed with me before. Mate could not make out what was wrong; they only told him there was *something*, and crossed themselves. Mate lost temper with one of them that day and struck him. Expected fierce quarrel, but all was quiet. On 16 July mate reported in the morning that one of crew, Petrofsky, was missing. Could not account for it. Took larboard watch eight bells last night; was relieved by Abramoff, but did not go to bunk. Men more downcast than ever. All said they expected something of the kind, but would not say more than there was *something* aboard. Mate getting very impatient with them; feared some trouble ahead.

On 17 July, yesterday, one of the men, Olgaren, came to my cabin, and in an awestruck way confided to me that he thought there was a strange man aboard the ship. He said that in his watch he had been sheltering behind the deck-house, as there was a rain-storm, when he saw a tall, thin man, who was not like any of the crew, come up the companion-way, and go along the deck forward, and disappear. He followed cautiously, but when he got to bows found no one, and the hatchways were all closed. He was in a panic of superstitious fear, and I am afraid the panic may spread. To allay it, I shall to-day search entire ship carefully from stem to stern.

Later in the day I got together the whole crew, and told them, as they evidently thought there was some one in the ship, we would search from stem to stern. First mate angry; said it was folly, and to yield to such foolish ideas would demoralize the men; said he would engage to keep them out of trouble with a handspike. I let him take the helm, while the rest began thorough search, all keeping abreast, with lanterns: we left no corner unsearched. As there were only the big wooden boxes, there were no odd corners where a man could hide. Men much relieved when search over, and went back to work cheerfully. First mate scowled, but said nothing. [. . .]

2 August, midnight.—Woke up from few minutes' sleep by hearing a cry, seemingly outside my port. Could see nothing in fog. Rushed on deck, and ran against mate. Tells me heard cry and ran, but no sign of man on watch. One more gone. Lord, help us! Mate says we must be past Straits of Dover, as in a moment of fog lifting he saw North Foreland, just as he heard the man cry out. If so we are now off in the North Sea, and only God can guide us in the fog, which seems to move with us; and God seems to have deserted us.

3 August.—At midnight I went to relieve the man at the wheel, and when I got to it found no one there. The wind was steady, and as we ran before it there was no yawing. I dared not leave it, so shouted for the mate. After a few seconds he rushed up on deck in his flannels. He looked wild-eyed and haggard, and I greatly fear his reason has given way.

He came close to me and whispered hoarsely, with his mouth to my ear, as though fearing the very air might hear: "*It is here; I know it, now. On the watch last night I saw It, like a man, tall and thin, and ghastly pale.*"

"It was in the bows, and looking out. I crept behind It, and gave It my knife; but the knife went through It, empty as the air." [. . .]

Then he went on: "But It is here, and I'll find It. It is in the hold, perhaps in one of those boxes. I'll unscrew them one by one and see. You work the helm." And, with a warning look and his finger on his lip, he went below. [. . .]

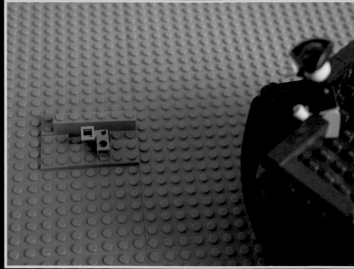

Just as I was beginning to hope that the mate would come out calmer—for I heard him knocking away at something in the hold, and work is good for him—there came up the hatchway a sudden, startled scream, which made my blood run cold, and up on the deck he came as if shot from a gun—a raging madman, with his eyes rolling and his face convulsed with fear. "Save me! save me!" he cried, and then looked round on the blanket of fog.

His horror turned to despair, and in a steady voice he said: "You had better come too, captain, before it is too late. *He* is there. I know the secret now. The sea will save me from Him, and it is all that is left!" Before I could say a word, or move forward to seize him, he sprang on the bulwark and deliberately threw himself into the sea.

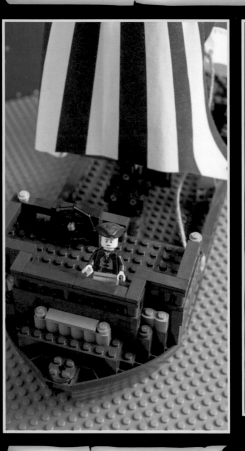

I suppose I know the secret too, now. It was this madman who had got rid of the men one by one, and now he has followed them himself. God help me! How am I to account for all these horrors *when* I get to port? When I get to port! Will that ever be? [. . .]

I dared not go below, I dared not leave the helm; so here all night I stayed, and in the dimness of the night I saw It—Him! God forgive me, but the mate was right to jump overboard. It was better to die like a man; to die like a sailor in blue water no man can object. But I am captain, and I must not leave my ship. But I shall baffle this fiend or monster, for I shall tie my hands to the wheel when my strength begins to fail, and along with them I shall tie that which He—It!—dare not touch; and then, come good wind or foul, I shall save my soul, and my honor as a captain. [. . .]

Mina Murray's Journal.

10 August.—The funeral of the poor sea-captain to-day was most touching. Every boat in the harbor seemed to be there, and the coffin was carried by captains all the way from Tate Hill Pier up to the churchyard. Lucy came with me, and we went early to our old seat, whilst the cortège of boats went up the river to the Viaduct and came down again. We had a lovely view, and saw the procession nearly all the way.

The poor fellow was laid to rest quite near our seat so that we stood on it when the time came and saw everything. Poor Lucy seemed much upset. She was restless and uneasy all the time, and I cannot but think that her dreaming at night is telling on her. She is quite odd in one thing: she will not admit to me that there is any cause for restlessness; or if there be, she does not understand it herself.

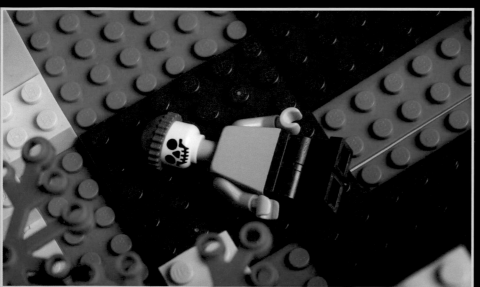

There is an additional cause in that poor old Mr. Swales was found dead this morning on our seat, his neck being broken. He had evidently, as the doctor said, fallen back in the seat in some sort of fright, for there was a look of fear and horror on his face that the men said made them shudder. Poor dear old man! Perhaps he had seen Death with his dying eyes! [. . .]

Chapter VIII — Mina Murray's Journal

Same day, 11 o'clock p. m.—Oh, but I am tired! If it were not that I had made my diary a duty I should not open it to-night. We had a lovely walk. [. . .] I am so happy to-night, because dear Lucy seems better. I really believe she has turned the corner, and that we are over her troubles with dreaming. I should be quite happy if I only knew if Jonathan. [. . .] God bless and keep him.

11 August, 3 a. m.—Diary again. No sleep now, so I may as well write. I am too agitated to sleep. We have had such an adventure, such an agonizing experience. I fell asleep as soon as I had closed my diary. [. . .]

Suddenly I became broad awake, and sat up, with a horrible sense of fear upon me, and of some feeling of emptiness around me. The room was dark, so I could not see Lucy's bed; I stole across and felt for her. The bed was empty. I lit a match and found that she was not in the room. [. . .]

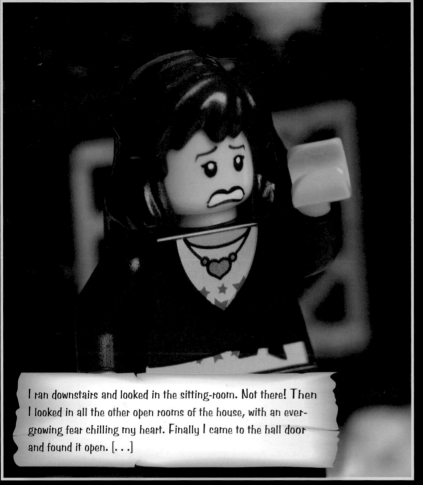

I ran downstairs and looked in the sitting-room. Not there! Then I looked in all the other open rooms of the house, with an ever-growing fear chilling my heart. Finally I came to the hall door and found it open. [. . .]

I took a big, heavy shawl and ran out. [. . .] [T]here, on our favorite seat, the silver light of the moon struck a half-reclining figure, snowy white. The coming of the cloud was too quick for me to see much, for shadow shut down on light almost immediately; but it seemed to me as though something dark stood behind the seat where the white figure shone, and bent over it. [. . .]

When I got almost to the top I could see the seat and the white figure, for I was now close enough to distinguish it even through the spells of shadow. There was undoubtedly something, long and black, bending over the half-reclining white figure.

I called in fright, "Lucy! Lucy!"

. . . and something raised a head, and from where I was I could see a white face and red, gleaming eyes. Lucy did not answer, and I ran on to the entrance of the churchyard.

When I came in view again the cloud had passed, and the moonlight struck so brilliantly that I could see Lucy half reclining with her head lying over the back of the seat. She was quite alone, and there was not a sign of any living thing about. When I bent over her I could see that she was still asleep. Her lips were parted, and she was breathing—not softly as usual with her, but in long, heavy gasps, as though striving to get her lungs full at every breath. [. . .]

I flung the warm shawl over her, and drew the edges tight round her neck, for I dreaded lest she should get some deadly chill from the night air, unclad as she was. I feared to wake her all at once, so, in order to have my hands free that I might help her, I fastened the shawl at her throat with a big safety-pin; but I must have been clumsy in my anxiety and pinched or pricked her with it, for by-and-by, when her breathing became quieter, she put her hand to her throat again and moaned. [. . .]

Same day, noon.—All goes well. Lucy slept till I woke her and seemed not to have even changed her side. The adventure of the night does not seem to have harmed her; on the contrary, it has benefited her, for she looks better this morning than she has done for weeks. I was sorry to notice that my clumsiness with the safety-pin hurt her. Indeed, it might have been serious, for the skin of her throat was pierced. I must have pinched up a piece of loose skin and have transfixed it, for there are two little red points like pin-pricks, and on the band of her nightdress was a drop of blood. [. . .]

12 August . . . twice during the night I was wakened by Lucy trying to get out. She seemed, even in her sleep, to be a little impatient at finding the door shut, and went back to bed under a sort of protest. [. . .]

13 August.—
Another quiet day, and to bed with the key on my wrist as before. Again I awoke in the night, and found Lucy sitting up in bed, still asleep, pointing to the window. I got up quietly, and pulling aside the blind, looked out. [. . .]

Between me and the moonlight flitted a great bat, coming and going in great whirling circles. Once or twice it came quite close, but was, I suppose, frightened at seeing me, and flitted away across the harbor towards the abbey. When I came back from the window Lucy had lain down again, and was sleeping peacefully. She did not stir again all night.

14 August.—On the East Cliff, reading and writing all day. [. . .] This afternoon Lucy made a funny remark. We were coming home for dinner, and had come to the top of the steps up from the West Pier and stopped to look at the view, as we generally do. [. . .] We were silent for a while, and suddenly Lucy murmured as if to herself:—"His red eyes again! They are just the same."

. . . I said nothing, but followed her eyes. She appeared to be looking over at our own seat, whereon was a dark figure seated alone. I was a little startled myself, for it seemed for an instant as if the stranger had great eyes like burning flames; but a second look dispelled the illusion. The red sunlight was shining on the windows of St. Mary's Church behind our seat, and as the sun dipped there was just sufficient change in the refraction and reflection to make it appear as if the light moved. [. . .]

Lucy had a headache and went early to bed. I saw her asleep, and went out for a little stroll myself; I walked along the cliffs to the westward, and was full of sweet sadness, for I was thinking of Jonathan.

When coming home—it was then bright moonlight, so bright that, though the front of our part of the Crescent was in shadow, everything could be well seen—I threw a glance up at our window, and saw Lucy's head leaning out. [. . .] There distinctly was Lucy with her head lying up against the side of the window-sill and her eyes shut. She was fast asleep, and by her, seated on the window-sill, was something that looked like a good-sized bird.

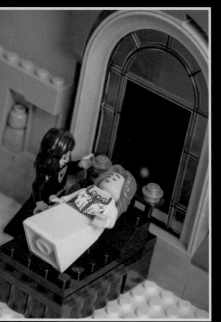

I was afraid she might get a chill, so I ran upstairs, but as I came into the room she was moving back to her bed, fast asleep, and breathing heavily; she was holding her hand to her throat, as though to protect it from cold. I did not wake her, but tucked her up warmly; I have taken care that the door is locked and the window securely fastened. [. . .]

17 August.—No diary for two whole days. I have not had the heart to write. Some sort of shadowy pall seems to be coming over our happiness. No news from Jonathan, and Lucy seems to be growing weaker . . .

I do not understand Lucy's fading away as she is doing. She eats well and sleeps well, and enjoys the fresh air; but all the time the roses in her cheeks are fading, and she gets weaker and more languid day by day; at night I hear her gasping as if for air. I keep the key of our door always fastened to my wrist at night, but she gets up and walks about the room, and sits at the open window.

Last night I found her leaning out when I woke up, and when I tried to wake her I could not; she was in a faint. When I managed to restore her she was as weak as water, and cried silently between long, painful struggles for breath. When I asked her how she came to be at the window she shook her head and turned away.

I trust her feeling ill may not be from that unlucky prick of the safety-pin. I looked at her throat just now as she lay asleep, and the tiny wounds seem not to have healed. They are still open, and, if anything, larger than before, and the edges of them are faintly white. They are like little white dots with red centers. Unless they heal within a day or two, I shall insist on the doctor seeing about them.

Letter, Samuel F. Billington & Son, Solicitors, to Messrs. Carter, Paterson & Co., London

"*17 August.* Dear Sirs,— Herewith please receive invoice of goods sent by Great Northern Railway. Same are to be delivered at Carfax, near Purfleet, immediately on receipt at goods station King's Cross. The house is at present empty, but enclosed please find keys, all of which are labeled. You will please deposit the boxes, fifty in number, which form the consignment, in the partially ruined building forming part of the house and marked 'A' on rough diagram enclosed. Your agent will easily recognize the locality, as it is the ancient chapel of the mansion. [. . .]

Mina Murray's Journal.

18 August.—I am happy to-day, and write sitting on the seat in the churchyard. Lucy is ever so much better. Last night she slept well all night, and did not disturb me once. The roses seem coming back already to her cheeks, though she is still sadly pale and wan-looking. If she were in any way anemic I could understand it, but she is not. She is in gay spirits and full of life and cheerfulness. [. . .]

19 August.—Joy, joy, joy! although not all joy. At last, news of Jonathan. The dear fellow has been ill; that is why he did not write. I am not afraid to think it or say it, now that I know. Mr. Hawkins sent me on the letter, and wrote himself, oh, so kindly. I am to leave in the morning and go over to Jonathan, and to help to nurse him if necessary, and to bring him home. [. . .]

I have cried over the good Sister's letter till I can feel it wet against my bosom, where it lies. It is of Jonathan, and must be next my heart, for he is *in* my heart. My journey is all mapped out, and my luggage ready. [. . .]

Letter, Sister Agatha, Hospital of St. Joseph and Ste. Mary, Buda-Pesth, to Miss Wilhemina Murray.

"*12 August.* Dear Madam,—I write by desire of Mr. Jonathan Harker, who is himself not strong enough to write, though progressing well, thanks to God and St. Joseph and Ste. Mary. He has been under our care for nearly six weeks, suffering from a violent brain fever. [. . .]

"Yours, with sympathy and all blessings, SISTER AGATHA. P. S.—My patient being asleep, I open this to let you know something more. He has told me all about you, and that you are shortly to be his wife. All blessings to you both! He has had some fearful shock—so says our doctor—and in his delirium his ravings have been dreadful; of wolves and poison and blood; of ghosts and demons; and I fear to say of what. Be careful with him always that there may be nothing to excite him of this kind for a long time to come; the traces of such an illness as his do not lightly die away. [. . .]"

Dr. Seward's Diary.

19 August.—Strange and sudden change in Renfield last night. About eight o'clock he began to get excited and sniff about as a dog does when setting. The attendant was struck by his manner, and knowing my interest in him, encouraged him to talk. He is usually respectful to the attendant and at times servile; but to-night, the man tells me, he was quite haughty. Would not condescend to talk with him at all. All he would say was:—"I don't want to talk to you: you don't count now; the Master is at hand." [. . .]

I had lain tossing about, and had heard the clock strike only twice, when the night-watchman came to me, sent up from the ward, to say that Renfield had escaped. I threw on my clothes and ran down at once; my patient is too dangerous a person to be roaming about. [. . .] I saw a white figure scale the high wall which separates our grounds from those of the deserted house. [. . .] I got a ladder myself, and crossing the wall, dropped down on the other side. I could see Renfield's figure just disappearing behind the angle of the house, so I ran after him. [. . .]

I heard him say:—"I am here to do Your bidding, Master. I am Your slave, and You will reward me, for I shall be faithful. I have worshipped You long and afar off. Now that You are near, I await Your commands, and You will not pass me by, will You, dear Master, in Your distribution of good things?"

Mina Murray's Journal (continued)

Letter, Mina Harker to Lucy Westenra.

"Buda-Pesth, 24 August. My dearest Lucy . . . I found my dear one, oh, so thin and pale and weak-looking. All the resolution has gone out of his dear eyes, and that quiet dignity which I told you was in his face has vanished. He is only a wreck of himself, and he does not remember anything that has happened to him for a long time past.

"At least, he wants me to believe so, and I shall never ask. He has had some terrible shock, and I fear it might tax his poor brain if he were to try to recall it. Sister Agatha, who is a good creature and a born nurse, tells me that he raved of dreadful things whilst he was off his head. I wanted her to tell me what they were; but she would only cross herself, and say she would never tell; that the ravings of the sick were the secrets of God, and that if a nurse through her vocation should hear them, she should respect her trust. [. . .]

"When he woke he asked me for his coat, as he wanted to get something from the pocket . . . 'Wilhelmina'—I knew then that he was in deadly earnest, for he has never called me by that name since he asked me to marry him . . . The secret is here, and I do not want to know it. I want to take up my life here, with our marriage.' For, my dear, we had decided to be married as soon as the formalities are complete. 'Are you willing, Wilhelmina, to share my ignorance? Here is the book. Take it and keep it, read it if you will, but never let me know; unless, indeed, some solemn duty should come upon me to go back to the bitter hours, asleep or awake, sane or mad, recorded here.'

He fell back exhausted, and I put the book under his pillow, and kissed him. I have asked Sister Agatha to beg the Superior to let our wedding be this afternoon, and am waiting her reply. [. . .]

Lucy, the time has come and gone. I feel very solemn, but very, very happy. Jonathan woke a little after the hour, and all was ready . . . He answered his 'I will' firmly and strongly. I could hardly speak; my heart was so full that even those words seemed to choke me."

Letter, Lucy Westenra to Mina Harker.

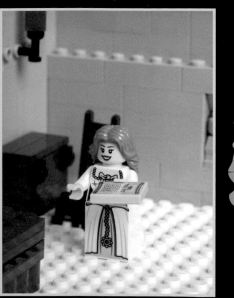

"*Whitby, 30 August.* My dearest Mina,—Oceans of love and millions of kisses, and may you soon be in your own home with your husband. I wish you could be coming home soon enough to stay with us here. The strong air would soon restore Jonathan; it has quite restored me. I have an appetite like a cormorant, am full of life, and sleep well. You will be glad to know that I have quite given up walking in my sleep. . . ."

Dr. Seward's Diary.

20 August.—The case of Renfield grows even more interesting. He has now so far quieted that there are spells of cessation from his passion. For the first week after his attack he was perpetually violent. Then one night, just as the moon rose, he grew quiet, and kept murmuring to himself: "Now I can wait; now I can wait." [. . .]

I wish I could get some clue to the cause. It would almost seem as if there was some influence which came and went. Happy thought! We shall to-night play sane wits against mad ones. He escaped before without our help; to-night he shall escape with it. We shall give him a chance, and have the men ready to follow in case they are required. [. . .]

23 August.—"The unexpected always happens." How well Disraeli knew life. Our bird when he found the cage open would not fly, so all our subtle arrangements were for nought. At any rate, we have proved one thing; that the spells of quietness last a reasonable time. [. . .]

Later.—Another night adventure. Renfield artfully waited until the attendant was entering the room to inspect. Then he dashed out past him and flew down the passage. I sent word for the attendants to follow. Again he went into the grounds of the deserted house, and we found him in the same place, pressed against the old chapel door. When he saw me he became furious, and had not the attendants seized him in time, he would have tried to kill me.

Lucy Westenra's Diary.

As we were holding him a strange thing happened. He suddenly redoubled his efforts, and then as suddenly grew calm. I looked round instinctively, but could see nothing. Then I caught the patient's eye and followed it, but could trace nothing as it looked into the moonlit sky except a big bat, which was flapping its silent and ghostly way to the west. Bats usually wheel and flit about, but this one seemed to go straight on, as if it knew where it was bound for or had some intention of its own. The patient grew calmer every instant, and presently said:—"You needn't tie me; I shall go quietly!" Without trouble we came back to the house. I feel there is something ominous in his calm, and shall not forget this night. [. . .]

25 August.—Another bad night. [. . .] I tried to keep awake, and succeeded for a while; but when the clock struck twelve it waked me from a doze, so I must have been falling asleep. There was a sort of scratching or flapping at the window, but I did not mind it, and as I remember no more, I suppose I must then have fallen asleep. More bad dreams. I wish I could remember them. This morning I am horribly weak. My face is ghastly pale, and my throat pains me. It must be something wrong with my lungs, for I don't seem ever to get air enough. [. . .]

Letter, Arthur Holmwood to Dr. Seward.

"*Albemarle Hotel, 31 August.* My dear Jack,—I want you to do me a favor. Lucy is ill; that is, she has no special disease, but she looks awful, and is getting worse every day. [. . .] I told her I should ask you to see her, and though she demurred at first—I know why, old fellow—she finally consented. [. . .] I am filled with anxiety, and want to consult with you alone as soon as I can after you have seen her. Do not fail! ARTHUR."

Letter from Dr. Seward to Arthur Holmwood.

"*2 September.* My dear old fellow,—With regard to Miss Westenra's health I hasten to let you know at once that in my opinion there is not any functional disturbance or any malady that I know of. At the same time, I am not by any means satisfied with her appearance; she is woefully different from what she was when I saw her last. [. . .] The qualitative analysis gives a quite normal condition, and shows, I should infer, in itself a vigorous state of health. In other physical matters I was quite satisfied that there is no need for anxiety; but as there must be a cause somewhere, I have come to the conclusion that it must be something mental. [. . .]

I am in doubt, and so have done the best thing I know of; I have written to my old friend and master, Professor Van Helsing, of Amsterdam, who knows as much about obscure diseases as any one in the world. I have asked him to come over. . . ."

Letter, Abraham Van Helsing, M. D., D. Ph., D. Lit., etc., etc., to Dr. Seward.

Letter, Dr. Seward to Hon. Arthur Holmwood.

"*2 September.* My good Friend,—When I have received your letter I am already coming to you. By good fortune I can leave just at once . . . Till then good-bye, my friend John. VAN HELSING."

"*3 September.* My dear Art . . . Van Helsing made a very careful examination of the patient. [. . .] He is, I fear, much concerned, but says he must think. [. . .]He would not give me any further clue. You must not be angry with me, Art, because his very reticence means that all his brains are working for her good. He will speak plainly enough when the time comes, be sure. [. . .]

"He looked grave, but said: 'I have made careful examination, but there is no functional cause. With you I agree that there has been much blood lost; it has been, but is not. But the conditions of her are in no way anemic. [. . .] And yet there is cause; there is always cause for everything. I must go back home and think. . . .' As I tell you, he would not say a word more, even when we were alone. And so now, Art, you know all I know. . . ."

Dr. Seward's Diary.

4 September.—Zoöphagous patient still keeps up our interest in him. [. . .] *Later . . .* At five o'clock I looked in on him, and found him seemingly as happy and contented as he used to be. He was catching flies and eating them, and was keeping note of his capture by making nail-marks on the edge of the door between the ridges of padding.

Midnight.—Another change in him. I had been to see Miss Westenra, whom I found much better, and had just returned, and was standing at our own gate looking at the sunset, when once more I heard him yelling. [. . .] I signaled to the attendants not to hold him, for I was anxious to see what he would do. He went straight over to the window and brushed out the crumbs of sugar; then he took his fly-box, and emptied it outside, and threw away the box; then he shut the window, and crossing over, sat down on his bed. All this surprised me, so I asked him: "Are you not going to keep flies any more?" "No," said he; "I am sick of all that rubbish!" [. . .]

Telegram, Sward, London, to Van Helsing, Amsterdam.

6 September.—Terrible change for the worse. Come at once; do not lose an hour. I hold over telegram to Holmwood till have seen you."

Chapter X – Dr. Seward's Diary

7 September.—Van Helsing and I were shown up to Lucy's room. If I was shocked when I saw her yesterday, I was horrified when I saw her to-day. She was ghastly, chalkily pale; the red seemed to have gone even from her lips and gums, and the bones of her face stood out prominently; her breathing was painful to see or hear. Van Helsing's face grew set as marble, and his eyebrows converged till they almost touched over his nose. [. . .]

"My God!" he said; "this is dreadful. There is no time to be lost. She will die for sheer want of blood to keep the heart's action as it should be. There must be transfusion of blood at once. Is it you or me?" "I am younger and stronger, Professor. It must be me." "Then get ready at once. I will bring up my bag. I am prepared."

. . . there was a knock at the door, and Arthur was stepping quickly in. He rushed up to me, saying in an eager whisper:—"Jack, I was so anxious. I read between the lines of your letter, and have been in an agony. The dad was better, so I ran down here to see for myself. Is not that gentleman Dr. Van Helsing? I am so thankful to you, sir, for coming." [. . .]

Without a pause the Professor said to him gravely as he held out his hand:—"Sir, you have come in time. You are the lover of our dear miss. She is bad, very, very bad. [. . .] You are to help her. You can do more than any that live, and your courage is your best help." "What can I do?" asked Arthur hoarsely. "Tell me, and I shall do it. My life is hers, and I would give the last drop of blood in my body for her."

The Professor has a strongly humorous side, and I could from old knowledge detect a trace of its origin in his answer:— "My young sir, I do not ask so much as that—not the last!" [. . .] Then with swiftness, but with absolute method, Van Helsing performed the operation.

As the transfusion went on something like life seemed to come back to poor Lucy's cheeks, and through Arthur's growing pallor the joy of his face seemed absolutely to shine. After a bit I began to grow anxious, for the loss of blood was telling on Arthur, strong man as he was. It gave me an idea of what a terrible strain Lucy's system must have undergone that what weakened Arthur only partially restored her. [. . .]

Just over the external jugular vein there were two punctures, not large, but not wholesome-looking. There was no sign of disease, but the edges were white and worn-looking, as if by some trituration. [. . .] "Well?" said Van Helsing. "Well," said I, "I can make nothing of it." The Professor stood up. "I must go back to Amsterdam to-night," he said. "There are books and things there which I want. You must remain here all the night, and you must not let your sight pass from her." [. . .]

8 September.—I sat up all night with Lucy. The opiate worked itself off towards dusk, and she waked naturally; she looked a different being from what she had been before the operation. Her spirits even were good, and she was full of a happy vivacity, but I could see evidences of the absolute prostration which she had undergone. [. . .] After a long spell she seemed sinking off to sleep, but with an effort seemed to pull herself together and shook it off. This was repeated several times, with greater effort and with shorter pauses as the time moved on.

It was apparent that she did not want to sleep, so I tackled the subject at once:—"You do not want to go to sleep?" "No; I am afraid." "Afraid to go to sleep! Why so? It is the boon we all crave for." "Ah, not if you were like me—if sleep was to you a presage of horror!" "A presage of horror! What on earth do you mean?" "I don't know; oh, I don't know. And that is what is so terrible. All this weakness comes to me in sleep; until I dread the very thought."

"But, my dear girl, you may sleep to-night. I am here watching you, and I can promise that nothing will happen." [. . .] And almost at the word she gave a deep sigh of relief, and sank back, asleep. [. . .]

10 September.—I was conscious of the Professor's hand on my head, and started awake all in a second. That is one of the things that we learn in an asylum, at any rate. "And how is our patient?" "Well, when I left her, or rather when she left me," I answered. "Come, let us see," he said. [. . .]

There on the bed, seemingly in a swoon, lay poor Lucy, more horribly white and wan-looking than ever. Even the lips were white, and the gums seemed to have shrunken back from the teeth, as we sometimes see in a corpse after a prolonged illness. [. . .] He felt her heart, and after a few moments of agonizing suspense said:—"It is not too late. It beats, though but feebly. All our work is undone; we must begin again. There is no young Arthur here now; I have to call on you yourself this time, friend John."

As he spoke, he was dipping into his bag and producing the instruments for transfusion; I had taken off my coat and rolled up my shirt-sleeve. There was no possibility of an opiate just at present, and no need of one; and so, without a moment's delay, we began the operation. [. . .] It was with a feeling of personal pride that I could see a faint tinge of color steal back into the pallid cheeks and lips. No man knows, till he experiences it, what it is to feel his own life-blood drawn away into the veins of the woman he loves. The Professor watched me critically. "That will do," he said. [. . .]

[H]e looked at me carefully, and then said:—"You are not much the worse. Go into the room, and lie on your sofa, and rest awhile; then have much breakfast, and come here to me." I followed out his orders, for I knew how right and wise they were. [. . .] I think I must have continued my wonder in my dreams, for, sleeping and waking, my thoughts always came back to the little punctures in her throat and the ragged, exhausted appearance of their edges—tiny though they were.

Lucy slept well into the day, and when she woke she was fairly well and strong, though not nearly so much so as the day before. When Van Helsing had seen her, he went out for a walk, leaving me in charge, with strict injunctions that I was not to leave her for a moment. I could hear his voice in the hall, asking the way to the nearest telegraph office. [. . .]

11 September.—This afternoon I went over to Hillingham. Found Van Helsing in excellent spirits, and Lucy much better. Shortly after I had arrived, a big parcel from abroad came for the Professor. He opened it with much impressment—assumed, of course—and showed a great bundle of white flowers.

"These are for you, Miss Lucy," he said. "For me? Oh, Dr. Van Helsing!" "Yes, my dear, but not for you to play with. These are medicines." Here Lucy made a wry face. "Nay, but they are not to take in a decoction or in nauseous form, so you need not snub that so charming nose, or I shall point out to my friend Arthur what woes he may have to endure in seeing so much beauty that he so loves so much distort. Aha, my pretty miss, that bring the so nice nose all straight again. This is medicinal, but you do not know how. I put him in your window, I make pretty wreath, and hang him round your neck, so that you sleep well. . . ."

[P]resently I said:—"Well, Professor, I know you always have a reason for what you do, but this certainly puzzles me. It is well we have no sceptic here, or he would say that you were working some spell to keep out an evil spirit." "Perhaps I am!" he answered quietly . . .

Chapter XI – Lucy Westenra's Diary

Dr. Seward's Diary.

12 September.—How good they all are to me. I quite love that dear Dr. Van Helsing. I wonder why he was so anxious about these flowers. He positively frightened me, he was so fierce. And yet he must have been right, for I feel comfort from them already. [. . .]

13 September . . . Let all be put down exactly. Van Helsing and I arrived at Hillingham at eight o'clock. [. . .] When we entered we met Mrs. Westenra coming out of the morning room. She is always an early riser. She greeted us warmly and said:—"You will be glad to know that Lucy is better. The dear child is still asleep. [. . .]

I was anxious about the dear child in the night, and went into her room. She was sleeping soundly—so soundly that even my coming did not wake her. But the room was awfully stuffy. There were a lot of those horrible, strong-smelling flowers about everywhere, and she had actually a bunch of them round her neck. I feared that the heavy odor would be too much for the dear child in her weak state, so I took them all away and opened a bit of the window to let in a little fresh air. You will be pleased with her, I am sure."

She moved off into her boudoir, where she usually breakfasted early. As she had spoken, I watched the Professor's face, and saw it turn ashen grey. [. . .] But the instant she had disappeared he pulled me, suddenly and forcibly, into the dining-room and closed the door. Then, for the first time in my life, I saw Van Helsing break down. He raised his hands over his head in a sort of mute despair, and then beat his palms together in a helpless way; finally he sat down on a chair, and putting his hands before his face, began to sob, with loud, dry sobs that seemed to come from the very racking of his heart. [. . .]

[T]ogether we went up to Lucy's room. Once again I drew up the blind, whilst Van Helsing went towards the bed. This time he did not start as he looked on the poor face with the same awful, waxen pallor as before. He wore a look of stern sadness and infinite pity. "As I expected," he murmured . . .

Without a word he went and locked the door, and then began to set out on the little table the instruments for yet another operation of transfusion of blood. [. . .] "To-day you must operate. I shall provide. You are weakened already." As he spoke he took off his coat and rolled up his shirt-sleeve. Again the operation; again some return of color to the ashy cheeks, and the regular breathing of healthy sleep. This time I watched whilst Van Helsing recruited himself and rested.

Presently he took an opportunity of telling Mrs. Westenra that she must not remove anything from Lucy's room without consulting him; that the flowers were of medicinal value, and that the breathing of their odor was a part of the system of cure. Then he took over the care of the case himself, saying that he would watch this night and the next and would send me word when to come. [. . .]

Dr. Seward's Diary.

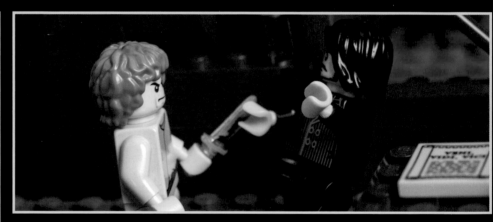

He was too quick and too strong for me, however; for before I could get my balance he had struck at me and cut my left wrist rather severely. [. . .] My wrist bled freely, and quite a little pool trickled on to the carpet. [. . .]

17 September.—I was engaged after dinner in my study . . . Suddenly the door was burst open, and in rushed my patient, with his face distorted with passion. [. . .] Without an instant's pause he made straight at me. He had a dinner-knife in his hand, and . . . I saw he was dangerous . . .

He was lying on his belly on the floor licking up, like a dog, the blood which had fallen from my wounded wrist. He was easily secured, and, to my surprise, went with the attendants quite placidly, simply repeating over and over again: "The blood is the life! The blood is the life!" [. . .]

Telegram, Van Helsing, Antwerp, to Seward, Carfax. (Sent to Carfax, Sussex, as no county given; delivered late by twenty-two hours.)

17 September.—Do not fail to be at Hillingham to-night. If not watching all the time frequently, visit and see that flowers are as placed; very important; do not fail. Shall be with you as soon as possible after arrival."

Memorandum left by Lucy Westenra.

17 September. Night.—I write this and leave it to be seen, so that no one may by any chance get into trouble through me. [. . .] I was waked by the flapping at the window . . . I was not afraid, but I did wish that Dr. Seward was in the next room—as Dr. Van Helsing said he would be—so that I might have called him. [. . .]

Then outside in the shrubbery I heard a sort of howl like a dog's, but more fierce and deeper. I went to the window and looked out, but could see nothing, except a big bat, which had evidently been buffeting its wings against the window. [. . .]

Presently the door opened, and mother looked in; seeing by my moving that I was not asleep, came in, and sat by me. She said to me even more sweetly and softly than her wont:—"I was uneasy about you, darling, and came in to see that you were all right." I feared she might catch cold sitting there, and asked her to come in and sleep with me, so she came into bed, and lay down beside me; she did not take off her dressing gown, for she said she would only stay a while and then go back to her own bed. [. . .]

After a while there was the low howl again out in the shrubbery, and shortly after there was a crash at the window, and a lot of broken glass was hurled on the floor.

The window blind blew back with the wind that rushed in, and in the aperture of the broken panes there was the head of a great, gaunt grey wolf.

Mother cried out in a fright, and struggled up into a sitting posture, and clutched wildly at anything that would help her.

Amongst other things, she clutched the wreath of flowers that Dr. Van Helsing insisted on my wearing round my neck, and tore it away from me.

For a second or two she sat up, pointing at the wolf, and there was a strange and horrible gurgling in her throat; then she fell over—as if struck with lightning . . .

The room and all round seemed to spin round. I kept my eyes fixed on the window, but the wolf drew his head back, and a whole myriad of little specks seemed to come blowing in through the broken window, and wheeling and circling round like the pillar of dust that travellers describe when there is a simoon in the desert. I tried to stir, but there was some spell upon me . . . and I remembered no more for a while. [. . .]

The sounds seemed to have awakened the maids, too, for I could hear their bare feet pattering outside my door. I called to them, and they came in, and when they saw what had happened, they screamed out. [. . .]

They were all so frightened and nervous that I directed them to go to the dining-room and have each a glass of wine. The door flew open for an instant and closed again. The maids shrieked, and then went in a body to the dining-room . . .

I was surprised that the maids did not come back. I called them, but got no answer, so I went to the dining-room to look for them. My heart sank when I saw what had happened.

They all four lay helpless on the floor, breathing heavily. The decanter of sherry was on the table half full, but there was a queer, acrid smell about. I was suspicious, and examined the decanter. It smelt of laudanum, and looking on the sideboard, I found that the bottle which mother's doctor uses for her—oh! did use—was empty.

What am I to do? what am I to do? I am back in the room with mother. I cannot leave her, and I am alone, save for the sleeping servants, whom some one has drugged. Alone with the dead! I dare not go out, for I can hear the low howl of the wolf through the broken window. [. . .] What am I to do? God shield me from harm this night! I shall hide this paper in my breast, where they shall find it when they come to lay me out. My dear mother gone! It is time that I go too. Good-bye, dear Arthur, if I should not survive this night. God keep you, dear, and God help me!

Chapter XII – Dr. Seward's Diary

18 September.—I drove at once to Hillingham and arrived early. Keeping my cab at the gate, I went up the avenue alone. I knocked gently and rang as quietly as possible, for I feared to disturb Lucy or her mother, and hoped to only bring a servant to the door. After a while, finding no response, I knocked and rang again; still no answer. [. . .] Hitherto I had blamed only the servants, but now a terrible fear began to assail me. [. . .]

[A] few seconds later I met Van Helsing running up the avenue. When he saw me, he gasped out:—"Then it was you, and just arrived. How is she? Are we too late? Did you not get my telegram?" I answered as quickly and coherently as I could that I had only got his telegram early in the morning, and had not lost a minute in coming here, and that I could not make any one in the house hear me. [. . .]

We went round to the back of the house, where there was a kitchen window. [. . .] I helped the Professor in, and followed him. [. . .] [We] found four servant-women lying on the floor. There was no need to think them dead, for their stertorous breathing and the acrid smell of laudanum in the room left no doubt as to their condition. [. . .]

Then we ascended to Lucy's room. [. . .] How shall I describe what we saw? [There] lay two women, Lucy and her mother . . . the latter showing the drawn, white face, with a look of terror fixed upon it.

By her side lay Lucy, with face white and still more drawn. The flowers which had been round her neck we found upon her mother's bosom, and her throat was bare, showing the two little wounds which we had noticed before, but looking horribly white and mangled. [. . .] [H]e cried out to me:—"It is not yet too late! Quick! quick! [. . .] You go wake those maids. Flick them in the face with a wet towel, and flick them hard. Make them get heat and fire and a warm bath. This poor soul is nearly as cold as that beside her. She will need be heated before we can do anything more."

I went at once, and found little difficulty in waking the women. [. . .] [A]s remembrance came back to them they cried and sobbed in a hysterical manner. [. . .] Fortunately, the kitchen and boiler fires were still alive, and there was no lack of hot water.

We got a bath and carried Lucy out as she was and placed her in it. Whilst we were busy chafing her limbs there was a knock at the hall door. One of the maids ran off, hurried on some more clothes, and opened it. Then she returned and whispered to us that there was a gentleman who had come with a message from Mr. Holmwood. I bade her simply tell him that he must wait, for we could see no one now. She went away with the message, and, engrossed with our work, I clean forgot all about him.

Van Helsing's sternness was somewhat relieved by a look of perplexity. He was evidently torturing his mind about something, so I waited for an instant, and he spoke:—"What are we to do now? Where are we to turn for help? We must have another transfusion of blood, and that soon, or that poor girl's life won't be worth an hour's purchase. You are exhausted already; I am exhausted too. I fear to trust those women, even if they would have courage to submit. What are we to do for some one who will open his veins for her?"

"What's the matter with me, anyhow?" The voice came across the room, and its tones brought relief and joy to my heart, for they were those of Quincey Morris. Van Helsing started angrily at the first sound, but his face softened and a glad look came into his eyes as I cried out: "Quincey Morris!" and rushed towards him with outstretched hands. "What brought you here?" I cried as our hands met. "I guess Art is the cause." He handed me a telegram:—"Have not heard from Seward for three days, and am terribly anxious. Cannot leave. Father still in same condition. Send me word how Lucy is. Do not delay.— HOLMWOOD." "I think I came just in the nick of time. You know you have only to tell me what to do." [. . .]

Once again we went through that ghastly operation. I have not the heart to go through with the details. Lucy had got a terrible shock and it told on her more than before, for though plenty of blood went into her veins, her body did not respond to the treatment as well as on the other occasions.

Her struggle back into life was something frightful to see and hear. However, the action of both heart and lungs improved, and Van Helsing made a subcutaneous injection of morphia, as before, and with good effect. Her faint became a profound slumber.

The Professor watched whilst I went downstairs with Quincey Morris. [. . .] When we were alone, he said to me:—"Jack Seward, I don't want to shove myself in anywhere where I've no right to be; but this is no ordinary case. You know I loved that girl and wanted to marry her; but, although that's all past and gone, I can't help feeling anxious about her all the same. What is it that's wrong with her? [. . .] I have not seen anything pulled down so quick since I was on the Pampas and had a mare that I was fond of go to grass all in a night. One of those big bats that they call vampires had got at her in the night, and what with his gorge and the vein left open, there wasn't enough blood in her to let her stand up, and I had to put a bullet through her as she lay. . . ."

Towards dusk she fell into a doze. Here a very odd thing occurred. Whilst still asleep she took the paper from her breast and tore it in two. Van Helsing stepped over and took the pieces from her. All the same, however, she went on with the action of tearing, as though the material were still in her hands; finally she lifted her hands and opened them as though scattering the fragments. Van Helsing seemed surprised, and his brows gathered as if in thought, but he said nothing.

September 19 . . . When the day came, its searching light showed the ravages in poor Lucy's strength. [. . .] At times she slept, and both Van Helsing and I noticed the difference in her, between sleeping and waking. Whilst asleep she looked stronger, although more haggard, and her breathing was softer; her open mouth showed the pale gums drawn back from the teeth, which thus looked positively longer and sharper than usual; when she woke the softness of her eyes evidently changed the expression, for she looked her own self, although a dying one.

In the afternoon she asked for Arthur, and we telegraphed for him. [. . .] When he arrived it was nearly six o'clock, and the sun was setting full and warm, and the red light streamed in through the window and gave more color to the pale cheeks. When he saw her, Arthur was simply choking with emotion, and none of us could speak. [. . .] Arthur's presence, however, seemed to act as a stimulant; she rallied a little, and spoke to him more brightly than she had done since we arrived. He too pulled himself together, and spoke as cheerily as he could, so that the best was made of everything. [. . .]

Letter, Mina Harker to Lucy Westenra. (Unopened by her.)

"17 September. My dearest Lucy, it seems an age since I heard from you, or indeed since I wrote. You will pardon me, I know, for all my faults when you have read all my budget of news. Well, I got my husband back all right; when we arrived at Exeter there was a carriage waiting for us, and in it, though he had an attack of gout, Mr. Hawkins. He took us to his house, where there were rooms for us all nice and comfortable, and we dined together. [...]"

Report from Patrick Hennessey, M. D., M. R. C. S. L. K. Q. C. P. I., etc., etc., to John Seward, M. D.

"20 September. My dear Sir, in accordance with your wishes, I enclose report of the conditions of everything left in my charge. [...] This afternoon a carrier's cart with two men made a call at the empty house whose grounds abut on ours—the house to which, you will remember, the patient twice ran away. The men stopped at our gate to ask the porter their way, as they were strangers. [...]

"As he passed the window of Renfield's room, the patient began to rate him from within, and called him all the foul names he could lay his tongue to. The man, who seemed a decent fellow enough, contented himself by telling him to 'shut up for a foul-mouthed beggar,' whereon our man accused him of robbing him and wanting to murder him and said that he would hinder him if he were to swing for it. [...]

[W]ithin half an hour . . . he had broken out through the window of his room, and was running down the avenue. I called to the attendants to follow me, and ran after him, for I feared he was intent on some mischief. My fear was justified when I saw the same [men who] had passed before coming down the road . . . Before I could get up to him the patient rushed at them, and pulling one of them [down], began to knock his head against the ground. If I had not seized him just at the moment I believe he would have killed the man there and then. . . ."

Letter, Mina Harker to Lucy Westenra. (Unopened by her.)

18 September . . . Mr. Hawkins has died very suddenly. [. . .] Jonathan is greatly distressed. It is not only that he feels sorrow, deep sorrow, for the dear, good man who has befriended him all his life, and now at the end has treated him like his own son and left him a fortune which to people of our modest bringing up is wealth beyond the dream of avarice. [. . .]

Dr. Seward's Diary.

20 September . . . I duly relieved Van Helsing in his watch over Lucy. [. . .] Lucy was breathing somewhat stertorously, and her face was at its worst, for the open mouth showed the pale gums. Her teeth, in the dim, uncertain light, seemed longer and sharper than they had been in the morning. [. . .] [T]here came a sort of dull flapping or buffeting at the window. I went over to it softly, and peeped out by the corner of the blind. There was a full moonlight, and I could see that the noise was made by a great bat, which wheeled round—doubtless attracted by the light, although so dim—and every now and again struck the window with its wings.

When I came back to my seat, I found that Lucy had moved slightly, and had torn away the garlic flowers from her throat. I replaced them as well as I could, and sat watching her. [. . .]

At six o'clock Van Helsing came to relieve me. [. . .] When he saw Lucy's face I could hear the sissing indraw of his breath, and he said to me in a sharp whisper: "Draw up the blind; I want light!" Then he bent down, and, with his face almost touching Lucy's, examined her carefully. [. . .] I bent over and looked, too, and as I noticed some queer chill came over me. The wounds on the throat had absolutely disappeared. For fully five minutes Van Helsing stood looking at her, with his face at its sternest. Then he turned to me and said calmly:—"She is dying. It will not be long now. Wake that poor boy, and let him come and see the last; he trusts us, and we have promised him."

I went . . . and waked him. [. . .] I assured him that Lucy was still asleep, but told him as gently as I could that both Van Helsing and I feared that the end was near. [. .] "Come," I said, "my dear old fellow, summon all your fortitude: it will be best and easiest for her."

When we came into the room she opened her eyes . . . Her breathing grew stertorous, the mouth opened, and the pale gums, drawn back, made the teeth look longer and sharper than ever. In a sort of sleep-waking, vague, unconscious way she opened her eyes, which were now dull and hard at once, and said in a soft, voluptuous voice, such as I had never heard from her lips:—"Arthur! Oh, my love, I am so glad you have come! Kiss me!" Arthur bent eagerly over to kiss her;

but at that instant Van Helsing, who, like me, had been startled by her voice, swooped upon him, and catching him by the neck with both hands, dragged him back with a fury of strength which I never thought he could have possessed, and actually hurled him almost across the room. "Not for your life!" he said; "not for your living soul and hers!" And he stood between them like a lion at bay. [. . .]

Very shortly after she opened her eyes in all their softness, and putting out her poor, pale, thin hand, took Van Helsing's great brown one; drawing it to her, she kissed it. "My true friend," she said, in a faint voice, but with untellable pathos, "My true friend, and his! Oh, guard him, and give me peace!" "I swear it!" he said solemnly, kneeling beside her and holding up his hand, as one who registers an oath. Then he turned to Arthur, and said to him: "Come, my child, take her hand in yours, and kiss her on the forehead, and only once." Their eyes met instead of their lips; and so they parted.

Lucy's eyes closed; and Van Helsing, who had been watching closely, took Arthur's arm, and drew him away. And then Lucy's breathing became stertorous again, and all at once it ceased. "It is all over," said Van Helsing. "She is dead!" [. . .] I went back to the room, and found Van Helsing looking at poor Lucy, and his face was sterner than ever. Some change had come over her body. Death had given back part of her beauty, for her brow and cheeks had recovered some of their flowing lines; even the lips had lost their deadly pallor. [. . .]

Chapter XIII – Dr. Seward's Diary (continued)

The funeral was arranged for the next succeeding day, so that Lucy and her mother might be buried together. [. . .]

Before turning in we went to look at poor Lucy. [. . .] The Professor . . . said to me: "Remain till I return," and left the room. He came back with a handful of wild garlic from the box waiting in the hall, but which had not been opened, and placed the flowers amongst the others on and around the bed. Then he took from his neck, inside his collar, a little gold crucifix, and placed it over the mouth. He restored the sheet to its place, and we came away.

I was undressing in my own room, when, with a premonitory tap at the door, he entered, and at once began to speak:—"To-morrow I want you to bring me, before night, a set of post-mortem knives." "Must we make an autopsy?" I asked. "Yes and no. I want to operate, but not as you think. Let me tell you now, but not a word to another. I want to cut off her head and take out her heart.

Ah! you a surgeon, and so shocked! [. . .]" "But why do it at all? The girl is dead. Why mutilate her poor body without need? And if there is no necessity for a post-mortem and nothing to gain by it—no good to her, to us, to science, to human knowledge—why do it? Without such it is monstrous."

For answer he put his hand on my shoulder, and said, with infinite tenderness:—". . . Were you not amazed, nay horrified, when I would not let Arthur kiss his love—though she was dying—and snatched him away by all my strength? Yes! And yet you saw how she thanked me, with her so beautiful dying eyes, her voice, too, so weak, and she kiss my rough old hand and bless me? Yes! And did you not hear me swear promise to her, that so she closed her eyes grateful? Yes! Well, I have good reason now for all I want to do. . . ."

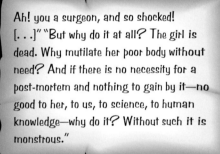

I must have slept long and soundly, for it was broad daylight when Van Helsing waked me by coming into my room. He came over to my bedside and said:—"You need not trouble about the knives; we shall not do it." "Why not?" I asked. For his solemnity of the night before had greatly impressed me. "Because," he said sternly, "it is too late—or too early. See!" Here he held up the little golden crucifix. "This was stolen in the night." [. . .]

The forenoon was a dreary time, but at noon [Arthur came, now Lord Godalming, since the sad passing of his father. He informed us that Lucy's whole estate, real and personal, was left absolutely to him] . . .

Poor fellow! He looked desperately sad and broken . . . he took my arm . . . saying huskily:—"You loved her too, old fellow; she told me all about it, and there was no friend had a closer place in her heart than you. I don't know how to thank you for all you have done for her. . . ."

God! how beautiful she was. Every hour seemed to be enhancing her loveliness. It frightened and amazed me somewhat; and as for Arthur, he fell a-trembling, and finally was shaken with doubt as with an ague. At last, after a long pause, he said to me in a faint whisper:— "Jack, is she really dead?" [. . .]

The Professor cleared his throat a couple of times, as though about to speak, and finally said:—"May I ask you something now? [. . .] I want you to give me permission to read all Miss Lucy's papers and letters. Believe me, it is no idle curiosity. [. . .] No word shall be lost; and in the good time I shall give them back to you. It's a hard thing I ask, but you will do it, will you not, for Lucy's sake?" Arthur spoke out heartily, like his old self:—"Dr. Van Helsing, you may do what you will. . . ."

Mina Harker's Journal.

It seems only yesterday that the last entry was made, and yet how much between then, in Whitby and all the world before me, Jonathan away and no news of him; and now, married to Jonathan, Jonathan a solicitor, a partner, rich, master of his business . . .

We came back to town quietly. [. . .] [W]e walked down Piccadilly. Jonathan was holding me by the arm, the way he used to in old days before I went to school. I felt it very improper, for you can't go on for some years teaching etiquette and decorum to other girls without the pedantry of it biting into yourself a bit; but it was Jonathan, and he was my husband, and we didn't know anybody who saw us—and we didn't care if they did—so on we walked. [. . .]

I felt Jonathan clutch my arm so tight that he hurt me, and he said under his breath: "My God!" [. . .] I turned to him quickly, and asked him what it was that disturbed him. He was very pale, and his eyes seemed bulging out as, half in terror and half in amazement, he gazed at a tall, thin man, with a beaky nose and black moustache and pointed beard. [. . .] His face was not a good face; it was hard, and cruel, and sensual, and his big white teeth, that looked all the whiter because his lips were so red, were pointed like an animal's. [. . .]

I asked Jonathan why he was disturbed, and he answered, evidently thinking that I knew as much about it as he did: "Do you see who it is?" "No, dear," I said; "I don't know him; who is it?" His answer seemed to shock and thrill me, for it was said as if he did not know that it was to me, Mina, to whom he was speaking:—"It is the man himself!" [. . .]

After a few minutes' staring at nothing, Jonathan's eyes closed, and he went quietly into a sleep, with his head on my shoulder. I thought it was the best thing for him, so did not disturb him. In about twenty minutes he woke up, and said to me quite cheerfully:—"Why, Mina, have I been asleep! Oh, do forgive me for being so rude. Come, and we'll have a cup of tea somewhere." He had evidently forgotten all about the dark stranger, as in his illness he had forgotten all that this episode had reminded him of.

I don't like this lapsing into forgetfulness; it may make or continue some injury to the brain. I must not ask him, for fear I shall do more harm than good; but I must somehow learn the facts of his journey abroad. The time is come, I fear, when I must open that parcel, and know what is written. Oh, Jonathan, you will, I know, forgive me if I do wrong, but it is for your own dear sake. [. . .]

During the past two or three days several cases have occurred of young children straying from home or neglecting to return from their playing on the Heath. In all these cases the children were too young to give any properly intelligible account of themselves, but the consensus of their excuses is that they had been with a "bloofer lady." [. . .]

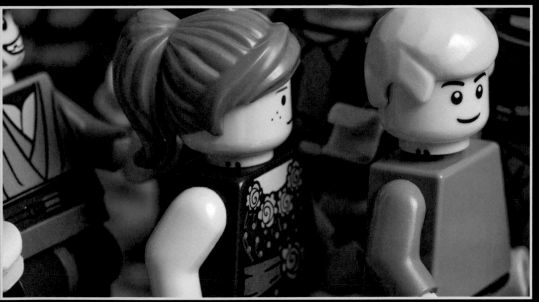

There is, however, possibly a serious side to the question, for some of the children, indeed all who have been missed at night, have been slightly torn or wounded in the throat. The wounds seem such as might be made by a rat or a small dog, and although of not much importance individually, would tend to show that whatever animal inflicts them has a system or method of its own.

The police of the division have been instructed to keep a sharp look-out for straying children, especially when very young, in and around Hampstead Heath, and for any stray dog which may be about.

Chapter XIV — Mina Harker's Journal

Letter, Van Helsing to Mrs. Harker.

Telegram, Mrs. Harker to Van Helsing.

"*24 September. (Confidence)* Dear Madam,— I pray you to pardon my writing, in that I am so far friend as that I sent to you sad news of Miss Lucy Westenra's death. [. . .] May it be that I see you? You can trust me. I am friend of Dr. John Seward and of Lord Godalming (that was Arthur of Miss Lucy). I must keep it private for the present from all. I should come to Exeter to see you at once if you tell me I am privilege to come, and where and when. I implore your pardon, madam. [. . .] I have read your letters to poor Lucy, and know how good you are and how your husband suffer; so I pray you, if it may be, enlighten him not, lest it may harm. Again your pardon, and forgive me. VAN HELSING."

"*25 September.*—Come to-day by quarter-past ten train if you can catch it. Can see you any time you call. WILHELMINA HARKER."

Mina Harker's Journal.

25 September . . . He has come and gone. Oh, what a strange meeting, and how it all makes my head whirl round! [. . .] I asked him what it was that he wanted to see me about, so he at once began:—"I have read your letters to Miss Lucy. Forgive me, but I had to begin to inquire somewhere, and there was none to ask. I know that you were with her at Whitby. She sometimes kept a diary—you need not look surprised, Madam Mina; it was begun after you had left, and was in imitation of you—and in that diary she traces by inference certain things to a sleep-walking in which she puts down that you saved her. In great perplexity then I come to you, and ask you out of your so much kindness to tell me all of it that you can remember." "I can tell you, I think, Dr. Van Helsing, all about it." "Ah, then you have good memory for facts, for details? It is not always so with young ladies." "No, doctor, but I wrote it all down at the time. I can show it to you if you like." [. . .]

I saw here an opening to ask him about Jonathan, so I said:—"He was almost recovered, but he has been greatly upset by Mr. Hawkins's death." He interrupted:— "Oh, yes, I know, I know. I have read your last two letters." I went on:—"I suppose this upset him, for when we were in town on Thursday last he had a sort of shock. He thought he saw some one who recalled something terrible, something which led to his brain fever." And here the whole thing seemed to overwhelm me in a rush. The pity for Jonathan, the horror which he experienced, the whole fearful mystery of his diary, and the fear that has been brooding over me ever since, all came in a tumult. I suppose I was hysterical, for I threw myself on my knees and held up my hands to him, and implored him to make my husband well again. [. . .]

"If you will let me, I shall give you a paper to read. It is long, but I have typewritten it out. It will tell you my trouble and Jonathan's. It is the copy of his journal when abroad, and all that happened. I dare not say anything of it; you will read for yourself and judge. And then when I see you, perhaps, you will be very kind and tell me what you think." "I promise," he said as I gave him the papers. [. . .]

Letter (by hand), Van Helsing to Mrs. Harker.

"25 September, 6 o'clock. Dear Madam Mina,— I have read your husband's so wonderful diary. You may sleep without doubt. Strange and terrible as it is, it is true! I will pledge my life on it. [. . .]"

Dr. Seward's Diary.

26 September . . . Renfield had become, to all intents, as sane as he ever was. He was already well ahead with his fly business; and he had just started in the spider line also; so he had not been of any trouble to me. . . .

To-day [Van Helsing] came back, and almost bounded into the room at about half-past five o'clock, and thrust last night's "Westminster Gazette" into my hand. "What do you think of that?" he asked as he stood back and folded his arms. I looked over the paper, for I really did not know what he meant; but he took it from me and pointed out a paragraph about children being decoyed away at Hampstead. It did not convey much to me, until I reached a passage where it described small punctured wounds on their throats. An idea struck me, and I looked up. "Well?" he said. "It is like poor Lucy's." "And what do you make of it?" "Simply that there is some cause in common. Whatever it was that injured her has injured them." I did not quite understand his answer:—"That is true indirectly, but not directly."

"How do you mean, Professor?" I asked. I was a little inclined to take his seriousness lightly—for, after all, four days of rest and freedom from burning, harrowing anxiety does help to restore one's spirits—but when I saw his face, it sobered me. Never, even in the midst of our despair about poor Lucy, had he looked more stern. "Tell me!" I said. "I can hazard no opinion. I do not know what to think, and I have no data on which to found a conjecture."

"Do you mean to tell me, friend John, that you have no suspicion as to what poor Lucy died of; not after all the hints given, not only by events, but by me? [. . .] You are clever man, friend John; you reason well, and your wit is bold; but you are too prejudiced. You do not let your eyes see nor your ears hear, and that which is outside your daily life is not of account to you. Do you not think that there are things which you cannot understand, and yet which are; that some people see things that others cannot? [. . .]"

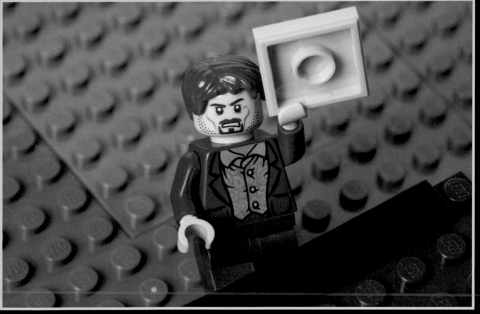

[H]e said . . . "I want you to believe." "To believe what?" "To believe in things that you cannot. Let me illustrate. I heard once of an American who so defined faith: 'that faculty which enables us to believe things which we know to be untrue.' For one, I follow that man. He meant that we shall have an open mind, and not let a little bit of truth check the rush of a big truth, like a small rock does a railway truck. [. . .]

Now that you are willing to understand, you have taken the first step to understand. You think then that those so small holes in the children's throats were made by the same that made the hole in Miss Lucy?" "I suppose so."

He stood up and said solemnly:—"Then you are wrong. Oh, would it were so! but alas! no. It is worse, far, far worse." "In God's name, Professor Van Helsing, what do you mean?" I cried. He threw himself with a despairing gesture into a chair, and placed his elbows on the table, covering his face with his hands as he spoke:—"They were made by Miss Lucy!"

Chapter XV – Dr. Seward's Diary

For a while sheer anger mastered me; it was as if he had during her life struck Lucy on the face. I smote the table hard and rose up as I said to him:—"Dr. Van Helsing, are you mad?"

He raised his head and looked at me, and somehow the tenderness of his face calmed me at once. "Would I were!" he said. "Madness were easy to bear compared with truth like this. [. . .] It is so hard to accept at once any abstract truth, that we may doubt such to be possible when we have always believed the 'no' of it; it is more hard still to accept so sad a concrete truth, and of such a one as Miss Lucy. To-night I go to prove it. Dare you come with me? [. . .]

"Come, I tell you what I propose: first, that we go off now and see that child in the hospital. Dr. Vincent, of the North Hospital, where the papers say the child is, is friend of mine, and I think of yours since you were in class at Amsterdam. [. . .] And then——" "And then?" He took a key from his pocket and held it up. "And then we spend the night, you and I, in the churchyard where Lucy lies. . . ."

We found the child awake. It had had a sleep and taken some food, and altogether was going on well.

Dr. Vincent took the bandage from its throat, and showed us the punctures. There was no mistaking the similarity to those which had been on Lucy's throat. They were smaller, and the edges looked fresher; that was all. [. . .]

Dr. Vincent says the children have made up a new fairytale, as they all talk of a "bloofer" (or "beautiful") lady. ". . . Even this poor little mite, when he woke up to-day, asked the nurse if he might go away. When she asked him why he wanted to go, he said he wanted to play with the 'bloofer lady.'"

"I hope," said Van Helsing, "that when you are sending the child home you will caution its parents to keep strict watch over it. These fancies to stray are most dangerous; and if the child were to remain out another night, it would probably be fatal. . . ."

At last we reached the wall of the churchyard, which we climbed over. With some little difficulty—for it was very dark, and the whole place seemed so strange to us—we found the Westenra tomb. [. . .]

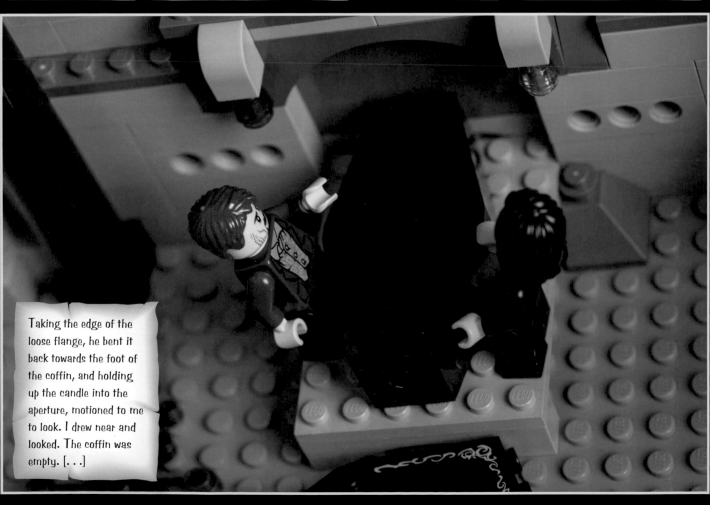

Taking the edge of the loose flange, he bent it back towards the foot of the coffin, and holding up the candle into the aperture, motioned to me to look. I drew near and looked. The coffin was empty. [. . .]

"Are you satisfied now, friend John?" he asked. I felt all the dogged argumentativeness of my nature awake within me as I answered him:—"I am satisfied that Lucy's body is not in that coffin; but that only proves one thing." "And what is that, friend John?" "That it is not there." "That is good logic," he said, "so far as it goes. But how do you—how can you—account for it not being there?" "Perhaps a body-snatcher," I suggested. "Some of the undertaker's people may have stolen it." I felt that I was speaking folly, and yet it was the only real cause which I could suggest. The Professor sighed. "Ah well!" he said, "we must have more proof. Come with me." [. . .]

Then he told me to watch at one side of the churchyard whilst he would watch at the other. I took up my place behind a yew-tree, and I saw his dark figure move until the intervening headstones and trees hid it from my sight.

It was a lonely vigil. [. . .] I was too cold and too sleepy to be keenly observant, and not sleepy enough to betray my trust so altogether I had a dreary, miserable time. Suddenly, as I turned round, I thought I saw something like a white streak, moving between two dark yew-trees at the side of the churchyard farthest from the tomb; at the same time a dark mass moved from the Professor's side of the ground, and hurriedly went towards it. [. . .]

The tomb itself was hidden by trees, and I could not see where the figure disappeared. I heard the rustle of actual movement where I had first seen the white figure, and coming over, found the Professor holding in his arms a tiny child.

When he saw me he held it out to me, and said:—"Are you satisfied now?" "No," I said, in a way that I felt was aggressive. "Do you not see the child?" "Yes, it is a child, but who brought it here? And is it wounded?" I asked. "We shall see," said the Professor, and with one impulse we took our way out of the churchyard, he carrying the sleeping child. [. . .] I cannot sleep, so I make this entry. But I must try to get a few hours' sleep, as Van Helsing is to call for me at noon. He insists that I shall go with him on another expedition.

27 September . . . The place was not so gruesome as last night, but oh, how unutterably mean-looking when the sunshine streamed in. Van Helsing walked over to Lucy's coffin, and I followed. He bent over and again forced back the leaden flange; and then a shock of surprise and dismay shot through me. There lay Lucy, seemingly just as we had seen her the night before her funeral. She was, if possible, more radiantly beautiful than ever; and I could not believe that she was dead. The lips were red, nay redder than before; and on the cheeks was a delicate bloom. [. . .]

"Are you convinced now?" said the Professor in response, and as he spoke he put over his hand, and in a way that made me shudder, pulled back the dead lips and showed the white teeth. [. . .] "She may have been placed here since last night." "Indeed? That is so, and by whom?" "I do not know. Some one has done it." "And yet she has been dead one week. Most peoples in that time would not look so." I had no answer for this, so was silent. [. . .]

Then he turned to me and said:—"Here, there is one thing which is different from all recorded; here is some dual life that is not as the common. She was bitten by the vampire when she was in a trance, sleep-walking . . . and in trance could he best come to take more blood. In trance she died, and in trance she is Un-Dead, too. So it is that she differ from all other. Usually when the Un-Dead sleep at home"—as he spoke he made a comprehensive sweep of his arm to designate what to a vampire was "home"—"their face show what they are, but this so sweet that was when she not Un-Dead she go back to the nothings of the common dead. There is no malign there, see, and so it make hard that I must kill her in her sleep."

This turned my blood cold, and it began to dawn upon me that I was accepting Van Helsing's theories; but if she were really dead, what was there of terror in the idea of killing her? He looked up at me, and evidently saw the change in my face, for he said almost joyously:— "Ah, you believe now?" I answered: "Do not press me too hard all at once. I am willing to accept. How will you do this bloody work?" "I shall cut off her head and fill her mouth with garlic, and I shall drive a stake through her body."

It made me shudder to think of so mutilating the body of the woman whom I had loved. And yet the feeling was not so strong as I had expected. I was, in fact, beginning to shudder at the presence of this being, this Un-Dead, as Van Helsing called it, and to loathe it. [. . .]

"My mind is made up. Let us go. You return home for to-night to your asylum, and see that all be well. As for me, I shall spend the night here in this churchyard in my own way. To-morrow night you will come to me to the Berkeley Hotel at ten of the clock. I shall send for Arthur to come too, and also that so fine young man of America that gave his blood. Later we shall all have work to do. [. . .]

Note left by Van Helsing in his portmanteau, Berkeley Hotel directed to John Seward, M. D. (Not delivered.)

"*27 September.* Friend John . . . I go alone to watch in that churchyard. It pleases me that the Un-Dead, Miss Lucy, shall not leave to-night, that so on the morrow night she may be more eager. Therefore I shall fix some things she like not—garlic and a crucifix—and so seal up the door of the tomb. She is young as Un-Dead, and will heed. [. . .]

Dr. Seward's Diary.

28 September.—It is wonderful what a good night's sleep will do for one. Yesterday I was almost willing to accept Van Helsing's monstrous ideas; but now they seem to start out lurid before me as outrages on common sense. I have no doubt that he believes it all. I wonder if his mind can have become in any way unhinged. Surely there must be some rational explanation of all these mysterious things. [. . .]

29 September, morning . . . Last night, at a little before ten o'clock, Arthur and Quincey came into Van Helsing's room; he told us all that he wanted us to do, but especially addressing himself to Arthur, as if all our wills were centred in his. [. . .] After a pause Van Helsing went on, evidently with an effort:—"Miss Lucy is dead; is it not so? Yes! Then there can be no wrong to her. [. . .] There are mysteries which men can only guess at, which age by age they may solve only in part. Believe me, we are now on the verge of one. But I have not done. May I cut off the head of dead Miss Lucy?" "Heavens and earth, no!" cried Arthur in a storm of passion. "Not for the wide world will I consent to any mutilation of her dead body. . . ."

Van Helsing rose up from where he had all the time been seated, and said, gravely and sternly:—"My Lord Godalming, I, too, have a duty to do, a duty to others, a duty to you, a duty to the dead; and, by God, I shall do it! All I ask you now is that you come with me, that you look and listen . . .

"But, I beseech you, do not go forth in anger with me. In a long life of acts which were often not pleasant to do, and which sometimes did wring my heart, I have never had so heavy a task as now. . . . I have come here from my own land to do what I can of good; at the first to please my friend John, and then to help a sweet young lady, whom, too, I came to love. For her . . . I gave what you gave; the blood of my veins; I gave it, I, who was not, like you, her lover, but only her physician and her friend. I gave to her my nights and days—before death, after death; and if my death can do her good even now, when she is the dead Un-Dead, she shall have it freely."

He said this with a very grave, sweet pride, and Arthur was much affected by it. He took the old man's hand and said in a broken voice:—"Oh, it is hard to think of it, and I cannot understand; but at least I shall go with you and wait."

Chapter XVI – Dr. Seward's Diary (continued)

It was just a quarter before twelve o'clock when we got into the churchyard over the low wall. The night was dark with occasional gleams of moonlight between the rents of the heavy clouds that scudded across the sky. We all kept somehow close together, with Van Helsing slightly in front as he led the way. [. . .]

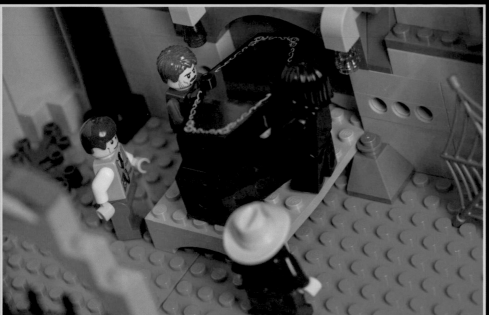

The Professor unlocked the door, and seeing a natural hesitation amongst us for various reasons, solved the difficulty by entering first himself. The rest of us followed, and he closed the door. He then lit a dark lantern and pointed to the coffin. Arthur stepped forward hesitatingly; Van Helsing said to me:—"You were with me here yesterday. Was the body of Miss Lucy in that coffin?" "It was."

The Professor turned to the rest saying:—"You hear; and yet there is no one who does not believe with me." He took his screwdriver and again took off the lid of the coffin. Arthur looked on, very pale but silent; when the lid was removed he stepped forward. [. . .] Van Helsing forced back the leaden flange, and we all looked in and recoiled. The coffin was empty!

For several minutes no one spoke a word. The silence was broken by Quincey Morris: "Professor, I answered for you. Your word is all I want. I wouldn't ask such a thing ordinarily—I wouldn't so dishonor you as to imply a doubt; but this is a mystery that goes beyond any honor or dishonor. Is this your doing?"

"I swear to you by all that I hold sacred that I have not removed nor touched her. What happened was this: Two nights ago my friend Seward and I came here—with good purpose, believe me. I opened that coffin, which was then sealed up, and we found it, as now, empty. We then waited, and saw something white come through the trees. The next day we came here in day-time, and she lay there. Did she not, friend John?" "Yes." [. . .]

He opened the door, and we filed out, he coming last and locking the door behind him. [. . .] Each in his own way was solemn and overcome. [. . .] As to Van Helsing, he was employed in a definite way. First he took from his bag a mass of what looked like thin, wafer-like biscuit, which was carefully rolled up in a white napkin; next he took out a double-handful of some whitish stuff, like dough or putty. He crumbled the wafer up fine and worked it into the mass between his hands. This he then took, and rolling it into thin strips, began to lay them into the crevices between the door and its setting in the tomb. I was somewhat puzzled at this, and being close, asked him what it was that he was doing. Arthur and Quincey drew near also, as they too were curious. He answered:—"I am closing the tomb, so that the Un-Dead may not enter." [. . .] "What is that which you are using?" This time the question was by Arthur. Van Helsing reverently lifted his hat as he answered:—"The Host. I brought it from Amsterdam. I have an Indulgence." [. . .]

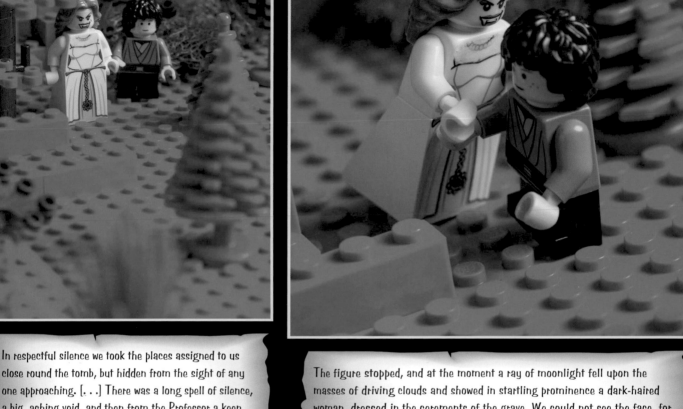

In respectful silence we took the places assigned to us close round the tomb, but hidden from the sight of any one approaching. [. . .] There was a long spell of silence, a big, aching void, and then from the Professor a keen "S-s-s-s!" He pointed; and far down the avenue of yews we saw a white figure advance—a dim white figure, which held something dark at its breast.

The figure stopped, and at the moment a ray of moonlight fell upon the masses of driving clouds and showed in startling prominence a dark-haired woman, dressed in the cerements of the grave. We could not see the face, for it was bent down over what we saw to be a fair-haired child. There was a pause and a sharp little cry, such as a child gives in sleep, or a dog as it lies before the fire and dreams. [. . .]

It was now near enough for us to see clearly, and the moonlight still held. My own heart grew cold as ice, and I could hear the gasp of Arthur, as we recognized the features of Lucy Westenra. Lucy Westenra, but yet how changed. [. . .]

The sweetness was turned to adamantine, heartless cruelty, and the purity to voluptuous wantonness. [. . .] Van Helsing raised his lantern and drew the slide; by the concentrated light that fell on Lucy's face we could see that the lips were crimson with fresh blood, and that the stream had trickled over her chin and stained the purity of her lawn death-robe. [. . .]

When Lucy—I call the thing that was before us Lucy because it bore her shape—saw us she drew back with an angry snarl, such as a cat gives when taken unawares; then her eyes ranged over us. Lucy's eyes in form and color; but Lucy's eyes unclean and full of hell-fire, instead of the pure, gentle orbs we knew. [. . .]

She still advanced, and with a languorous, voluptuous grace, said:—"Come to me, Arthur. Leave these others and come to me. My arms are hungry for you. Come, and we can rest together. Come, my husband, come!"

There was something diabolically sweet in her tones—something of the tingling of glass when struck—which rang through the brains even of us who heard the words addressed to another. As for Arthur, he seemed under a spell; moving his hands from his face, he opened wide his arms. [. . .]

She recoiled from it, and, with a suddenly distorted face, full of rage, dashed past him as if to enter the tomb. When within a foot or two of the door, however, she stopped, as if arrested by some irresistible force.

She was leaping for them, when Van Helsing sprang forward and held between them his little golden crucifix.

Then she turned, and her face was shown in the clear burst of moonlight and by the lamp, which had now no quiver from Van Helsing's iron nerves. Never did I see such baffled malice on a face; and never, I trust, shall such ever be seen again by mortal eyes. The beautiful color became livid, the eyes seemed to throw out sparks of hell-fire, the brows were wrinkled as though the folds of the flesh were the coils of Medusa's snakes, and the lovely, blood-stained mouth grew to an open square, as in the passion masks of the Greeks and Japanese. If ever a face meant death—if looks could kill—we saw it at that moment. [. . .]

Van Helsing broke the silence by asking Arthur:— "Answer me, oh my friend! Am I to proceed in my work?" Arthur threw himself on his knees, and hid his face in his hands, as he answered:—"Do as you will, friend; do as you will. There can be no horror like this ever any more;" and he groaned in spirit. [. . .] We could hear the click of the closing lantern as Van Helsing held it down; coming close to the tomb, he began to remove from the chinks some of the sacred emblem which he had placed there.

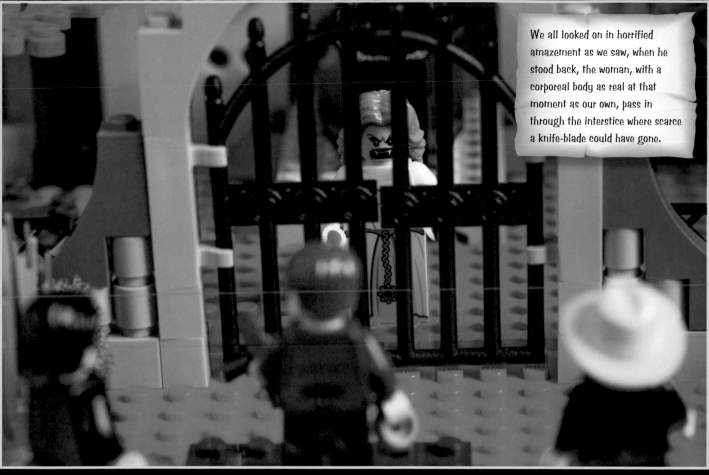

We all looked on in horrified amazement as we saw, when he stood back, the woman, with a corporeal body as real at that moment as our own, pass in through the interstice where scarce a knife-blade could have gone.

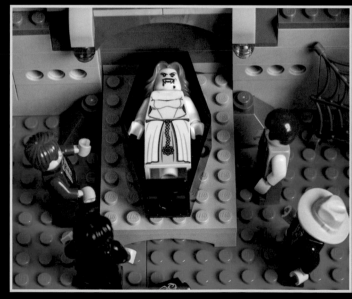

We all felt a glad sense of relief when we saw the Professor calmly restoring the strings of putty to the edges of the door. When this was done, he lifted the child and said: "Come now, my friends; we can do no more till to-morrow. [. . .]"

29 September, night . . . We got to the churchyard by half-past one, and strolled about, keeping out of official observation . . . When we were alone and had heard the last of the footsteps die out up the road, we silently, and as if by ordered intention, followed the Professor to the tomb. [. . .] When he again lifted the lid off Lucy's coffin we all looked—Arthur trembling like an aspen—and saw that the body lay there in all its death-beauty. But there was no love in my own heart, nothing but loathing for the foul Thing which had taken Lucy's shape without her soul. [. . .]

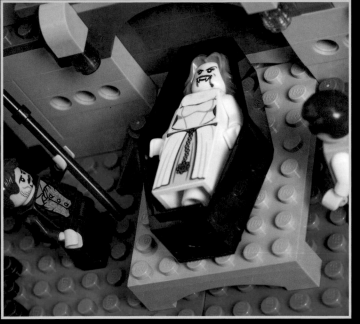

When all was ready, Van Helsing said:—". . . [W]hen this now Un-Dead be made to rest as true dead, then the soul of the poor lady whom we love shall again be free. Instead of working wickedness by night and growing more debased in the assimilating of it by day, she shall take her place with the other Angels. So that, my friend, it will be a blessed hand for her that shall strike the blow that sets her free. . . ."

We all looked at Arthur. He saw, too, what we all did, the infinite kindness which suggested that his should be the hand which would restore Lucy to us as a holy, and not an unholy, memory; he stepped forward and said bravely, though his hand trembled, and his face was as pale as snow:—"My true friend, from the bottom of my broken heart I thank you. Tell me what I am to do, and I shall not falter!" [. . .]

Arthur took the stake and the hammer, and when once his mind was set on action his hands never trembled nor even quivered. [. . .] Arthur placed the point over the heart, and as I looked I could see its dint in the white flesh. Then he struck with all his might. The Thing in the coffin writhed; and a hideous, blood-curdling screech came from the opened red lips. The body shook and quivered and twisted in wild contortions; the sharp white teeth champed together till the lips were cut, and the mouth was smeared with a crimson foam. But Arthur never faltered. He looked like a figure of Thor as his untrembling arm rose and fell, driving deeper and deeper the mercy-bearing stake, whilst the blood from the pierced heart welled and spurted up around it. His face was set, and high duty seemed to shine through it; the sight of it gave us courage so that our voices seemed to ring through the little vault. And then the writhing and quivering of the body became less, and the teeth seemed to champ, and the face to quiver. Finally it lay still. The terrible task was over. [. . .]

There, in the coffin lay no longer the foul Thing that we had so dreaded and grown to hate that the work of her destruction was yielded as a privilege to the one best entitled to it, but Lucy as we had seen her in her life, with her face of unequalled sweetness and purity. [...]

Van Helsing came and laid his hand on Arthur's shoulder, and said to him:—"And now, Arthur my friend, dear lad, am I not forgiven?" The reaction of the terrible strain came as he took the old man's hand in his, and raising it to his lips, pressed it, and said:—"Forgiven! God bless you that you have given my dear one her soul again, and me peace." [...]

Before we moved away Van Helsing said:—"Now, my friends, one step of our work is done, one the most harrowing to ourselves. But there remains a greater task: to find out the author of all this our sorrow and to stamp him out. [...] Two nights hence you shall meet with me and dine together at seven of the clock with friend John. [...] Then our promise shall be made to each other anew; for there is a terrible task before us, and once our feet are on the ploughshare we must not draw back."

Chapter XVII — Dr. Seward's Diary (continued)

When we arrived at the Berkeley Hotel, Van Helsing found a telegram waiting for him:— "Am coming up by train. Jonathan at Whitby. Important news.—MINA HARKER." The Professor was delighted. "Ah, that wonderful Madam Mina," he said, "pearl among women! She arrive, but I cannot stay. She must go to your house, friend John. You must meet her at the station. Telegraph her en route, so that she may be prepared." When the wire was dispatched he had a cup of tea; over it he told me of a diary kept by Jonathan Harker when abroad, and gave me a typewritten copy of it, as also of Mrs. Harker's diary at Whitby. "Take these," he said, "and study them well. When I have returned you will be master of all the facts, and we can then better enter on our inquisition. Keep them safe, for there is in them much of treasure. . . ."

Mina Harker's Journal.

He then made ready for his departure, and shortly after drove off to Liverpool Street. I took my way to Paddington, [to meet Mrs. Harker at her train] . . . I got her luggage, which included a typewriter, and we took the Underground to Fenchurch Street, after I had sent a wire to my housekeeper to have a sitting-room and bedroom prepared at once for Mrs. Harker. In due time we arrived. She knew, of course, that the place was a lunatic asylum, but I could see that she was unable to repress a shudder when we entered. [. . .]

29 September.—After I had tidied myself, I went down to Dr. Seward's study. [. . .] [I said to him,] "You helped to attend dear Lucy at the end. Let me hear how she died; for all that I know of her, I shall be very grateful. She was very, very dear to me." To my surprise, he answered, with a horrorstruck look in his face:— "Tell you of her death? Not for the wide world!"

"Why not?" I asked, for some grave, terrible feeling was coming over me. [. . .] By this time my mind was made up that the diary of a doctor who attended Lucy might have something to add to the sum of our knowledge of that terrible Being, and I said boldly:— "Then, Dr. Seward, you had better let me copy it out for you on my typewriter." He grew to a positively deathly pallor as he said:— "No! no! no! For all the world, I wouldn't let you know that terrible story!" [. . .] "You do not know me," I said. "When you have read those papers—my own diary and my husband's also, which I have typed—you will know me better. . . ."

Dr. Seward's Diary.

30 September . . . Strange that it never struck me that the very next house might be the Count's hiding-place! Goodness knows that we had enough clues from the conduct of the patient Renfield! The bundle of letters relating to the purchase of the house were with the typescript. Oh, if we had only had them earlier we might have saved poor Lucy! Harker has gone back, and is again collating his material. He says that by dinner-time they will be able to show a whole connected narrative. He thinks that in the meantime I should see Renfield, as hitherto he has been a sort of index to the coming and going of the Count. [. . .]

I found Renfield sitting placidly in his room with his hands folded, smiling benignly. At the moment he seemed as sane as any one I ever saw. I sat down and talked with him on a lot of subjects, all of which he treated naturally. He then, of his own accord, spoke of going home, a subject he has never mentioned to my knowledge during his sojourn here. In fact, he spoke quite confidently of getting his discharge at once. I believe that, had I not had the chat with Harker and read the letters and the dates of his outbursts, I should have been prepared to sign for him after a brief time of observation. As it is, I am darkly suspicious. All those outbreaks were in some way linked with the proximity of the Count. What then does this absolute content mean? Can it be that his instinct is satisfied as to the vampire's ultimate triumph? [. . .]

Jonathan Harker's Journal.

29 September, in train to London . . . It was now my object to trace that horrid cargo of the Count's to its place in London. [. . .] I saw the invoice, and took note of it: "Fifty cases of common earth, to be used for experimental purposes." [. . .] [N]o one could add to the simple description "Fifty cases of common earth."

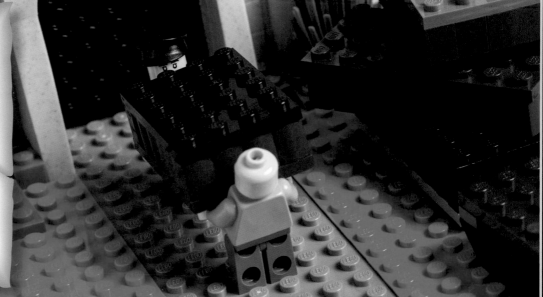

30 September . . . Of one thing I am now satisfied: that *all* the boxes which arrived at Whitby from Varna in the Demeter were safely deposited in the old chapel at Carfax. There should be fifty of them there, unless any have since been removed—as from Dr. Seward's diary I fear. I shall try to see the carter who took away the boxes from Carfax when Renfield attacked them. By following up this clue we may learn a good deal. [. . .]

Mina Harker's Journal.

30 September.—I am so glad that I hardly know how to contain myself. It is, I suppose, the reaction from the haunting fear which I have had: that this terrible affair and the reopening of his old wound might act detrimentally on Jonathan. The effort has, however, done him good. He was never so resolute, never so strong, never so full of volcanic energy, as at present. [. . .]

Later.—Lord Godalming and Mr. Morris arrived earlier than we expected. Dr. Seward was out on business, and had taken Jonathan with him, so I had to see them. It was to me a painful meeting, for it brought back all poor dear Lucy's hopes of only a few months ago. Of course they had heard Lucy speak of me, and it seemed that Dr. Van Helsing, too, has been quite "blowing my trumpet," as Mr. Morris expressed it. [. . .]

[W]hen Lord Godalming found himself alone with me he sat down on the sofa and gave way utterly and openly. I sat down beside him and took his hand. [. . .] I said to him, for I could see that his heart was breaking:— "I loved dear Lucy, and I know what she was to you, and what you were to her. She and I were like sisters; and now she is gone, will you not let me be like a sister to you in your trouble? I know what sorrows you have had, though I cannot measure the depth of them. If sympathy and pity can help in your affliction, won't you let me be of some little service—for Lucy's sake?" In an instant the poor dear fellow was overwhelmed with grief. It seemed to me that all that he had of late been suffering in silence found a vent at once. He grew quite hysterical, and raising his open hands, beat his palms together in a perfect agony of grief. He stood up and then sat down again, and the tears rained down his cheeks. I felt an infinite pity for him, and opened my arms unthinkingly. With a sob he laid his head on my shoulder and cried like a wearied child, whilst he shook with emotion. [. . .]

Chapter XVIII – Dr. Seward's Diary

When I went into the room, I told the man that a lady would like to see him . . . "Oh, very well," he said; "let her come in, by all means; but just wait a minute till I tidy up the place." His method of tidying was peculiar: he simply swallowed all the flies and spiders in the boxes before I could stop him. It was quite evident that he feared, or was jealous of, some interference. When he had got through his disgusting task, he said cheerfully: "Let the lady come in," and sat down on the edge of his bed with his head down, but with his eyelids raised so that he could see her as she entered. [. . .]

30 September . . . [Mrs. Harker came see me today. She] said:— "Dr. Seward, may I ask a favour? I want to see your patient, Mr. Renfield. Do let me see him. What you have said of him in your diary interests me so much!" She looked so appealing and so pretty that I could not refuse her, and there was no possible reason why I should; so I took her with me.

We continued to talk for some time; and, seeing that he was seemingly quite reasonable, she ventured, looking at me questioningly as she began, to lead him to his favourite topic. I was again astonished, for he addressed himself to the question with the impartiality of the completest sanity; he even took himself as an example when he mentioned certain things.

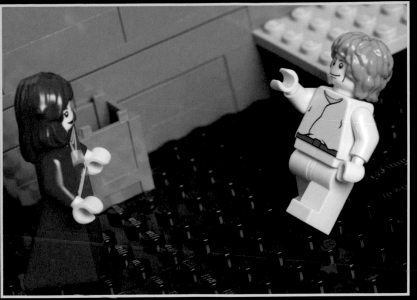

"Why, I myself am an instance of a man who had a strange belief. Indeed, it was no wonder that my friends were alarmed, and insisted on my being put under control. I used to fancy that life was a positive and perpetual entity, and that by consuming a multitude of live things, no matter how low in the scale of creation, one might indefinitely prolong life. At times I held the belief so strongly that I actually tried to take human life. . . ." Looking at my watch, I saw that I should go to the station to meet Van Helsing, so I told Mrs. Harker that it was time to leave. She came at once, after saying pleasantly to Mr. Renfield: "Good-bye, and I hope I may see you often, under auspices pleasanter to yourself," to which, to my astonishment, he replied:— "Good-bye, my dear. I pray God I may never see your sweet face again. May He bless and keep you!" [. . .]

And so now, up to this very hour, all the records we have are complete and in order. The Professor took away one copy to study after dinner, and before our meeting, which is fixed for nine o'clock. The rest of us have already read everything; so when we meet in the study we shall all be informed as to facts, and can arrange our plan of battle with this terrible and mysterious enemy.

Mina Harker's Journal.

30 September.—When we met in Dr. Seward's study two hours after dinner, which had been at six o'clock, we unconsciously formed a sort of board or committee. Professor Van Helsing took the head of the table, to which Dr. Seward motioned him as he came into the room. He made me sit next to him on his right, and asked me to act as secretary; Jonathan sat next to me. Opposite us were Lord Godalming, Dr. Seward, and Mr. Morris—Lord Godalming being next the Professor, and Dr. Seward in the center.

"There are such beings as vampires; some of us have evidence that they exist. [. . .] The *nosferatu* do not die like the bee when he sting once. He is only stronger; and being stronger, have yet more power to work evil. This vampire which is amongst us is of himself so strong in person as twenty men; he is of cunning more than mortal, for his cunning be the growth of ages; he have still the aids of necromancy, which is, as his etymology imply, the divination by the dead, and all the dead that he can come nigh to are for him at command . . .

"My friends, this is much; it is a terrible task that we undertake, and there may be consequence to make the brave shudder. For if we fail in this our fight he must surely win; and then where end we? Life is nothings; I heed him not. But to fail here, is not mere life or death. It is that we become as him; that we henceforward become foul things of the night like him—without heart or conscience, preying on the bodies and the souls of those we love best. To us for ever are the gates of heaven shut; for who shall open them to us again? [. . .] What say you?" [. . .] When the Professor had done speaking my husband looked in my eyes, and I in his; there was no need for speaking between us. "I answer for Mina and myself," he said. "Count me in, Professor," said Mr. Quincey Morris, laconically as usual. "I am with you," said Lord Godalming, "for Lucy's sake, if for no other reason." Dr. Seward simply nodded. The Professor stood up and, after laying his golden crucifix on the table, held out his hand on either side. I took his right hand, and Lord Godalming his left; Jonathan held my right with his left and stretched across to Mr. Morris. So as we all took hands our solemn compact was made. [. . .]

"[L]et us consider the limitations of the vampire in general, and of this one in particular. All we have to go upon are traditions and superstitions. [. . .] He throws no shadow; he make in the mirror no reflect, as again Jonathan observe. He has the strength of many of his hand—witness again Jonathan when he shut the door against the wolfs, and when he help him from the diligence too. He can transform himself to wolf, as we gather from the ship arrival in Whitby . . .

"he can be as bat, as Madam Mina saw him on the window at Whitby, and as friend John saw him fly from this so near house, and as my friend Quincey saw him at the window of Miss Lucy. [. . .]

"Ah, but hear me through. He can do all these things, yet he is not free. [. . .] He cannot go where he lists; he who is not of nature has yet to obey some of nature's laws—why we know not. He may not enter anywhere at the first, unless there be some one of the household who bid him to come; though afterwards he can come as he please.

"His power ceases, as does that of all evil things, at the coming of the day. Only at certain times can he have limited freedom. If he be not at the place whither he is bound, he can only change himself at noon or at exact sunrise or sunset. [. . .]

145

"Then there are things which so afflict him that he has no power, as the garlic that we know of; and as for things sacred, as this symbol, my crucifix, that was amongst us even now when we resolve, to them he is nothing, but in their presence he take his place far off and silent with respect. There are others, too, which I shall tell you of, lest in our seeking we may need them. The branch of wild rose on his coffin keep him that he move not from it; a sacred bullet fired into the coffin kill him so that he be true dead; and as for the stake through him, we know already of its peace; or the cut-off head that giveth rest. We have seen it with our eyes. . . ."

Whilst we were talking Mr. Morris was looking steadily at the window, and he now got up quietly, and went out of the room. [. . .] Here we were interrupted in a very startling way. Outside the house came the sound of a pistol-shot; the glass of the window was shattered with a bullet, which, ricocheting from the top of the embrasure, struck the far wall of the room. [. . .]

A minute later he came in and said:— "It was an idiotic thing of me to do, and I ask your pardon, Mrs. Harker, most sincerely; I fear I must have frightened you terribly. But the fact is that whilst the Professor was talking there came a big bat and sat on the window-sill. I have got such a horror of the damned brutes from recent events that I cannot stand them, and I went out to have a shot, as I have been doing of late of evenings, whenever I have seen one. . . ." "Did you hit it?" asked Dr. Van Helsing. "I don't know; I fancy not, for it flew away into the wood."

Without saying any more he took his seat, and the Professor began to resume his statement:— "We must trace each of these boxes; and when we are ready, we must either capture or kill this monster in his lair; or we must, so to speak, sterilize the earth, so that no more he can seek safety in it. . . ."

Dr. Seward's Diary.

1 October, 4 a. m.—Just as we were about to leave the house, an urgent message was brought to me from Renfield to know if I would see him at once, as he had something of the utmost importance to say to me. [. . .] I said: "All right; I'll go now"; and I asked the others to join me, as I went to see my "patient." [. . .]

We found him in a state of considerable excitement, but far more rational in his speech and manner than I had ever seen him. [. . .] His request was that I would at once release him from the asylum and send him home. This he backed up with arguments regarding his complete recovery, and adduced his own existing sanity. [. . .]

I felt under a strong impulse to tell him that I was satisfied as to his sanity, and would see about the necessary formalities for his release in the morning. I thought it better to wait, however, before making so grave a statement, for of old I knew the sudden changes to which this particular patient was liable. So I contented myself with making a general statement that he appeared to be improving very rapidly; that I would have a longer chat with him in the morning, and would then see what I could do in the direction of meeting his wishes. This did not at all satisfy him, for he said quickly:— "But I fear, Dr. Seward, that you hardly apprehend my wish. I desire to go at once—here—now—this very hour—this very moment, if I may. . . ."

Van Helsing was gazing at him with a look of utmost intensity, his bushy eyebrows almost meeting with the fixed concentration of his look. He said to Renfield . . . "Can you not tell frankly your real reason for wishing to be free to-night? I will undertake that if you will satisfy even me—a stranger, without prejudice, and with the habit of keeping an open mind—Dr. Seward will give you, at his own risk and on his own responsibility, the privilege you seek." [. . .]

147

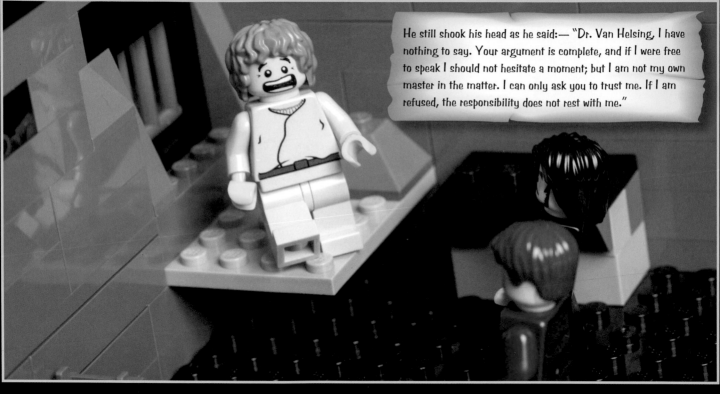

He still shook his head as he said:— "Dr. Van Helsing, I have nothing to say. Your argument is complete, and if I were free to speak I should not hesitate a moment; but I am not my own master in the matter. I can only ask you to trust me. If I am refused, the responsibility does not rest with me."

I thought it was now time to end the scene, which was becoming too comically grave, so I went towards the door, simply saying:— "Come, my friends, we have work to do. Good-night." [. . .] He threw himself on his knees, and held up his hands, wringing them in plaintive supplication, and poured forth a torrent of entreaty, with the tears rolling down his cheeks, and his whole face and form expressive of the deepest emotion:— "Let me entreat you, Dr. Seward, oh, let me implore you, to let me out of this house at once. [. . .] You don't know what you do by keeping me here. I am speaking from the depths of my heart—of my very soul. You don't know whom you wrong, or how; and I may not tell. Woe is me! I may not tell. By all you hold sacred—by all you hold dear—by your love that is lost—by your hope that lives—for the sake of the Almighty, take me out of this and save my soul from guilt! Can't you hear me, man? Can't you understand? Will you never learn? Don't you know that I am sane and earnest now; that I am no lunatic in a mad fit, but a sane man fighting for his soul? Oh, hear me! hear me! Let me go! let me go! let me go!" [. . .]

Chapter XIX — Jonathan Harker's Journal

1 October, 5 a. m.—I went with the party to the search with an easy mind, for I think I never saw Mina so absolutely strong and well. I am so glad that she consented to hold back and let us men do the work. [. . .] When we got to the porch the Professor opened his bag and took out a lot of things, which he laid on the step, sorting them into four little groups, evidently one for each. Then he spoke:— "My friends, we are going into a terrible danger, and we need arms of many kinds. [. . .] We must, therefore, guard ourselves from his touch. Keep this near your heart"—as he spoke he lifted a little silver crucifix and held it out to me, I being nearest to him—"put these flowers round your neck"—here he handed to me a wreath of withered garlic blossoms—"for other enemies more mundane, this revolver and this knife; and for aid in all, these so small electric lamps, which you can fasten to your breast; and for all, and above all at the last, this, which we must not desecrate needless." This was a portion of Sacred Wafer, which he put in an envelope and handed to me. Each of the others was similarly equipped. [. . .]

I could not for my life get away from the feeling that there was some one else amongst us. I suppose it was the recollection, so powerfully brought home to me by the grim surroundings, of that terrible experience in Transylvania. I think the feeling was common to us all, for I noticed that the others kept looking over their shoulders at every sound and every new shadow, just as I felt myself doing. [. . .]

There was an earthy smell, as of some dry miasma, which came through the fouler air. But as to the odour itself, how shall I describe it? It was not alone that it was composed of all the ills of mortality and with the pungent, acrid smell of blood, but it seemed as though corruption had become itself corrupt. Faugh! it sickens me to think of it. Every breath exhaled by that monster seemed to have clung to the place and intensified its loathsomeness. [. . .]

We made an accurate examination of the place, the Professor saying as we began:— "The first thing is to see how many of the boxes are left; we must then examine every hole and corner and cranny and see if we cannot get some clue as to what has become of the rest." A glance was sufficient to show how many remained, for the great earth chests were bulky, and there was no mistaking them. There were only twenty-nine left out of the fifty! [. . .]

A few minutes later I saw Morris step suddenly back from a corner, which he was examining. We all followed his movements with our eyes, for undoubtedly some nervousness was growing on us, and we saw a whole mass of phosphorescence, which twinkled like stars. We all instinctively drew back. The whole place was becoming alive with rats.

For a moment or two we stood appalled, all save Lord Godalming, who was seemingly prepared for such an emergency. [. . .] [T]aking his little silver whistle from his pocket, he blew a low, shrill call. It was answered from behind Dr. Seward's house by the yelping of dogs, and after about a minute three terriers came dashing round the corner of the house. [. . .] The rats were multiplying in thousands, and we moved out. Lord Godalming lifted one of the dogs, and carrying him in, placed him on the floor. The instant his feet touched the ground he seemed to recover his courage, and rushed at his natural enemies. They fled before him so fast that before he had shaken the life out of a score, the other dogs, who had by now been lifted in the same manner, had but small prey ere the whole mass had vanished.

With their going it seemed as if some evil presence had departed, for the dogs frisked about and barked merrily as they made sudden darts at their prostrate foes, and turned them over and over and tossed them in the air with vicious shakes. We all seemed to find our spirits rise. Whether it was the purifying of the deadly atmosphere by the opening of the chapel door, or the relief which we experienced by finding ourselves in the open I know not; but most certainly the shadow of dread seemed to slip from us like a robe, and the occasion of our coming lost something of its grim significance, though we did not slacken a whit in our resolution. [. . .]

Dr. Seward's Diary.

1 October.—It was towards noon when I was awakened by the Professor walking into my room. [. . .] After going over the adventure of the night he suddenly said:— "Your patient interests me much. May it be that with you I visit him this morning . . . ?" I had some work to do which pressed, so I told him that if he would go alone I would be glad, as then I should not have to keep him waiting . . .

It seemed that the time had been very short indeed, but there was Van Helsing back in the study. [. . .] "I fear that he does not appraise me at much. Our interview was short. [. . .] I spoke to him as cheerfully as I could, and with such a measure of respect as I could assume. He made no reply whatever. 'Don't you know me?' I asked. His answer was not reassuring: 'I know you well enough; you are the old fool Van Helsing. I wish you would take yourself and your idiotic brain theories somewhere else. Damn all thick-headed Dutchmen!' Not a word more would he say, but sat in his implacable sullenness as indifferent to me as though I had not been in the room at all. . . ."

Mina Harker's Journal.

1 October.—It is strange to me to be kept in the dark as I am to-day; after Jonathan's full confidence for so many years, to see him manifestly avoid certain matters, and those the most vital of all. He spoke to me before he went out, never more sweetly or tenderly, but he never mentioned a word of what had happened in the visit to the Count's house. And yet he must have known how terribly anxious I was. Poor dear fellow! I suppose it must have distressed him even more than it did me. [. . .]

I can't quite remember how I fell asleep last night. I remember hearing the sudden barking of the dogs and a lot of queer sounds, like praying on a very tumultuous scale, from Mr. Renfield's room, which is somewhere under this.

And then there was silence over everything, silence so profound that it startled me, and I got up and looked out of the window. All was dark and silent, the black shadows thrown by the moonlight seeming full of a silent mystery of their own. [. . .]

The poor man was more loud than ever, and though I could not distinguish a word he said, I could in some way recognize in his tones some passionate entreaty on his part. Then there was the sound of a struggle, and I knew that the attendants were dealing with him. I was so frightened that I crept into bed, and pulled the clothes over my head, putting my fingers in my ears. I was not then a bit sleepy, at least so I thought; but I must have fallen asleep, for, except dreams, I do not remember anything until the morning, when Jonathan woke me. [. . .]

I thought that I was asleep, and waiting for Jonathan to come back. [. . .] I put back the clothes from my face, and found, to my surprise, that all was dim around. The gaslight which I had left lit for Jonathan, but turned down, came only like a tiny red spark through the fog, which had evidently grown thicker and poured into the room. Then it occurred to me that I had shut the window before I had come to bed. I would have got out to make certain on the point, but some leaden lethargy seemed to chain my limbs and even my will. [. . .]

The mist grew thicker and thicker and I could see now how it came in, for I could see it like smoke—or with the white energy of boiling water—pouring in through the window. It got thicker and thicker, till it seemed as if it became concentrated into a sort of pillar of cloud in the room, through the top of which I could see the light of the gas shining like a red eye.

Things began to whirl through my brain just as the cloudy column was now whirling in the room, and through it all came the scriptural words "a pillar of cloud by day and of fire by night." [. . .] But the pillar was composed of both the day and the night-guiding, for the fire was in the red eye, which at the thought got a new fascination for me; till, as I looked, the fire divided, and seemed to shine on me through the fog like two red eyes, such as Lucy told me of in her momentary mental wandering when, on the cliff, the dying sunlight struck the windows of St. Mary's Church. [. . .]

Suddenly the horror burst upon me that it was thus that Jonathan had seen those awful women growing into reality though the whirling mist in the moonlight, and in my dream I must have fainted, for all became black darkness.

The last conscious effort which imagination made was to show me a livid white face bending over me out of the mist. I must be careful of such dreams, for they would unseat one's reason if there were too much of them.

I should get Dr. Van Helsing or Dr. Seward to prescribe something for me which would make me sleep, only that I fear to alarm them. Such a dream at the present time would become woven into their fears for me. To-night I shall strive hard to sleep naturally. If I do not, I shall to-morrow night get them to give me a dose of chloral; that cannot hurt me for once, and it will give me a good night's sleep. Last night tired me more than if I had not slept at all.

2 October 10 p. m . . . . I spent all yesterday trying to read, or lying down dozing. In the afternoon Mr. Renfield asked if he might see me. [. . .]

Poor man, he was very gentle, and when I came away he kissed my hand and bade God bless me. Some way it affected me much; I am crying when I think of him. [. . .]

Chapter XX — Jonathan Harker's Journal

1 October, evening . . . I drove to Walworth, and found Mr. Joseph Smollet, who delivered the boxes, at home and in his shirtsleeves . . . he gave me the destinations of the boxes. There were, he said, six in the cartload which he took from Carfax and left at 197, Chicksand Street, Mile End New Town, and another six which he deposited at Jamaica Lane, Bermondsey. If then the Count meant to scatter these ghastly refuges of his over London, these places were chosen as the first of delivery, so that later he might distribute more fully. [. . .]

2 October, evening . . . When I had promised to pay for [Sam Bloxam's] information and given him an earnest, he told me that he had made two journeys between Carfax and a house in Piccadilly, and had taken from this house to the latter nine great boxes—"main heavy ones"—with a horse and cart hired by him for this purpose. [. . .]

I found all the others at home. Mina was looking tired and pale, but she made a gallant effort to be bright and cheerful, it wrung my heart to think that I had had to keep anything from her and so caused her inquietude. [. . .] I took Mina to her room and left her to go to bed. [. . .]

When I came down again I found the others all gathered round the fire in the study. [. . .] We all sat silent awhile and all at once Mr. Morris spoke:— "Say! how are we going to get into that house?" "We got into the other," answered Lord Godalming quickly. "But, Art, this is different. We broke house at Carfax, but we had night and a walled park to protect us. It will be a mighty different thing to commit burglary in Piccadilly, either by day or night. I confess I don't see how we are going to get in unless that agency duck can find us a key of some sort; perhaps we shall know when you get his letter in the morning." [. . .]

Dr. Seward's Diary.

1 October.—I am puzzled afresh about Renfield. His moods change so rapidly that I find it difficult to keep touch of them, and as they always mean something more than his own well-being, they form a more than interesting study.

This morning, when I went to see him after his repulse of Van Helsing, his manner was that of a man commanding destiny. [. . .] He did not really care for any of the things of mere earth; he was in the clouds and looked down on all the weaknesses and wants of us poor mortals. I thought I would improve the occasion and learn something, so I asked him:— "What about the flies these times?"

He smiled on me in quite a superior sort of way as he answered me . . . "The fly, my dear sir, has one striking feature; its wings are typical of the aerial powers of the psychic faculties. The ancients did well when they typified the soul as a butterfly!" I thought I would push his analogy to its utmost logically, so I said quickly:— "Oh, it is a soul you are after now, is it?" His madness foiled his reason, and a puzzled look spread over his face as, shaking his head with a decision which I had but seldom seen in him, he said:— "Oh, no, oh no! I want no souls. Life is all I want." [. . .]

"So you don't care about life and you don't want souls. Why not?" I put my question quickly and somewhat sternly, on purpose to disconcert him. [. . .] He replied:— "I don't want any souls, indeed, indeed! I don't. I couldn't use them if I had them; they would be no manner of use to me. I couldn't eat them or——" He suddenly stopped and the old cunning look spread over his face, like a wind-sweep on the surface of the water. "And doctor, as to life, what is it after all? When you've got all you require, and you know that you will never want, that is all. . . ."

The matter seemed preying on his mind, and so I determined to use it—to "be cruel only to be kind." So I said:— "You like life, and you want life?" "Oh yes! but that is all right; you needn't worry about that!" "But," I asked, "how are we to get the life without getting the soul also?" This seemed to puzzle him, so I followed it up:— "A nice time you'll have some time when you're flying out there, with the souls of thousands of flies and spiders and birds and cats buzzing and twittering and miauing all round you. You've got their lives, you know, and you must put up with their souls!" [. . .]

"Would you like some sugar to get your flies round again?" He seemed to wake up all at once, and shook his head. With a laugh he replied:— "Not much! flies are poor things, after all!" After a pause he added, "But I don't want their souls buzzing round me, all the same." "Or spiders?" I went on. "Blow spiders! What's the use of spiders? There isn't anything in them to eat or"—he stopped suddenly, as though reminded of a forbidden topic. "So, so!" I thought to myself, "this is the second time he has suddenly stopped at the word 'drink'; what does it mean?" [. . .]

For a few moments he sat despondently. Suddenly he jumped to his feet, with his eyes blazing and all the signs of intense cerebral excitement. "To hell with you and your souls!" he shouted. "Why do you plague me about souls? Haven't I got enough to worry, and pain, and distract me already, without thinking of souls!" [...]

There is certainly something to ponder over in this man's state. Several points seem to make what the American interviewer calls "a story," if one could only get them in proper order. Here they are:— Will not mention "drinking." Fears the thought of being burdened with the "soul" of anything. Has no dread of wanting "life" in the future. Despises the meaner forms of life altogether, though he dreads being haunted by their souls. Logically all these things point one way! he has assurance of some kind that he will acquire some higher life. He dreads the consequence—the burden of a soul. Then it is a human life he looks to! And the assurance—? Merciful God! the Count has been to him, and there is some new scheme of terror afoot! [...]

2 October.—I placed a man in the corridor last night, and told him to make an accurate note of any sound he might hear from Renfield's room, and gave him instructions that if there should be anything strange he was to call me.

After dinner, when we had all gathered round the fire in the study—Mrs. Harker having gone to bed—we discussed the attempts and discoveries of the day. [. . .] We must sterilise all the imported earth between sunrise and sunset; we shall thus catch the Count at his weakest, and without a refuge to fly to. [. . .]

Later . . . We seem at last to be on the track, and our work of to-morrow may be the beginning of the end. I wonder if Renfield's quiet has anything to do with this. His moods have so followed the doings of the Count, that the coming destruction of the monster may be carried to him in some subtle way. If we could only get some hint as to what passed in his mind, between the time of my argument with him to-day and his resumption of fly-catching, it might afford us a valuable clue. He is now seemingly quiet for a spell. . . . Is he?—— That wild yell seemed to come from his room. [. . .]

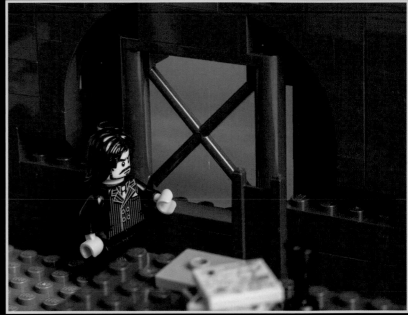

The attendant came bursting into my room and told me that Renfield had somehow met with some accident. He had heard him yell; and when he went to him found him lying on his face on the floor, all covered with blood. I must go at once. [. . .]

Chapter XXI — Dr. Seward's Diary

3 October . . . When I came to Renfield's room I found him lying on the floor on his left side in a glittering pool of blood. When I went to move him, it became at once apparent that he had received some terrible injuries . . .

The attendant who was kneeling beside the body said to me as we turned him over:— "I think, sir, his back is broken. See, both his right arm and leg and the whole side of his face are paralysed."

How such a thing could have happened puzzled the attendant beyond measure. He seemed quite bewildered, and his brows were gathered in as he said:— "I can't understand the two things. He could mark his face like that by beating his own head on the floor. I saw a young woman do it once at the Eversfield Asylum before anyone could lay hands on her. And I suppose he might have broke his neck by falling out of bed, if he got in an awkward kink. But for the life of me I can't imagine how the two things occurred. If his back was broke, he couldn't beat his head; and if his face was like that before the fall out of bed, there would be marks of it." [. . .]

[W]ithin a few minutes the Professor . . . appeared. When he saw Renfield on the ground, he looked keenly at him a moment, and then turned to me. I think he recognized my thought in my eyes, for he said very quietly, manifestly for the ears of the attendant:— "Ah, a sad accident! He will need very careful watching, and much attention. . . ."

[H]e whispered to me:— "Send the attendant away. We must be alone with him when he becomes conscious, after the operation." [. . .] The man withdrew, and we went into a strict examination of the patient. [. . .]

His face was sternly set as he spoke:— "There is no time to lose. His words may be worth many lives; I have been thinking so, as I stood here. It may be there is a soul at stake! We shall operate just above the ear." Without another word he made the operation. For a few moments the breathing continued to be stertorous. Then there came a breath so prolonged that it seemed as though it would tear open his chest.

Suddenly his eyes opened, and became fixed in a wild, helpless stare. [. . .] He moved convulsively, and as he did so, said:— "I'll be quiet, Doctor. Tell them to take off the strait-waistcoat. I have had a terrible dream, and it has left me so weak that I cannot move. What's wrong with my face? it feels all swollen, and it smarts dreadfully." He tried to turn his head; but even with the effort his eyes seemed to grow glassy again so I gently put it back. [. . .] "I must not deceive myself; it was no dream, but all a grim reality." [. . .]

For an instant his eyes closed—not with pain or sleep but voluntarily, as though he were bringing all his faculties to bear; when he opened them he said, hurriedly, and with more energy than he had yet displayed:— "Quick, Doctor, quick. I am dying! I feel that I have but a few minutes; and then I must go back to death—or worse! [. . .] I have something that I must say before I die; or before my poor crushed brain dies anyhow. [. . .]

It was that night after you left me, when I implored you to let me go away. I couldn't speak then, for I felt my tongue was tied; but I was as sane then, except in that way, as I am now. [. . .] He came up to the window in the mist, as I had seen him often before; but he was solid then—not a ghost, and his eyes were fierce like a man's when angry. He was laughing with his red mouth; the sharp white teeth glinted in the moonlight when he turned to look back over the belt of trees, to where the dogs were barking.

I wouldn't ask him to come in at first, though I knew he wanted to—just as he had wanted all along. Then he began promising me things— not in words but by doing them." [. . .]

"How?" "By making them happen; just as he used to send in the flies when the sun was shining. [. . .]

"Great big fat ones with steel and sapphire on their wings; and big moths, in the night, with skull and cross-bones on their backs." [. . .]

165

The patient went on without stopping. "Then he began to whisper: 'Rats, rats, rats! Hundreds, thousands, millions of them, and every one a life; and dogs to eat them, and cats too. All lives! all red blood, with years of life in it; and not merely buzzing flies!' . . . He held up his hand, and they all stopped; and I thought he seemed to be saying: 'All these lives will I give you, ay, and many more and greater, through countless ages, if you will fall down and worship me!'

"And then a red cloud, like the color of blood, seemed to close over my eyes; and before I knew what I was doing, I found myself opening the sash and saying to Him: 'Come in, Lord and Master!' The rats were all gone, but He slid into the room through the sash, though it was only open an inch wide—just as the Moon herself has often come in through the tiniest crack and has stood before me in all her size and splendor. [. . .]

"All day I waited to hear from him, but he did not send me anything, not even a blow-fly, and when the moon got up I was pretty angry with him. [. . .]

"When Mrs. Harker came in to see me this afternoon she wasn't the same . . . I didn't know that she was here till she spoke; and she didn't look the same. I don't care for the pale people; I like them with lots of blood in them, and hers had all seemed to have run out. I didn't think of it at the time; but when she went away I began to think, and it made me mad to know that He had been taking the life out of her. [. . .]

"So when He came to-night I was ready for Him. I saw the mist stealing in, and I grabbed it tight. I had heard that madmen have unnatural strength; and as I knew I was a madman—at times anyhow—I resolved to use my power. Ay, and He felt it too, for He had to come out of the mist to struggle with me. I held tight; and I thought I was going to win, for I didn't mean Him to take any more of her life, till I saw His eyes."

"They burned into me, and my strength became like water. He slipped through it, and when I tried to cling to Him, He raised me up and flung me down. There was a red cloud before me, and a noise like thunder, and the mist seemed to steal away under the door." [. . .]

Van Helsing stood up instinctively. "We know the worst now," he said. "He is here, and we know his purpose. It may not be too late.

"Let us be armed—the same as we were the other night, but lose no time; there is not an instant to spare." There was no need to put our fear, nay our conviction, into words—we shared them in common. We all hurried and took from our rooms the same things that we had when we entered the Count's house. [. . .]

Outside the Harkers' door we paused. Art and Quincey held back, and the latter said:— "Should we disturb her?" "We must," said Van Helsing grimly. "If the door be locked, I shall break it in." [. . .] He turned the handle as he spoke, but the door did not yield. We threw ourselves against it; with a crash it burst open, and we almost fell headlong into the room. [. . .]

On the bed beside the window lay Jonathan Harker, his face flushed and breathing heavily as though in a stupor.

Kneeling on the near edge of the bed facing outwards was the white-clad figure of his wife. By her side stood a tall, thin man, clad in black. His face was turned from us, but the instant we saw we all recognized the Count—in every way, even to the scar on his forehead. With his left hand he held both Mrs. Harker's hands, keeping them away with her arms at full tension; his right hand gripped her by the back of the neck, forcing her face down on his bosom. [. . .]

As we burst into the room, the Count turned his face, and the hellish look that I had heard described seemed to leap into it. His eyes flamed red with devilish passion; the great nostrils of the white aquiline nose opened wide and quivered at the edge; and the white sharp teeth, behind the full lips of the blood-dripping mouth, champed together like those of a wild beast.

With a wrench, which threw his victim back upon the bed as though hurled from a height, he turned and sprang at us.

But by this time the Professor had gained his feet, and was holding towards him the envelope which contained the Sacred Wafer. The Count suddenly stopped, just as poor Lucy had done outside the tomb, and cowered back. [. . .]

Further and further back he cowered, as we, lifting our crucifixes, advanced. The moonlight suddenly failed, as a great black cloud sailed across the sky;

And when the gaslight sprang up under Quincey's match, we saw nothing but a faint vapour. [. . .]

Van Helsing, Art, and I moved forward to Mrs. Harker, who by this time had drawn her breath and with it had given a scream so wild, so ear-piercing, so despairing that it seems to me now that it will ring in my ears till my dying day. [. . .] Then she put before her face her poor crushed hands, which bore on their whiteness the red mark of the Count's terrible grip, and from behind them came a low desolate wail which made the terrible scream seem only the quick expression of an endless grief. [. . .]

I raised the blind, and looked out of the window. There was much moonshine; and as I looked I could see Quincey Morris run across the lawn and hide himself in the shadow of a great yew-tree. [. . .]

I heard Harker's quick exclamation as he woke to partial consciousness, and turned to the bed. On his face, as there might well be, was a look of wild amazement. He seemed dazed for a few seconds, and then full consciousness seemed to burst upon him all at once, and he started up. His wife was aroused by the quick movement, and turned to him with her arms stretched out, as though to embrace him; instantly, however, she drew them in again, and putting her elbows together, held her hands before her face, and shuddered till the bed beneath her shook. "In God's name what does this mean?" Harker cried out. [. . .]

Lord Godalming answered:— "I could not see him anywhere in the passage, or in any of our rooms. I looked in the study but, though he had been there, he had gone. [. . .]

"He had been there, and though it could only have been for a few seconds, he made rare hay of the place. All the manuscript had been burned, and the blue flames were flickering amongst the white ashes; the cylinders of your phonograph too were thrown on the fire, and the wax had helped the flames."

Here I interrupted. "Thank God there is the other copy in the safe!" [. . .]

"And you, friend Quincey, have you any to tell?" "A little," he answered. "It may be much eventually, but at present I can't say. I thought it well to know if possible where the Count would go when he left the house. I did not see him; but I saw a bat rise from Renfield's window, and flap westward. I expected to see him in some shape go back to Carfax; but he evidently sought some other lair. He will not be back to-night; for the sky is reddening in the east, and the dawn is close. We must work to-morrow!" [. . .]

[T]hen Van Helsing said, placing his hand very tenderly on Mrs. Harker's head:— "And now, Madam Mina—poor, dear, dear Madam Mina—tell us exactly what happened." [. . .] After a pause in which she was evidently ordering her thoughts, she began:— "I took the sleeping draught which you had so kindly given me, but for a long time it did not act. [. . .] Well, I saw I must try to help the medicine to its work with my will, if it was to do me any good, so I resolutely set myself to sleep. Sure enough sleep must soon have come to me, for I remember no more.

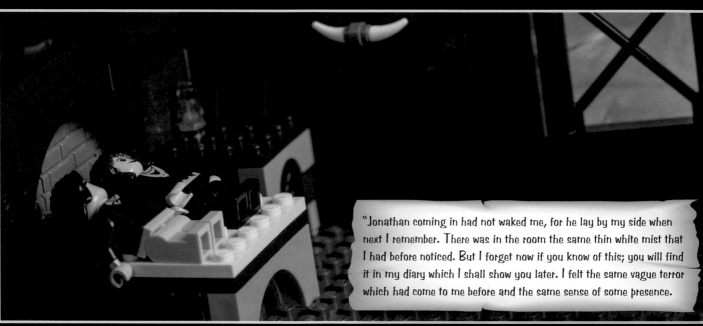

"Jonathan coming in had not waked me, for he lay by my side when next I remember. There was in the room the same thin white mist that I had before noticed. But I forget now if you know of this; you will find it in my diary which I shall show you later. I felt the same vague terror which had come to me before and the same sense of some presence.

"I turned to wake Jonathan, but found that he slept so soundly that it seemed as if it was he who had taken the sleeping draught, and not I. I tried, but I could not wake him. This caused me a great fear, and I looked around terrified.

"Then indeed, my heart sank within me: beside the bed, as if he had stepped out of the mist—or rather as if the mist had turned into his figure, for it had entirely disappeared—stood a tall, thin man, all in black.

"I knew him at once from the description of the others. The waxen face; the high aquiline nose, on which the light fell in a thin white line; the parted red lips, with the sharp white teeth showing between; and the red eyes that I had seemed to see in the sunset on the windows of St. Mary's Church at Whitby. I knew, too, the red scar on his forehead where Jonathan had struck him.

"For an instant my heart stood still, and I would have screamed out, only that I was paralysed. In the pause he spoke in a sort of keen, cutting whisper, pointing as he spoke to Jonathan:— 'Silence! If you make a sound I shall take him and dash his brains out before your very eyes.' . . .

"Then he spoke to me mockingly, 'And so you, like the others, would play your brains against mine. You would help these men to hunt me and frustrate me in my designs! You know now, and they know in part already, and will know in full before long, what it is to cross my path. They should have kept their energies for use closer to home.

"'Whilst they played wits against me—against me who commanded nations, and intrigued for them, and fought for them, hundreds of years before they were born—I was countermining them.

"'And you, their best beloved one, are now to me, flesh of my flesh; blood of my blood; kin of my kin; my bountiful wine-press for a while; and shall be later on my companion and my helper. You shall be avenged in turn; for not one of them but shall minister to your needs. But as yet you are to be punished for what you have done. You have aided in thwarting me; now you shall come to my call. When my brain says 'Come!' to you, you shall cross land or sea to do my bidding; and to that end this!'

"With that he pulled open his shirt, and with his long sharp nails opened a vein in his breast. When the blood began to spurt out, he took my hands in one of his, holding them tight, and with the other seized my neck and pressed my mouth to the wound, so that I must either suffocate or swallow some of the—— Oh my God! my God! what have I done? What have I done to deserve such a fate, I who have tried to walk in meekness and righteousness all my days. God pity me . . . !"

Chapter XXII — Jonathan Harker's Journal

3 October . . . Van Helsing was looking at [Mina] fixedly as she spoke, and said, suddenly but quietly:— "But dear Madam Mina, are you not afraid; not for yourself, but for others from yourself, after what has happened?" Her face grew set in its lines, but her eyes shone with the devotion of a martyr as she answered:— "Ah no! for my mind is made up!" "To what?" he asked gently, whilst we were all very still; for each in our own way we had a sort of vague idea of what she meant. Her answer came with direct simplicity, as though she were simply stating a fact:— "Because if I find in myself—and I shall watch keenly for it—a sign of harm to any that I love, I shall die!" "You would not kill yourself?" he asked, hoarsely. "I would; if there were no friend who loved me, who would save me such a pain, and so desperate an effort!" [. . .]

He was sitting down; but now he rose and came close to her and put his hand on her head as he said solemnly: "My child, there is such an one if it were for your good. [. . .] There are here some who would stand between you and death. You must not die. You must not die by any hand; but least of all by your own. Until the other, who has fouled your sweet life, is true dead you must not die; for if he is still with the quick Un-Dead, your death would make you even as he is. [. . .]

"It is perhaps well," he said, "that at our meeting after our visit to Carfax we decided not to do anything with the earth-boxes that lay there. Had we done so, the Count must have guessed our purpose, and would doubtless have taken measures in advance to frustrate such an effort with regard to the others; but now he does not know our intentions. [. . .] And so we have this day to hunt out all his lairs and sterilise them. So we shall, if we have not yet catch him and destroy him, drive him to bay in some place where the catching and the destroying shall be, in time, sure. [. . .]"

"I have thought and thought, and it seems to me that the simplest way is the best of all. Now we wish to get into the house, but we have no key; is it not so?" I nodded. "Now suppose that you were, in truth, the owner of that house, and could not still get it; and think there was to you no conscience of the housebreaker, what would you do?" "I should get a respectable locksmith, and set him to work to pick the lock for me." "And your police, they would interfere, would they not?" "Oh, no! not if they knew the man was properly employed." [. . .]

Mina took a growing interest in everything and I was rejoiced to see that the exigency of affairs was helping her to forget for a time the terrible experience of the night. She was very, very pale—almost ghastly, and so thin that her lips were drawn away, showing her teeth in somewhat of prominence. I did not mention this last, lest it should give her needless pain; but it made my blood run cold in my veins to think of what had occurred with poor Lucy when the Count had sucked her blood. [. . .]

177

Van Helsing stood up and said . . . "Madam Mina, you are in any case *quite* safe here until the sunset; and before then we shall return—if—— We shall return! But before we go let me see you armed against personal attack. I have myself, since you came down, prepared your chamber by the placing of things of which we know, so that He may not enter. [. . .]

"Now let me guard yourself. On your forehead I touch this piece of Sacred Wafer in the name of the Father, the Son, and——" There was a fearful scream which almost froze our hearts to hear. As he had placed the Wafer on Mina's forehead, it had seared it—had burned into the flesh as though it had been a piece of white-hot metal. [. . .]

Pulling her beautiful hair over her face, as the leper of old his mantle, she wailed out:— "Unclean! Unclean! Even the Almighty shuns my polluted flesh! I must bear this mark of shame upon my forehead until the Judgment Day. . . ." It was then time to start. So I said farewell to Mina, a parting which neither of us shall forget to our dying day; and we set out. [. . .]

We entered Carfax without trouble and found all things the same as on the first occasion. It was hard to believe that amongst so prosaic surroundings of neglect and dust and decay there was any ground for such fear as already we knew. [. . .] We found no papers, or any sign of use in the house; and in the old chapel the great boxes looked just as we had seen them last.

Dr. Van Helsing said to us solemnly as we stood before them:— "And now, my friends, we have a duty here to do. We must sterilise this earth, so sacred of holy memories, that he has brought from a far distant land for such fell use. He has chosen this earth because it has been holy. Thus we defeat him with his own weapon, for we make it more holy still. It was sanctified to such use of man, now we sanctify it to God." As he spoke he took from his bag a screwdriver and a wrench, and very soon the top of one of the cases was thrown open. The earth smelled musty and close; but we did not somehow seem to mind, for our attention was concentrated on the Professor. Taking from his box a piece of the Sacred Wafer he laid it reverently on the earth, and then shutting down the lid began to screw it home, we aiding him as he worked.

One by one we treated in the same way each of the great boxes, and left them as we had found them to all appearance; but in each was a portion of the Host. [. . .]

Piccadilly, 12:30 o'clock.—Just before we reached Fenchurch Street Lord Godalming said to me:—"Quincey and I will find a locksmith." [. . .] Godalming and Morris hurried off in a cab, we following in another. [. . .] We waited patiently as we saw the workman come out and bring in his bag. Then he held the door partly open, steadying it with his knees, whilst he fitted a key to the lock. [. . .] When the man had fairly gone, we three crossed the street and knocked at the door. It was immediately opened by Quincey Morris, beside whom stood Lord Godalming lighting a cigar. [. . .]

We moved to explore the house, all keeping together in case of attack; for we knew we had a strong and wily enemy to deal with, and as yet we did not know whether the Count might not be in the house.

In the dining-room, which lay at the back of the hall, we found eight boxes of earth. Eight boxes only out of the nine, which we sought! Our work was not over, and would never be until we should have found the missing box. [. . .]

We did not lose any time in examining the chests. With the tools which we had brought with us we opened them, one by one, and treated them as we had treated those others in the old chapel. [. . .]

There were title deeds of the Piccadilly house in a great bundle; deeds of the purchase of the houses at Mile End and Bermondsey; note-paper, envelopes, and pens and ink. All were covered up in thin wrapping paper to keep them from the dust. There were also a clothes brush, a brush and comb, and a jug and basin—the latter containing dirty water which was reddened as if with blood. Last of all was a little heap of keys of all sorts and sizes, probably those belonging to the other houses. [. . .]

When we had examined this last find, Lord Godalming and Quincey Morris taking accurate notes of the various addresses of the houses in the East and the South, took with them the keys in a great bunch, and set out to destroy the boxes in these places. [. . .]

Chapter XXIII – Dr. Seward's Diary

3 October . . . "Do you not see how, of late, this monster has been creeping into knowledge experimentally. How he has been making use of the zoäphagous patient to effect his entry into friend John's home; for your Vampire, though in all afterwards he can come when and how he will, must at the first make entry only when asked thereto by an inmate.

"But these are not his most important experiments. Do we not see how at the first all these so great boxes were moved by others. He knew not then but that must be so. But all the time that so great child-brain of his was growing, and he began to consider whether he might not himself move the box. So he began to help; and then, when he found that this be all-right, he try to move them all alone. And so he progress, and he scatter these graves of him; and none but he know where they are hidden. [. . .] But, my child, do not despair; this knowledge come to him just too late! Already all of his lairs but one be sterilise as for him; and before the sunset this shall be so. Then he have no place where he can move and hide. . . ."

Whilst he was speaking we were startled by a knock at the hall door, the double postman's knock of the telegraph boy. [. . .] The Professor closed the door again, and, after looking at the direction, opened it and read aloud. "Look out for D. He has just now, 12:45, come from Carfax hurriedly and hastened towards the South. He seems to be going the round and may want to see you: Mina."

There was a pause, broken by Jonathan Harker's voice:— "Now, God be thanked, we shall soon meet!" [...]

About half an hour after we had received Mrs. Harker's telegram, there came a quiet, resolute knock at the hall door. [...] The gladness of our hearts must have shown upon our faces when on the step, close to the door, we saw Lord Godalming and Quincey Morris. They came quickly in and closed the door behind them, the former saying, as they moved along the hall:— "It is all right. We found both places; six boxes in each and we destroyed them all!" [...]

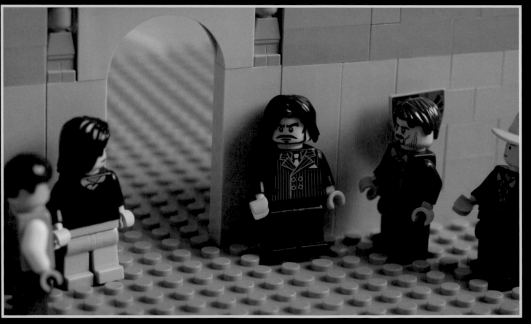

Quincey said:— "There's nothing to do but to wait here. If, however, he doesn't turn up by five o'clock, we must start off; for it won't do to leave Mrs. Harker alone after sunset." "He will be here before long now," said Van Helsing . . . "We should have ready some plan of attack, so that we may throw away no chance. Hush, there is no time now. Have all your arms! Be ready!" He held up a warning hand as he spoke, for we all could hear a key softly inserted in the lock of the hall door. [...]

Suddenly with a single bound he leaped into the room, winning a way past us before any of us could raise a hand to stay him.

There was something so panther-like in the movement—something so unhuman, that it seemed to sober us all from the shock of his coming. [. . .]

[W]ith a single impulse, we all advanced upon him. It was a pity that we had not some better organized plan of attack, for even at the moment I wondered what we were to do. I did not myself know whether our lethal weapons would avail us anything. Harker evidently meant to try the matter, for he had ready his great Kukri knife and made a fierce and sudden cut at him. The blow was a powerful one; only the diabolical quickness of the Count's leap back saved him. A second less and the trenchant blade had shorne through his heart. [. . .]

Instinctively I moved forward with a protective impulse, holding the Crucifix and Wafer in my left hand. I felt a mighty power fly along my arm; and it was without surprise that I saw the monster cower back before a similar movement made spontaneously by each one of us. [. . .]

The next instant, with a sinuous dive he swept under Harker's arm, ere his blow could fall, and, grasping a handful of the money from the floor, dashed across the room, threw himself at the window. Amid the crash and glitter of the falling glass, he tumbled into the flagged area below. [. . .]

We ran over and saw him spring unhurt from the ground. [. . .] There he turned and spoke to us:— "You think to baffle me, you—with your pale faces all in a row, like sheep in a butcher's. You shall be sorry yet, each one of you! You think you have left me without a place to rest; but I have more.

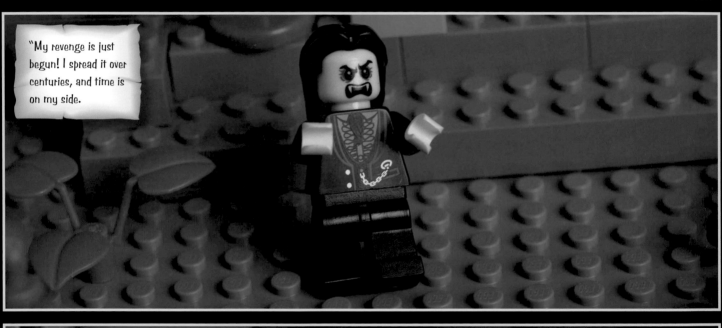

"My revenge is just begun! I spread it over centuries, and time is on my side.

"Your girls that you all love are mine already; and through them you and others shall yet be mine—my creatures, to do my bidding and to be my jackals when I want to feed. Bah!" With a contemptuous sneer, he passed quickly through the door, and we heard the rusty bolt creak as he fastened it behind him. A door beyond opened and shut.

The first of us to speak was the Professor, as, realising the difficulty of following him through the stable, we moved toward the hall. "We have learnt something—much! Notwithstanding his brave words, he fears us; he fear time, he fear want! For if not, why he hurry so? His very tone betray him, or my ears deceive. Why take that money? [. . .]"

With sad hearts we came back to my house, where we found Mrs. Harker waiting us, with an appearance of cheerfulness which did honor to her bravery and unselfishness. [. . .]

We had a sort of perfunctory supper together, and I think it cheered us all up somewhat. [. . .] True to our promise, we told Mrs. Harker everything which had passed; and although she grew snowy white at times when danger had seemed to threaten her husband, and red at others when his devotion to her was manifested, she listened bravely and with calmness. [. . .] "Jonathan dear, and you all my true, true friends, I want you to bear something in mind through all this dreadful time. I know that you must fight—that you must destroy even as you destroyed the false Lucy so that the true Lucy might live hereafter; but it is not a work of hate. That poor soul who has wrought all this misery is the saddest case of all. Just think what will be his joy when he, too, is destroyed in his worser part that his better part may have spiritual immortality. You must be pitiful to him, too, though it may not hold your hands from his destruction."

As she spoke I could see her husband's face darken and draw together, as though the passion in him were shriveling his being to its core. Instinctively the clasp on his wife's hand grew closer, till his knuckles looked white. [. . .] "May God give him into my hand just for long enough to destroy that earthly life of him which we are aiming at. If beyond it I could send his soul for ever and ever to burning hell I would do it!"

"Oh, hush! oh, hush! in the name of the good God. Don't say such things, Jonathan, my husband; or you will crush me with fear and horror. Just think, my dear—I have been thinking all this long, long day of it—that . . . perhaps . . . some day . . . I, too, may need such pity; and that some other like you—and with equal cause for anger—may deny it to me! [. . .]"

Jonathan Harker's Journal.

We men were all in tears now. There was no resisting them, and we wept openly. She wept, too, to see that her sweeter counsels had prevailed. [. . .]

3-4 October, close to midnight . . . Before we parted, we discussed what our next step was to be, but we could arrive at no result. All we knew was that one earth-box remained, and that the Count alone knew where it was. If he chooses to lie hidden, he may baffle us for years; and in the meantime!—the thought is too horrible, I dare not think of it even now. [. . .]

4 October, morning.—Once again during the night I was wakened by Mina. This time we had all had a good sleep, for the grey of the coming dawn was making the windows into sharp oblongs, and the gas flame was like a speck rather than a disc of light. She said to me hurriedly:— "Go, call the Professor. I want to see him at once." "Why?" I asked. "I have an idea. I suppose it must have come in the night, and matured without my knowing it. He must hypnotise me before the dawn, and then I shall be able to speak. Go quick, dearest; the time is getting close." [. . .]

[Van Helsing] said, cheerfully: "And what am I do for you? For at this hour you do not want me for nothings." "I want you to hypnotise me!" she said. "Do it before the dawn, for I feel that then I can speak, and speak freely. Be quick, for the time is short!" Without a word he motioned her to sit up in bed. Looking fixedly at her, he commenced to make passes in front of her, from over the top of her head downward, with each hand in turn. Mina gazed at him fixedly for a few minutes, during which my own heart beat like a trip hammer, for I felt that some crisis was at hand. Gradually her eyes closed, and she sat, stock still; only by the gentle heaving of her bosom could one know that she was alive. [. . .]

"Where are you now?" The answer came dreamily, but with intention; it were as though she were interpreting something. I have heard her use the same tone when reading her shorthand notes. "I do not know. It is all strange to me!" "What do you see?" "I can see nothing; it is all dark." "What do you hear?" I could detect the strain in the Professor's patient voice. "The lapping of water. It is gurgling by, and little waves leap. I can hear them on the outside."

"Then you are on a ship?" We all looked at each other, trying to glean something each from the other. We were afraid to think. The answer came quick:— "Oh, yes!"

"What else do you hear?" "The sound of men stamping overhead as they run about. There is the creaking of a chain, and the loud tinkle as the check of the capstan falls into the rachet." "What are you doing?" "I am still—oh, so still. It is like death!" The voice faded away into a deep breath as of one sleeping, and the open eyes closed again. [. . .]

The Professor repeated the conversation, and she said:— "Then there is not a moment to lose: it may not be yet too late!" Mr. Morris and Lord Godalming started for the door but the Professor's calm voice called them back:— "Stay, my friends. That ship, wherever it was, was weighing anchor whilst she spoke. There are many ships weighing anchor at the moment in your so great Port of London. . . ."

Chapter XXIV — Dr. Seward's Diary

Mina Harker's Journal.

Dr. Van Helsing described what steps were taken during the day to discover on what boat and whither bound Count Dracula made his escape:—
"As I knew that he wanted to get back to Transylvania, I felt sure that he must go by the Danube mouth; or by somewhere in the Black Sea, since by that way he come. [. . .]

"There we find that only one Black-Sea-bound ship go out with the tide. She is the *Czarina Catherine*, and she sail from Doolittle's Wharf for Varna, and thence on to other parts and up the Danube. ÔSoh!' said I, Ôthis is the ship whereon is the Count.' . . .

"They make known to us among them, how last afternoon at about five o'clock comes a man so hurry.

"A tall man, thin and pale, with high nose and teeth so white, and eyes that seem to be burning. That he be all in black, except that he have a hat of straw which suit not him or the time. That he scatter his money in making quick inquiry as to what ship sails for the Black Sea and for where. [. . .]

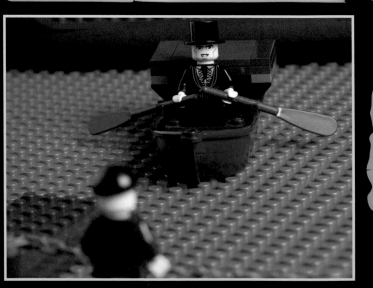

"He go there and soon he come again, himself driving cart on which a great box; this he himself lift down, though it take several to put it on truck for the ship. He give much talk to captain as to how and where his box is to be place; but the captain like it not and swear at him in many tongues, and tell him that if he like he can come and see where it shall be. [. . .]

"And so, my dear Madam Mina, it is that we have to rest for a time, for our enemy is on the sea, with the fog at his command, on his way to the Danube mouth. To sail a ship takes time, go she never so quick; and when we start we go on land more quick, and we meet him there. Our best hope is to come on him when in the box between sunrise and sunset; for then he can make no struggle, and we may deal with him as we should. . . ."

When Dr. Van Helsing had done speaking, I asked him if he were certain that the Count had remained on board the ship. He replied: "We have the best proof of that: your own evidence, when in the hypnotic trance this morning." I asked him again if it were really necessary that they should pursue the Count, for oh! I dread Jonathan leaving me, and I know that he would surely go if the others went.

He answered in growing passion, at first quietly. As he went on, however, he grew more angry and more forceful, till in the end we could not but see wherein was at least some of that personal dominance which made him so long a master amongst men:— "Yes, it is necessary—necessary—necessary! For your sake in the first, and then for the sake of humanity. . . ."

Dr. Seward's Diary.

5 October . . . I see only one immediate difficulty, I know it by instinct rather than reason: we shall all have to speak frankly; and yet I fear that in some mysterious way poor Mrs. Harker's tongue is tied. I *know* that she forms conclusions of her own, and from all that has been I can guess how brilliant and how true they must be; but she will not, or cannot, give them utterance. I have mentioned this to Van Helsing, and he and I are to talk it over when we are alone. I suppose it is some of that horrid poison which has got into her veins beginning to work. The Count had his own purposes when he gave her what Van Helsing called "the Vampire's baptism of blood." [. . .]

One thing I know: that if my instinct be true regarding poor Mrs. Harker's silences, then there is a terrible difficulty—an unknown danger—in the work before us. The same power that compels her silence may compel her speech. [. . .]

Later . . . "Madam Mina, our poor, dear Madam Mina is changing." A cold shiver ran through me to find my worst fears thus endorsed. [. . .] "I can see the characteristics of the vampire coming in her face. It is now but very, very slight; but it is to be seen if we have eyes to notice without to prejudge. Her teeth are some sharper, and at times her eyes are more hard. [. . .]

"If it be that she can, by our hypnotic trance, tell what the Count see and hear, is it not more true that he who have hypnotize her first, and who have drink of her very blood and make her drink of his, should, if he will, compel her mind to disclose to him that which she know?" I nodded acquiescence; he went on:— "Then, what we must do is to prevent this; we must keep her ignorant of our intent, and so she cannot tell what she know not. This is a painful task! Oh, so painful that it heart-break me to think of; but it must be. . . ."

Later.—At the very outset of our meeting a great personal relief was experienced by both Van Helsing and myself. Mrs. Harker had sent a message by her husband to say that she would not join us at present, as she thought it better that we should be free to discuss our movements without her presence to embarrass us. The Professor and I looked at each other for an instant, and somehow we both seemed relieved. For my own part, I thought that if Mrs. Harker realized the danger herself, it was much pain as well as much danger averted. [. . .]

Van Helsing roughly put the facts before us first:— "The *Czarina Catherine* left the Thames yesterday morning. It will take her at the quickest speed she has ever made at least three weeks to reach Varna; but we can travel overland to the same place in three days. [. . .] Thus, in order to be quite safe, we must leave here on 17th at latest. Then we shall at any rate be in Varna a day before the ship arrives, and able to make such preparations as may be necessary. [. . .]

"In the meantime we can do nothing here; and as I think that Varna is not familiar to any of us, why not go there more soon? It is as long to wait here as there. To-night and to-morrow we can get ready, and then, if all be well, we four can set out on our journey." "We four?" said Harker interrogatively, looking from one to another of us. "Of course!" answered the Professor quickly, "you must remain to take care of your so sweet wife!" Harker was silent for awhile and then said in a hollow voice:— "Let us talk of that part of it in the morning. I want to consult with Mina." . . .

Later . . . "Promise me that you will not tell me anything of the plans formed for the campaign against the Count. Not by word, or inference, or implication; not at any time whilst this remains to me!" and she solemnly pointed to the scar. I saw that she was in earnest, and said solemnly:— "I promise!" and as I said it I felt that from that instant a door had been shut between us. [. . .]

6 October, morning.—Another surprise. Mina woke me early, about the same time as yesterday, and asked me to bring Dr. Van Helsing. [. . .] He came at once; as he passed into the room, he asked Mina if the others might come, too. "No," she said quite simply, "it will not be necessary. You can tell them just as well. I must go with you on your journey." Dr. Van Helsing was as startled as I was. After a moment's pause he asked:— "But why?" "You must take me with you. I am safer with you, and you shall be safer, too." [. . .]

Chapter XXV – Dr. Seward's Diary

15 October.—We left Charing Cross on the morning of the 12th, got to Paris the same night, and took the places secured for us in the Orient Express. [. . .] Thank God! Mina is well, and looks to be getting stronger; her color is coming back. She sleeps a great deal; throughout the journey she slept nearly all the time. Before sunrise and sunset, however, she is very wakeful and alert; and it has become a habit for Van Helsing to hypnotize her at such times. [. . .] He always asks her what she can see and hear. She answers to the first:— "Nothing; all is dark." And to the second:— "I can hear the waves lapping against the ship, and the water rushing by. . . ."

We had dinner and went to bed early. To-morrow we are to see the Vice-Consul, and to arrange, if we can, about getting on board the ship as soon as she arrives. Van Helsing says that our chance will be to get on the boat between sunrise and sunset. The Count, even if he takes the form of a bat, cannot cross the running water of his own volition, and so cannot leave the ship. [. . .]

Dr. Seward's Diary.

25 October, noon . . . Van Helsing and I were a little alarmed about Mrs. Harker to-day. About noon she got into a sort of lethargy which we did not like; although we kept silence to the others, we were neither of us happy about it.

28 October.— Telegram. Rufus Smith, London, to Lord Godalming, care H. B. M. Vice Consul, Varna.

"*Czarina Catherine* reported entering Galatz at one o'clock to-day."

Dr. Seward's Diary.

28 October . . . "He has so used your mind; and by it he has left us here in Varna, whilst the ship that carried him rushed through enveloping fog up to Galatz, where, doubtless, he had made preparation for escaping from us. But his child-mind only saw so far; and it may be that, as ever is in God's Providence, the very thing that the evil-doer most reckoned on for his selfish good, turns out to be his chiefest harm. [. . .]

"For now that he think he is free from every trace of us all, and that he has escaped us with so many hours to him, then his selfish child-brain will whisper him to sleep. He think, too, that as he cut himself off from knowing your mind, there can be no knowledge of him to you; there is where he fail! That terrible baptism of blood which he give you makes you free to go to him in spirit, as you have as yet done in your times of freedom, when the sun rise and set. At such times you go by my volition and not by his; and this power to good of you and others, as you have won from your suffering at his hands. This is now all the more precious that he know it not, and to guard himself have even cut himself off from his knowledge of our where. [. . .]"

Chapter XXVI – Dr. Seward's Diary

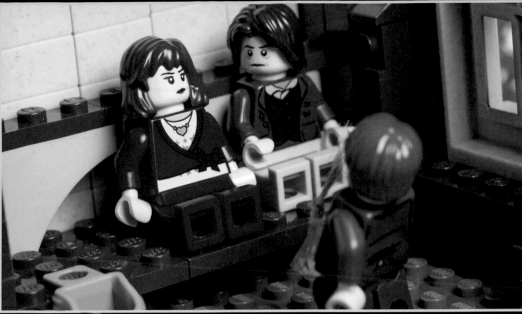

29 October.—This is written in the train from Varna to Galatz. Last night we all assembled a little before the time of sunset. Each of us had done his work as well as he could; so far as thought, and endeavor, and opportunity go, we are prepared for the whole of our journey, and for our work when we get to Galatz.

When the usual time came round Mrs. Harker prepared herself for her hypnotic effort; and after a longer and more serious effort on the part of Van Helsing than has been usually necessary, she sank into the trance. Usually she speaks on a hint; but this time the Professor had to ask her questions, and to ask them pretty resolutely, before we could learn anything; at last her answer came:—

"I can see nothing; we are still; there are no waves lapping, but only a steady swirl of water softly running against the hawser. I can hear men's voices calling, near and far, and the roll and creak of oars in the rowlocks. A gun is fired somewhere; the echo of it seems far away. There is tramping of feet overhead, and ropes and chains are dragged along. What is this? There is a gleam of light; I can feel the air blowing upon me." [. . .]

[W]hen she had gone Van Helsing said:— "You see, my friends. He is close to land: he has left his earth-chest. But he has yet to get on shore. In the night he may lie hidden somewhere; but if he be not carried on shore, or if the ship do not touch it, he cannot achieve the land.

"In such case he can, if it be in the night, change his form and can jump or fly on shore, as he did at Whitby. But if the day come before he get on shore, then, unless he be carried he cannot escape. And if he be carried, then the customs men may discover what the box contain. Thus, in fine, if he escape not on shore to-night, or before dawn, there will be the whole day lost to him. We may then arrive in time; for if he escape not at night we shall come on him in daytime, boxed up and at our mercy; for he dare not be his true self, awake and visible, lest he be discovered." [. . .]

Later . . . Mrs. Harker yielded to the hypnotic influence even less readily than this morning. I am in fear that her power of reading the Count's sensations may die away, just when we want it most. [. . .]

Jonathan Harker's Journal.

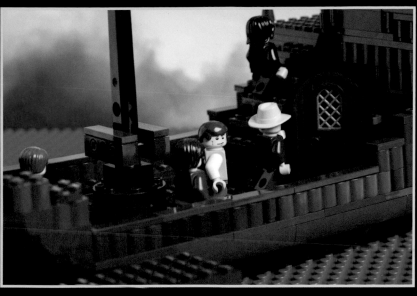

30 October.—At nine o'clock Dr. Van Helsing, Dr. Seward, and I called on Messrs. Mackenzie & Steinkoff, the agents of the London firm of Hapgood. [. . .] They were more than kind and courteous, and took us at once on board the *Czarina Catherine*, which lay at anchor out in the river harbor. There we saw the Captain, Donelson by name, who told us of his voyage. [. . .]

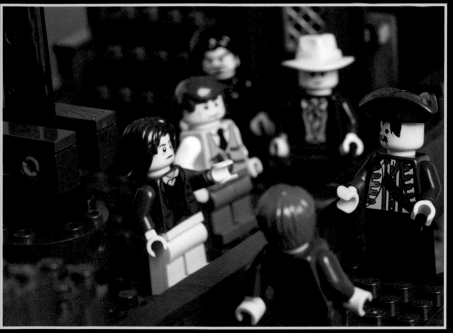

"They had, mind ye, taken the box on the deck ready to fling in, and as it was marked Galatz *via* Varna, I thocht I'd let it lie till we discharged in the port an' get rid o't althegither. We didn't do much clearin' that day, an' had to remain the nicht at anchor; but in the mornin', braw an' airly, an hour before sun-up, a man came aboard wi' an order, written to him from England, to receive a box marked for one Count Dracula. . . ." "What was the name of the man who took it?" asked Dr. Van Helsing with restrained eagerness. "I'll be tellin' ye quick!" he answered, and, stepping down to his cabin, produced a receipt signed "Immanuel Hildesheim." Burgen-strasse 16 was the address. We found out that this was all the Captain knew; so with thanks we came away.

We found Hildesheim in his office . . . He had received a letter from Mr. de Ville of London, telling him to receive, if possible before sunrise so as to avoid customs, a box which would arrive at Galatz in the *Czarina Catherine*. This he was to give in charge to a certain Petrof Skinsky, who dealt with the Slovaks who traded down the river to the port. He had been paid for his work by an English bank note, which had been duly cashed for gold at the Danube International Bank. When Skinsky had come to him, he had taken him to the ship and handed over the box, so as to save porterage. That was all he knew.

We then sought for Skinsky, but were unable to find him. One of his neighbors, who did not seem to bear him any affection, said that he had gone away two days before, no one knew whither. [. . .] Whilst we were talking one came running and breathlessly gasped out that the body of Skinsky had been found inside the wall of the churchyard of St. Peter, and that the throat had been torn open as if by some wild animal. [. . .]

Mina Harker's Journal.

30 October, evening.—They were so tired and worn out and dispirited that there was nothing to be done till they had some rest; so I asked them all to lie down for half an hour whilst I should enter everything up to the moment. [. . .] I do believe that under God's providence I have made a discovery. I shall get the maps and look over them. [. . .] Mina Harker's Memorandum. (Entered in her Journal) . . . We know from the record that he was on the water; so what we have to do is to ascertain what water. [. . .] My surmise is, this: that in London the Count decided to get back to his castle by water, as the most safe and secret way. He was brought from the castle by Szgany, and probably they delivered their cargo to Slovaks who took the boxes to Varna, for there they were shipped for London. Thus the Count had knowledge of the persons who could arrange this service. [. . .]

I have examined the map and find that the river most suitable for the Slovaks to have ascended is either the Pruth or the Sereth. I read in the typescript that in my trance I heard cows low and water swirling level with my ears and the creaking of wood. The Count in his box, then, was on a river in an open boat—propelled probably either by oars or poles, for the banks are near and it is working against stream. There would be no such sound if floating down stream. Of course it may not be either the Sereth or the Pruth, but we may possibly investigate further. Now of these two, the Pruth is the more easily navigated, but the Sereth is, at Fundu, joined by the Bistritza which runs up round the Borgo Pass. The loop it makes is manifestly as close to Dracula's castle as can be got by water.

Mina Harker's Journal—continued.

"Now men, to our Council of War; for, here and now, we must plan what each and all shall do."

"I shall get a steam launch and follow [Count Dracula]," said Lord Godalming.

"And I, horses to follow on the bank lest by chance he land," said Mr. Morris. [. . .] Dr. Seward said:— "I think I had better go with Quincey. We have been accustomed to hunt together, and we two, well armed, will be a match for whatever may come along. . . ."

He looked at Jonathan as he spoke, and Jonathan looked at me. I could see that the poor dear was torn about in his mind. Of course he wanted to be with me; but then the boat service would, most likely, be the one which would destroy the . . . the . . . the . . . Vampire. (Why did I hesitate to write the word?)

"Now let me say that what I would is this: while you, my Lord Godalming and friend Jonathan go in your so swift little steamboat up the river, and whilst John and Quincey guard the bank where perchance he might be landed, I will take Madam Mina right into the heart of the enemy's country. [. . .] [W]e shall go in the track where Jonathan went,—from Bistritz over the Borgo, and find our way to the Castle of Dracula. Here, Madam Mina's hypnotic power will surely help, and we shall find our way—all dark and unknown otherwise—after the first sunrise when we are near that fateful place. . . ."

Here Jonathan interrupted him hotly:— "Do you mean to say, Professor Van Helsing, that you would bring Mina, in her sad case and tainted as she is with that devil's illness, right into the jaws of his death-trap? Not for the world! Not for Heaven or Hell!" [. . .]

The Professor's voice, as he spoke in clear, sweet tones, which seemed to vibrate in the air, calmed us all:— "Oh, my friend, it is because I would save Madam Mina from that awful place that I would go. God forbid that I should take her into that place. There is work—wild work—to be done there, that her eyes may not see. . . ."

Later . . . It is not three hours since it was arranged what part each of us was to do; and now Lord Godalming and Jonathan have a lovely steam launch, with steam up ready to start at a moment's notice. [. . .] We have all got arms, even for me a large-bore revolver; Jonathan would not be happy unless I was armed like the rest. [. . .] It took all my courage to say good-bye to my darling. We may never meet again. Courage, Mina! the Professor is looking at you keenly; his look is a warning. There must be no tears now—unless it may be that God will let them fall in gladness.

Jonathan Harker's Journal.

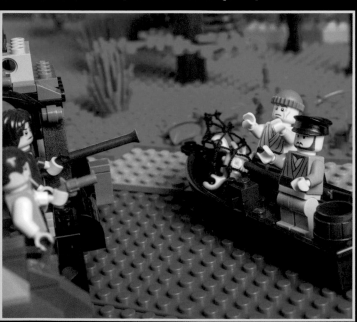

31 October.—Still hurrying along. The day has come, and Godalming is sleeping. I am on watch. The morning is bitterly cold; the furnace heat is grateful, though we have heavy fur coats. As yet we have passed only a few open boats, but none of them had on board any box or package of anything like the size of the one we seek. The men were scared every time we turned our electric lamp on them, and fell on their knees and prayed.

1 November . . . Some of the Slovaks tell us that a big boat passed them, going at more than usual speed as she had a double crew on board. This was before they came to Fundu, so they could not tell us whether the boat turned into the Bistritza or continued on up the Sereth. At Fundu we could not hear of any such boat, so she must have passed there in the night. [. . .]

Dr. Seward's Diary.

2 November.—Three days on the road. No news, and no time to write it if there had been, for every moment is precious. We have had only the rest needful for the horses; but we are both bearing it wonderfully. Those adventurous days of ours are turning up useful. We must push on . . .

Mina Harker's Journal.

31 October . . . We have something more than 70 miles before us. The country is lovely, and most interesting; if only we were under different conditions, how delightful it would be to see it all. If Jonathan and I were driving through it alone what a pleasure it would be. To stop and see people, and learn something of their life, and to fill our minds and memories with all the color and picturesqueness of the whole wild, beautiful country and the quaint people! But, alas!—

Later.—Dr. Van Helsing has returned. He has got the carriage and horses; we are to have some dinner, and to start in an hour. [. . .]

Chapter XXVII – Mina Harker's Journal

1 November.—All day long we have travelled, and at a good speed. The horses seem to know that they are being kindly treated, for they go willingly their full stage at best speed. [. . .] It is a lovely country; full of beauties of all imaginable kinds, and the people are brave, and strong, and simple, and seem full of nice qualities. They are *very, very* superstitious.

In the first house where we stopped, when the woman who served us saw the scar on my forehead, she crossed herself and put out two fingers towards me, to keep off the evil eye. I believe they went to the trouble of putting an extra amount of garlic into our food; and I can't abide garlic. [. . .]

Memorandum by Abraham Van Helsing.

2 November . . . we took turns driving all [night . . .]

4 November.—This to my old and true friend John Seward, M.D., of Purfleet, London, in case I may not see him. It may explain. It is morning, and I write by a fire which all the night I have kept alive—Madam Mina aiding me. It is cold, cold; so cold that the grey heavy sky is full of snow, which when it falls will settle for all winter as the ground is hardening to receive it. It seems to have affected Madam Mina; she has been so heavy of head all day that she was not like herself. She sleeps, and sleeps, and sleeps! [. . .]

We got to the Borgo Pass just after sunrise yesterday morning. [. . .]

So we came down this road; when we meet other ways—not always were we sure that they were roads at all, for they be neglect and light snow have fallen—the horses know and they only. I give rein to them, and they go on so patient. By-and-by we find all the things which Jonathan have note in that wonderful diary of him. Then we go on for long, long hours and hours. [. . .]

Then I arouse Madam Mina. This time she wake with not much trouble, and then I try to put her to hypnotic sleep. But she sleep not, being as though I were not.

Still I try and try, till all at once I find her and myself in dark; so I look round, and find that the sun have gone down. [. . .]

5 November . . . I got ready food: but she would not eat, simply saying that she had not hunger. [. . .]

Then, with the fear on me of what might be, I drew a ring so big for her comfort, round where Madam Mina sat; and over the ring I passed some of the wafer, and I broke it fine so that all was well guarded. [. . .]

I wished to make a test of what she could. She rose obedient, but when she have made a step she stopped, and stood as one stricken. "Why not go on?" I asked. She shook her head, and, coming back, sat down in her place. Then, looking at me with open eyes, as of one waked from sleep, she said simply:— "I cannot!" and remained silent. I rejoiced, for I knew that what she could not, none of those that we dreaded could. Though there might be danger to her body, yet her soul was safe!

Presently the horses began to scream, and tore at their tethers till I came to them and quieted them. When they did feel my hands on them, they whinnied low as in joy, and licked at my hands and were quiet for a time. [. . .]

I began to fear—horrible fears; but then came to me the sense of safety in that ring wherein I stood. I began, too, to think that my imaginings were of the night, and the gloom, and the unrest that I have gone through, and all the terrible anxiety. It was as though my memories of all Jonathan's horrid experience were befooling me; for the snow flakes and the mist began to wheel and circle round, till I could get as though a shadowy glimpse of those women that would have kissed him. And then the horses cowered lower and lower, and moaned in terror as men do in pain. Even the madness of fright was not to them, so that they could break away. I feared for my dear Madam Mina when these weird figures drew near and circled round.

I looked at her, but she sat calm, and smiled at me; when I would have stepped to the fire to replenish it, she caught me and held me back, and whispered, like a voice that one hears in a dream, so low it was:— "No! No! Do not go without. Here you are safe!" I turned to her, and looking in her eyes, said:— "But you? It is for you that I fear!"

whereat she laughed—a laugh, low and unreal, and said:— "Fear for *me*! Why fear for me? None safer in all the world from them than I am," and as I wondered at the meaning of her words, a puff of wind made the flame leap up, and I see the red scar on her forehead. Then, alas! I knew.

Did I not, I would soon have learned, for the wheeling figures of mist and snow came closer, but keeping ever without the Holy circle. Then they began to materialize till—if God have not take away my reason, for I saw it through my eyes—there were before me in actual flesh the same three women that Jonathan saw in the room, when they would have kissed his throat. [. . .]

They smiled ever at poor dear Madam Mina; and as their laugh came through the silence of the night, they twined their arms and pointed to her, and said in those so sweet tingling tones that Jonathan said were of the intolerable sweetness of the water-glasses:— "Come, sister. Come to us. Come! Come!" [. . .]

God be thanked she was not, yet, of them. I seized some of the firewood which was by me, and holding out some of the Wafer, advanced on them towards the fire. They drew back before me, and laughed their low horrid laugh. I fed the fire, and feared them not; for I knew that we were safe within our protections. They could not approach, me, whilst so armed, nor Madam Mina whilst she remained within the ring, which she could not leave no more than they could enter.

The horses had ceased to moan, and lay still on the ground; the snow fell on them softly, and they grew whiter. I knew that there was for the poor beasts no more of terror.

And so we remained till the red of the dawn to fall through the snow-gloom. I was desolate and afraid, and full of woe and terror; but when that beautiful sun began to climb the horizon life was to me again. At the first coming of the dawn the horrid figures melted in the whirling mist and snow; the wreaths of transparent gloom moved away towards the castle, and were lost. [. . .]

5 November, afternoon . . . I left Madam Mina sleeping within the Holy circle, [and] I took my way to the castle. [. . .]

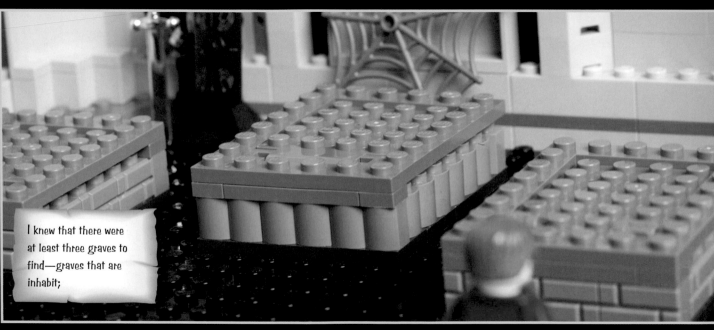

I knew that there were at least three graves to find—graves that are inhabit;

so I search, and search, and I find one of them. She lay in her Vampire sleep, so full of life and voluptuous beauty that I shudder as though I have come to do murder. [. . .]

Then I braced myself again to my horrid task, and found by wrenching away tomb-tops one other of the sisters, the other dark one. I dared not pause to look on her as I had on her sister, lest once more I should begin to be enthrall;

but I go on searching until, presently, I find in a high great tomb as if made to one much beloved that other fair sister which, like Jonathan I had seen to gather herself out of the atoms of the mist. She was so fair to look on, so radiantly beautiful, so exquisitely voluptuous, that the very instinct of man in me, which calls some of my sex to love and to protect one of hers, made my head whirl with new emotion. But God be thanked, that soul-wail of my dear Madam Mina had not died out of my ears; and, before the spell could be wrought further upon me, I had nerved myself to my wild work. [. . .]

There was one great tomb more lordly than all the rest; huge it was, and nobly proportioned. On it was but one word[:] DRACULA. [. . .]

I laid in Dracula's tomb some of the Wafer, and so banished him from it, Un-Dead, for ever. [. . .]

Before I left the castle I so fixed its entrances that never more can the Count enter there Un-Dead.

When I stepped into the circle where Madam Mina slept, she woke from her sleep, and, seeing, me, cried out in pain that I had endured too much. "Come!" she said, "come away from this awful place! Let us go to meet my husband who is, I know, coming towards us." She was looking thin and pale and weak; but her eyes were pure and glowed with fervor. I was glad to see her paleness and her illness, for my mind was full of the fresh horror of that ruddy vampire sleep. And so with trust and hope, and yet full of fear, we go eastward to meet our friends—and *him*—whom Madam Mina tell me that she know are coming to meet us.

Mina Harker's Journal.

6 November.—It was late in the afternoon when the Professor and I took our way towards the east whence I knew Jonathan was coming. We did not go fast, though the way was steeply downhill, for we had to take heavy rugs and wraps with us; we dared not face the possibility of being left without warmth in the cold and the snow. [. . .] We could hear the distant howling of wolves. They were far off, but the sound, even though coming muffled through the deadening snowfall, was full of terror.

I knew from the way Dr. Van Helsing was searching about that he was trying to seek some strategic point, where we would be less exposed in case of attack. The rough roadway still led downwards; we could trace it through the drifted snow. In a little while the Professor signaled to me, so I got up and joined him. He had found a wonderful spot, a sort of natural hollow in a rock, with an entrance like a doorway between two boulders. He took me by the hand and drew me in: "See!" he said, "here you will be in shelter; and if the wolves do come I can meet them one by one." [. . .]

Suddenly he called out:— "Look! Madam Mina, look! look!" I sprang up and stood beside him on the rock; he handed me his glasses and pointed. [. . .]

Straight in front of us and not far off—in fact, so near that I wondered we had not noticed before—came a group of mounted men hurrying along. In the midst of them was a cart, a long leiter-wagon which swept from side to side, like a dog's tail wagging, with each stern inequality of the road. Outlined against the snow as they were, I could see from the men's clothes that they were peasants or gypsies of some kind. On the cart was a great square chest. [. . .]

He paused and went on in a hollow voice:— "They are racing for the sunset. We may be too late. God's will be done!" Down came another blinding rush of driving snow, and the whole landscape was blotted out. [. . .]

Then came a sudden cry:— "Look! Look! Look! See, two horsemen follow fast, coming up from the south. It must be Quincey and John. . . ."

[L]ooking around I saw on the north side of the coming party two other men, riding at break-neck speed. One of them I knew was Jonathan, and the other I took, of course, to be Lord Godalming. They, too, were pursuing the party with the cart. [. . .]

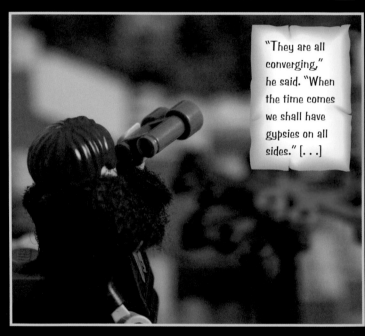

"They are all converging," he said. "When the time comes we shall have gypsies on all sides." [. . .]

We could distinguish clearly the individuals of each party, the pursued and the pursuers. Strangely enough those pursued did not seem to realize, or at least to care, that they were pursued; they seemed, however, to hasten with redoubled speed as the sun dropped lower and lower on the mountain tops. [. . .]

All at once two voices shouted out to: "Halt!" One was my Jonathan's, raised in a high key of passion; the other Mr. Morris' strong resolute tone of quiet command.

The gypsies may not have known the language, but there was no mistaking the tone, in whatever tongue the words were spoken. Instinctively they reined in, and at the instant Lord Godalming and Jonathan dashed up at one side and Dr. Seward and Mr. Morris on the other. The leader of the gypsies, a splendid-looking fellow who sat his horse like a centaur, waved them back, and in a fierce voice gave to his companions some word to proceed.

They lashed the horses which sprang forward; but the four men raised their Winchester rifles, and in an unmistakable way commanded them to stop. At the same moment Dr. Van Helsing and I rose behind the rock and pointed our weapons at them. [. . .]

For answer, all four men of our party threw themselves from their horses and dashed towards the cart. I should have felt terrible fear at seeing Jonathan in such danger, but that the ardor of battle must have been upon me as well as the rest of them; I felt no fear, but only a wild, surging desire to do something. [. . .]

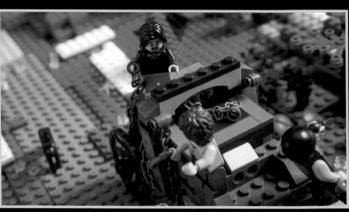

In the midst of this I could see that Jonathan on one side of the ring of men, and Quincey on the other, were forcing a way to the cart; it was evident that they were bent on finishing their task before the sun should set. [. . .]

In an instant he had jumped upon the cart, and, with a strength which seemed incredible, raised the great box, and flung it over the wheel to the ground.

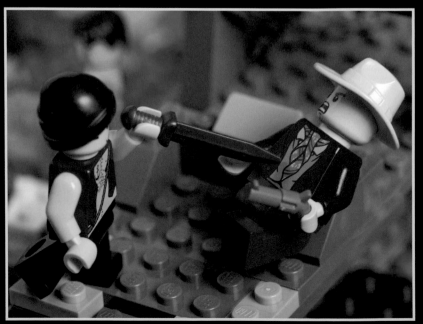

In the meantime, Mr. Morris had had to use force to pass through his side of the ring of Szgany. All the time I had been breathlessly watching Jonathan I had, with the tail of my eye, seen him pressing desperately forward, and had seen the knives of the gypsies flash as he won a way through them, and they cut at him. He had parried with his great bowie knife, and at first I thought that he too had come through in safety; but as he sprang beside Jonathan, who had by now jumped from the cart, I could see that with his left hand he was clutching at his side, and that the blood was spurting through his fingers. [. . .]

He did not delay notwithstanding this, for as Jonathan, with desperate energy, attacked one end of the chest, attempting to prize off the lid with his great Kukri knife, he attacked the other frantically with his bowie. Under the efforts of both men the lid began to yield; the nails drew with a quick screeching sound, and the top of the box was thrown back.

By this time the gypsies, seeing themselves covered by the Winchesters, and at the mercy of Lord Godalming and Dr. Seward, had given in and made no resistance. [. . .]

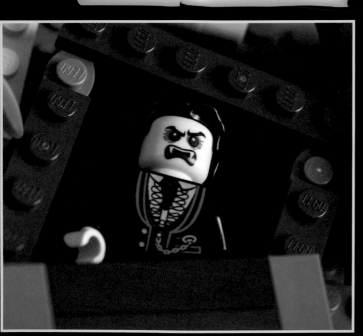

I saw the Count lying within the box upon the earth, some of which the rude falling from the cart had scattered over him. He was deathly pale, just like a waxen image, and the red eyes glared with the horrible vindictive look which I knew too well. As I looked, the eyes saw the sinking sun, and the look of hate in them turned to triumph.

But, on the instant, came the sweep and flash of Jonathan's great knife. I shrieked as I saw it shear through the throat; whilst at the same moment Mr. Morris's bowie knife plunged into the heart. [. . .]

It was like a miracle; but before our very eyes, and almost in the drawing of a breath, the whole body crumble into dust and passed from our sight.

I shall be glad as long as I live that even in that moment of final dissolution,

there was in the face a look of peace, such as I never could have imagined might have rested there. [. . .]

The gypsies, taking us as in some way the cause of the extraordinary disappearance of the dead man, turned, without a word, and rode away as if for their lives. Those who were unmounted jumped upon the leiter-wagon and shouted to the horsemen not to desert them. The wolves, which had withdrawn to a safe distance, followed in their wake, leaving us alone.

Mr. Morris, who had sunk to the ground, leaned on his elbow, holding his hand pressed to his side; the blood still gushed through his fingers. I flew to him, for the Holy circle did not now keep me back; so did the two doctors. [. . .]

He must have seen the anguish of my heart in my face, for he smiled at me and said:— "I am only too happy to have been of any service! Oh, God!" he cried suddenly, struggling up to a sitting posture and pointing to me, "It was worth for this to die! Look! look!" The sun was now right down upon the mountain top, and the red gleams fell upon my face, so that it was bathed in rosy light. With one impulse the men sank on their knees and a deep and earnest "Amen" broke from all as their eyes followed the pointing of his finger. The dying man spoke:— "Now God be thanked that all has not been in vain! See! the snow is not more stainless than her forehead! The curse has passed away!"

And, to our bitter grief, with a smile and in silence, he died, a gallant gentleman.

NOTE (Post-Script)

Seven years ago we all went through the flames; and the happiness of some of us since then is, we think, well worth the pain we endured. It is an added joy to Mina and to me that our boy's birthday is the same day as that on which Quincey Morris died. His mother holds, I know, the secret belief that some of our brave friend's spirit has passed into him. His bundle of names links all our little band of men together; but we call him Quincey.

In the summer of this year we made a journey to Transylvania, and went over the old ground which was, and is, to us so full of vivid and terrible memories. It was almost impossible to believe that the things which we had seen with our own eyes and heard with our own ears were living truths. Every trace of all that had been was blotted out. The castle stood as before, reared high above a waste of desolation.

When we got home we were talking of the old time—which we could all look back on without despair, for Godalming and Seward are both happily married.

I took the papers from the safe where they had been ever since our return so long ago. We were struck with the fact, that in all the mass of material of which the record is composed, there is hardly one authentic document; nothing but a mass of typewriting, except the later note-books of Mina and Seward and myself, and Van Helsing's memorandum. We could hardly ask any one, even did we wish to, to accept these as proofs of so wild a story. Van Helsing summed it all up as he said, with our boy on his knee:— "We want no proofs; we ask none to believe us! This boy will some day know what a brave and gallant woman his mother is. Already he knows her sweetness and loving care; later on he will understand how some men so loved her, that they did dare much for her sake." JONATHAN HARKER.

Frankenstein

CONTENTS

Horror stories terrify us, not because they are fantastical or unlikely, but because they show us our greatest weaknesses and what makes us vulnerable. They span our deepest fears and our darkest secrets, which is why many of these stories explore themes of death and dying, immortality, and the creation of life. The laws of nature are often tested by nefarious means, whether by the supernatural or the scientific. Among the most prolific of these kinds of tales is *Frankenstein*. First penned by English author Mary Wollstonecraft Shelley, the novel was written in a friendly competition of ghost stories while on a trip in Geneva, Switzerland. It was soon published anonymously in London in 1818 and again under Shelley's name in France in 1823.

Frankenstein's original subtitle, *The Modern Prometheus*, explains the book's main character concisely. Prometheus was an ancient Greek Titan who was tasked by Zeus with creating mankind and who, later—against Zeus's wishes—gave fire to humanity, allowing them to flourish and become civilized. Prometheus quickly discovered that undermining the great god came with great consequences. Like Prometheus, Shelley's Victor Frankenstein meddles with the mysteries of life and nature, and his creation only causes him suffering. The sinister tale of *Frankenstein* also comments on the Biblical creation story. The Creature reads John Milton's *Paradise Lost*, an epic poem about the fall of man. He alludes to Victor Frankenstein's role as his own God and creator, and in his struggles to garner purpose and familial love from Frankenstein, he finds himself doing horrific things, devolving from Frankenstein's "Adam" to his "fallen angel."

Frankenstein, like *Dracula*, is an epistolary novel, written as a series of letters. We begin our brick adaptation with an ambitious sea Captain named Robert Walton. Walton writes to his sister that he has just rescued a mysterious stranger from the frigid waters near the North Pole. This stranger, who we soon learn is our title character, tells the story of the great science experiment that tortures him.

Letters

Letter 1:

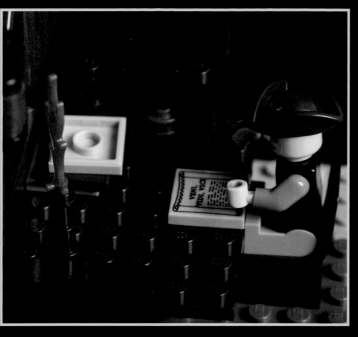

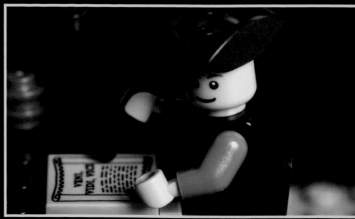

St. Petersburgh, Dec. 11th, 17—, To Mrs. Saville, England. You will rejoice to hear that no disaster has accompanied the commencement of an enterprise which you have regarded with such evil forebodings. [. . .]

Six years have passed since I resolved on my present undertaking. I can, even now, remember the hour from which I dedicated myself to this great enterprise. I commenced by inuring my body to hardship. I accompanied the whale-fishers on several expeditions to the North Sea; I often worked harder than the common sailors during the day and devoted my nights to the study of mathematics, the theory of medicine, and those branches of physical science from which a naval adventurer might derive the greatest practical advantage.

Your affectionate brother,
R. Walton

Letter 2:

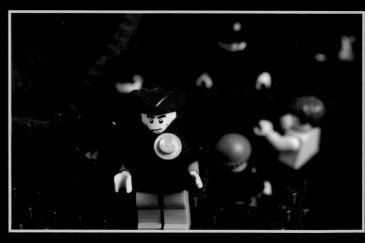

To Mrs. Saville, England. (Archangel, 28th March, 17—). How slowly the time passes here, encompassed as I am by frost and snow! Yet a second step is taken towards my enterprise. I have hired a vessel and am occupied in collecting my sailors; those on whom I can depend and are certainly possessed of dauntless courage.

But I have one want which I have never yet been able to satisfy, and the absence of the object of which I now feel as a most severe evil. I have no friend, Margaret: when I am glowing with the enthusiasm of success, there will be none to participate my joy; if I am assailed by disappointment, no one will endeavour to sustain me in dejection. I shall commit my thoughts to paper, it is true; but that is a poor medium for the communication of feeling. [. . .]

Your affectionate brother,
Robert Walton

Letter 4:

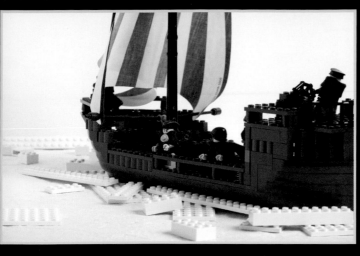

To Mrs. Saville, England (Archangel, 28th March, 17—). Last Monday (July 31st) we were nearly surrounded by ice, which closed in the ship on all sides, scarcely leaving her the sea-room in which she floated.

Our situation was somewhat dangerous, especially as we were compassed round by a very thick fog. [. . .]

Some of my comrades groaned, and my own mind began to grow watchful with anxious thoughts, when a strange sight suddenly attracted our attention and diverted our solicitude from our own situation. We perceived a low carriage, fixed on a sledge and drawn by dogs, pass on towards the north, at the distance of half a mile; a being which had the shape of a man, but apparently of gigantic stature, sat in the sledge and guided the dogs. We watched the rapid progress of the traveller with our telescopes until he was lost among the distant inequalities of the ice. [. . .]

In the morning, however, as soon as it was light, I went upon the deck and found all the sailors busy on one side of the vessel, apparently talking to someone in the sea.

It was, in fact, a sledge, like that we had seen before, which had drifted towards us in the night on a large fragment of ice. Only one dog remained alive, but there was a human being within it whom the sailors were persuading to enter the vessel. [. . .]

"Before I come on board your vessel," said he, "will you have the kindness to inform me whither you are bound?"

You may conceive my astonishment on hearing such a question addressed to me from a man on the brink of destruction and to whom I should have supposed that my vessel would have been a resource which would not have exchanged for the most precious wealth the earth can afford. I replied, however, that we were on a voyage of discovery towards the northern pole.

Upon hearing this he appeared satisfied and consented to come on board. Good God! Margaret, if you had seen the man who thus capitulated for his safety, your surprise would have been boundless. His limbs were nearly frozen, and his body dreadfully emaciated by fatigue and suffering. [. . .]

When my guest was a little recovered I had great trouble to keep off the men, who wished to ask him a thousand questions; but I would not allow him to be tormented by their idle curiosity, in a state of body and mind whose restoration evidently depended upon entire repose. Once, however, the lieutenant asked why he had come so far upon the ice in so strange a vehicle. His countenance instantly assumed an aspect of the deepest gloom, and he replied, "To seek one who fled from me." [. . .]

"Then I fancy we have seen him, for the day before we picked you up we saw some dogs drawing a sledge, with a man in it, across the ice." This aroused the stranger's attention, and he asked a multitude of questions concerning the route which the demon, as he called him, had pursued. [. . .]

From this time a new spirit of life animated the decaying frame of the stranger. He manifested the greatest eagerness to be upon deck to watch for the sledge which had before appeared; but I have persuaded him to remain in the cabin, for he is far too weak to sustain the rawness of the atmosphere. I have promised that someone should watch for him and give him instant notice if any new object should appear in sight. [. . .]

August 13, 17—

My affection for my guest increases every day. He excites at once my great admiration and my pity to an astonishing degree. How can I see so noble a creature destroyed by misery without feeling the most poignant grief? He is so gentle, yet so wise; his mind is so cultivated, and when he speaks, although his words are culled with the choicest art, yet they flow with rapidity and unparalleled eloquence. [. . .]

Yet, although unhappy, he is not so utterly occupied by his own misery but that he interests himself deeply in the projects of others. He has frequently conversed with me on mine, which I have communicated to him without disguise. He entered attentively into all my arguments in favour of my eventual success and into every minute detail of the measures I had taken to secure it.

I was easily led by the sympathy which he evinced to use the language of my heart, to give utterance to the burning ardour of my soul, and to say, with all the fervour that warmed me, how gladly I would sacrifice my fortune, my existence, my every hope, to the furtherance of my enterprise. One man's life or death were but a small price to pay for the acquirement of the knowledge which I sought, for the dominion I should acquire and transmit over the elemental foes of our race.

As I spoke, a dark gloom spread over my listener's countenance. At first I perceived that he tried to suppress his emotion; he placed his hands before his eyes, and my voice quivered and failed me as I beheld tears trickle fast from between his fingers; a groan burst from his heaving breast. I paused; at length he spoke, in broken accents: "Unhappy man! So you share my madness? Have you drunk also the intoxicating draught? Hear me; let me reveal my tale, and you will dash the cup from your lips!" [. . .]

August 19, 17—

"I do not know that the relation of my disasters will be useful to you; yet, when I reflect that you are pursuing the same course, exposing yourself to the same dangers which have rendered me what I am, I imagine that you may deduce an apt moral from my tale, one that may direct you if you succeed in your undertaking and console you in case of failure. . . ."

I felt the greatest eagerness to hear the promised narrative, partly from curiosity and partly from a strong desire to ameliorate his fate if it were in my power. [. . .]

"I thank you," he replied, "for your sympathy, but it is useless; my fate is nearly fulfilled. I wait but for one event, and then I shall repose in peace. I understand your feeling," continued he, perceiving that I wished to interrupt him; "but you are mistaken, my friend, if thus you will allow me to name you; nothing can alter my destiny; listen to my history, and you will perceive how irrevocably it is determined." [. . .]

Chapter 1 – Victor Frankenstein's Early Life

I am by birth a Genevese, and my family is one of the most distinguished of that republic. My ancestors had been for many years counsellors and syndics, and my father had filled several public situations with honour and reputation. He was respected by all who knew him for his integrity and indefatigable attention to public business. He passed his younger days perpetually occupied by the affairs of his country; a variety of circumstance had prevented his marrying early, nor was it until the decline of life that he became a husband and the father of a family. [. . .]

Much as they were attached to each other, they seemed to draw inexhaustible stores of affection from a very mine of love to bestow them on me. My mother's tender caresses and my father's smile of benevolent pleasure while regarding me are my first recollections. I was their plaything and their idol, and something better—their child, the innocent and helpless creature bestowed on them by heaven, whom to bring up to good, and whose future lot it was in their hands to direct the happiness or misery, according as they fulfilled their duties towards me. [. . .]

Their benevolent disposition often made them enter the cottages of the poor. This, to my mother, was more than a duty; it was a necessity, a passion . . . for her to act in her turn the guardian angel to the afflicted. [. . .]

One day, when my father had gone by himself to Milan, my mother, accompanied by me, visited this abode. She found a peasant and his wife, hard working, bent down by care and labour, distributing a scanty meal to five hungry babes. Among these there was one which attracted my mother far above all rest. She appeared of a different stock. The four others were dark-eyed, hardy little vagrants; this child was thin and very fair. Her hair was the brightest living gold, and despite the poverty of her clothing, seemed to set crown of distinction on her head. Her brow was clear and ample, her blue eyes cloudless, and her lips and the moulding of her face so expressive of sensibility and sweetness that none could behold her without looking on her as of a distinct species, a being heaven-sent, and bearing a celestial stamp on all her features. [. . .]

She was not [the peasants'] child, but the daughter of a Milanese nobleman. Her mother was a German and had died on giving her birth. [. . .]

With [my father's] permission my mother prevailed on her rustic guardians to yield their charge to her. [. . .] They consulted their village priest, and the result was that Elizabeth Lavenza became the inmate of my parents' house—my more than sister—the beautiful and adored companion of all my occupations and my pleasures.

Everyone loved Elizabeth. The passionate and almost reverential attachment with which all regarded her became, while I shared it, my pride and my delight.

No word, no expression could body forth the kind of relation in which she stood to me—my more than sister, since till death she was to be mine only.

Chapter 2 – Youthful Studies and Electricity

Elizabeth was of a calmer and more concentrated disposition; but, with all my ardour, I was capable of a more intense application and was more deeply smitten with the thirst for knowledge. She busied herself with following the aerial creations of the poets; and in the majestic and wondrous scenes which surrounded our Swiss home—the sublime shapes of the mountains, the changes of the seasons, tempest and calm, the silence of winter, and the life and turbulence of our Alpine summers—she found ample scope for admiration and delight. [. . .]

On the birth of a second son, my junior by seven years, my parents gave up entirely their wandering life and fixed themselves in their native country. [. . .]

It was my temper to avoid a crowd and to attach myself fervently to a few. I was indifferent, therefore, to my school-fellows in general; but I united myself in the bonds of the closest friendship to one among them.

Henry Clerval was the son of a merchant of Geneva. He was a boy of singular talent and fancy. He loved enterprise, hardship, and even danger for its own sake. [. . .]

No human being could have passed a happier childhood than myself. [. . .] When I mingled with other families I distinctly discerned how peculiarly fortunate my lot was, and gratitude assisted the development of filial love. [. . .]

The saintly soul of Elizabeth shone like a shrine-dedicated lamp in our peaceful home. Her sympathy was ours; her smile, her soft voice, the sweet glance of her celestial eyes, were ever there to bless and animate us. She was the living spirit of love to soften and attract;

I might have become sullen in my study,

rought through the ardour of my nature, but that she was there to subdue me to a semblance of her own gentleness. And Clerval—could aught ill entrench on the noble spirit of Clerval?

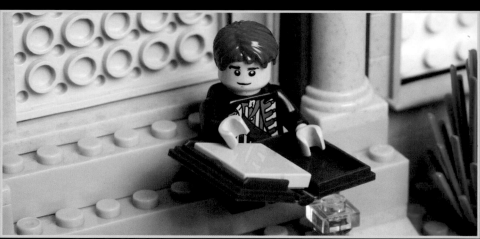

Yet he might not have been so perfectly humane, so thoughtful in his generosity, so full of kindness and tenderness amidst his passion for adventurous exploit, had she not unfolded to him the real loveliness of beneficence and made the doing good the end and aim of his soaring ambition.

When I was thirteen years of age we all went on a party of pleasure to the baths near Thonon; the inclemency of the weather obliged us to remain a day confined to the inn. In this house I chanced to find a volume of the works of Cornelius Agrippa. [. . .] A new light seemed to dawn upon my mind, and bounding with joy, I communicated my discovery to my father. My father looked carelessly at the title page of my book and said, "Ah! Cornelius Agrippa! My dear Victor, do not waste your time upon this; it is sad trash." [. . .]

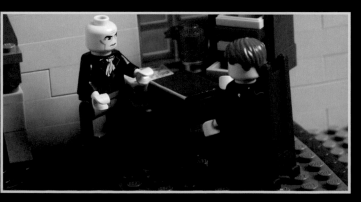

But the cursory glance my father had taken of my volume by no means assured me that he was acquainted with its contents, and I continued to read with the greatest avidity. When I returned home my first care was to procure the whole works of this author, and afterwards of Paracelsus and Albertus Magnus. I read and studied the wild fancies of these writers with delight; they appeared to me treasures known to few besides myself. I have described myself as always having been imbued with a fervent longing to penetrate the secrets of nature. [. . .]

But here were books, and here were men who had penetrated deeper and knew more. I took their word for all that they averred, and I became their disciple. [. . .] Under the guidance of my new preceptors I entered with the greatest diligence into the search of the philosopher's stone and the elixir of life; but the latter soon obtained my undivided attention. [. . .]

When I was about fifteen years old we had retired to our house near Belrive, when we witnessed a most violent and terrible thunderstorm. [. . .] I stood at the door, on a sudden I beheld a stream of fire issue from an old and beautiful oak which stood about twenty yards from our house; and so soon as the dazzling light vanished, the oak had disappeared, and nothing remained but a blasted stump.

When we visited it the next morning, we found the tree shattered in a singular manner. It was not splintered by the shock, but entirely reduced to thin ribbons of wood. I never beheld anything so utterly destroyed.

Before this I was not unacquainted with the more obvious laws of electricity. On this occasion a man of great research in natural philosophy was with us, and excited by this catastrophe, he entered on the explanation of a theory which he had formed on the subject of electricity and galvanism, which was at once new and astonishing to me.

All that he said threw greatly into the shade Cornelius Agrippa, Albertus Magnus, and Paracelsus, the lords of my imagination; but by some fatality the overthrow of these men disinclined me to pursue my accustomed studies. It seemed to me as if nothing would or could ever be known. All that had so long engaged my attention suddenly grew despicable. [. . .]

Chapter 3 – University and the "Deepest Mysteries of Creation"

When I had attained the age of seventeen my parents resolved that I should become a student at the university of Ingolstadt. [. . .]

My departure was therefore fixed at an early date, but before the day resolved upon could arrive, the first misfortune of my life occurred—an omen, as it were, of my future misery. Elizabeth had caught the scarlet fever; her illness was severe, and she was in the greatest danger.

During her illness many arguments had been urged to persuade my mother to refrain from attending upon her. She had at first yielded to our entreaties, but when she heard that the life of her favourite was menaced, she could no longer control her anxiety. She attended her sickbed; her watchful attentions triumphed over the malignity of the distemper—

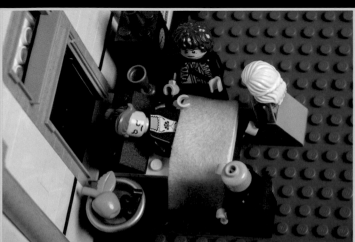

Elizabeth was saved, but the consequences of this imprudence were fatal to her preserver. [. . .]

She joined the hands of Elizabeth and myself. "My children," she said, "my firmest hopes of future happiness were placed on the prospect of your union." [. . .]

"I will endeavour to resign myself cheerfully to death and will indulge a hope of meeting you in another world." [. . .]

My departure for Ingolstadt, which had been deferred by these events, was now again determined upon. [. . .]

We could not tear ourselves away from each other nor persuade ourselves to say the word "Farewell!" It was said, and we retired under the pretence of seeking repose, each fancying that the other was deceived; but when at morning's dawn I descended to the carriage which was to convey me away, they were all there—my father again to bless me, Clerval to press my hand once more, my Elizabeth to renew her entreaties that I would write often and to bestow the last feminine attentions on her playmate and friend. [. . .]

I loved my brothers, Elizabeth, and Clerval; these were "old familiar faces," but I believed myself totally unfitted for the company of strangers.

Such were my reflections as I commenced my journey; but as I proceeded, my spirits and hopes rose.

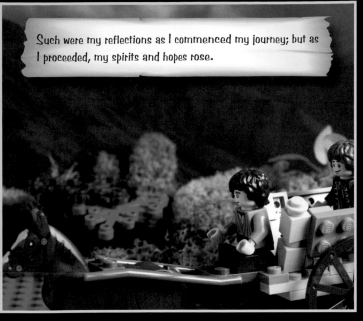

I ardently desired the acquisition of knowledge. [. . .]

Partly from curiosity and partly from idleness, I went into the lecturing room, which M. Waldman entered shortly after. [. . .] He began his lecture by a recapitulation of the history of chemistry and the various improvements made by different men of learning, pronouncing with fervour the names of the most distinguished discoverers. [. . .]

"The ancient teachers of this science," said he, "promised impossibilities and performed nothing. The modern masters promise very little; they know that metals cannot be transmuted and that the elixir of life is a chimera but these philosophers, whose hands seem only made to dabble in dirt, and their eyes to pore over the microscope or crucible, have indeed performed miracles. They penetrate into the recesses of nature and show how she works in her hiding-places. They ascend into the heavens; they have discovered how the blood circulates, and the nature of the air we breathe. They have acquired new and almost unlimited powers; they can command the thunders of heaven, mimic the earthquake, and even mock the invisible world with its own shadows." Such were the professor's words—rather let me say such the words of the fate—enounced to destroy me.

As he went on I felt as if my soul were grappling with a palpable enemy; one by one the various keys were touched which formed the mechanism of my being; chord after chord was sounded, and soon my mind was filled with one thought, one conception, one purpose.

So much has been done, exclaimed the soul of Frankenstein—more, far more, will I achieve; treading in the steps already marked, I will pioneer a new way, explore unknown powers, and unfold to the world the deepest mysteries of creation. [. . .]

"I am happy," said M. Waldman, "to have gained a disciple; and if your application equals your ability, I have no doubt of your success. Chemistry is that branch of natural philosophy in which the greatest improvements have been and may be made; it is on that account that I have made it my peculiar study; but at the same time, I have not neglected the other branches of science. A man would make but a very sorry chemist if he attended to that department of human knowledge alone. If your wish is to become really a man of science and not merely a petty experimentalist, I should advise you to apply to every branch of natural philosophy, including mathematics." [. . .]

Chapter 4 – The Secret of Life

In M. Waldman I found a true friend. His gentleness was never tinged by dogmatism, and his instructions were given with an air of frankness and good nature that banished every idea of pedantry. [. . .]

As I applied so closely, it may be easily conceived that my progress was rapid.

My ardour was indeed the astonishment of the students, and my proficiency that of the masters. [. . .]

Two years passed in this manner, during which I paid no visit to Geneva, but was engaged, heart and soul, in the pursuit of some discoveries which I hoped to make. [. . .]

When I found so astonishing a power placed within my hands, I hesitated a long time concerning the manner in which I should employ it. Although I possessed the capacity of bestowing animation, yet to prepare a frame for the reception of it, with all its intricacies of fibres, muscles, and veins, still remained a work of inconceivable difficulty and labour. I doubted at first whether I should attempt the creation of a being like myself, or one of simpler organization . . .

One secret which I alone possessed was the hope to which I dedicated myself; and the moon gazed on my midnight labours, while, with unrelaxed and breathless eagerness, I pursued nature to her hiding-places. Who shall conceive the horrors of my secret toil as I dabbled among the unhallowed damps of the grave or tortured the living animal to animate the lifeless clay? My limbs now tremble, and my eyes swim with the remembrance; but then a resistless and almost frantic impulse urged me forward; I seemed to have lost all soul or sensation but for this one pursuit. [. . .]

I collected the bones from charnel-houses

and disturbed, with profane fingers,

the tremendous secrets of the human frame. [. . .]

Every night I was oppressed by a slow fever, and I became nervous to a most painful degree;

the fall of a leaf startled me,

and I shunned my fellow creatures as if I had been guilty of a crime.

Sometimes I grew alarmed at the wreck I perceived that I had become;

the energy of my purpose alone sustained me:

my labours would soon end, and I believed that exercise and amusement would the drive away incipient disease;

and I promised myself both of these when my creation should be complete.

Chapter 5 – The Spark of Life: It's Alive

It was on a dreary night of November that I beheld the accomplishment of my toils.

With an anxiety that almost amounted accounted to agony, I collected the instruments of life around me,

that I might infuse a spark of being into the lifeless thing that lay at my feet.

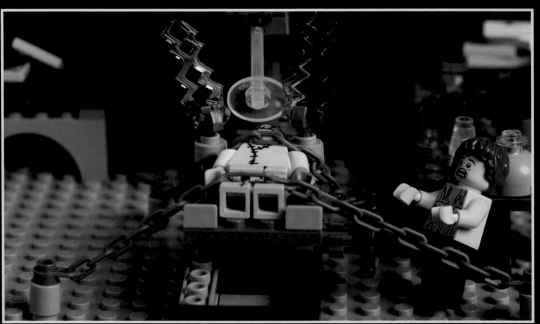

How can I describe my emotions at this catastrophe, or how delineate the wretch whom with such infinite pains and care I had endeavoured to form?

His limbs were in proportion, and I had selected his features as beautiful! Beautiful! Great God!

His yellow skin scarcely covered the work of muscles and arteries beneath;

his hair was of a lustrous black, and flowing; his teeth of a pearly whiteness; but these luxuriances only formed a more horrid contrast with his watery eyes,

that seemed almost the same colour as the dun-white sockets in which they were set, his shrivelled complexion and straight black lips.

Unable to endure the aspect of the being I had created, I rushed out of the room

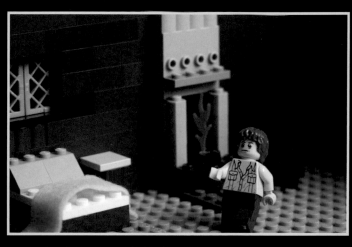

and continued a long time traversing my bedchamber, unable to compose my mind to sleep. At length lassitude succeeded to the tumult I had before endured,

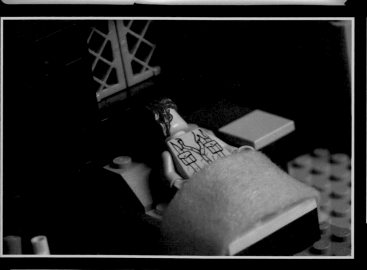

and I threw myself on the bed in my clothes, endeavouring to seek a few moments of forgetfulness. [. . .]

I started from my sleep with horror; a cold dew covered my forehead, my teeth chattered, and every limb became convulsed; when, by the dim and yellow light of the moon, as it forced its way through the window shutters,

I beheld the wretch—the miserable monster whom I had created. He held the curtain of the bed; and his eyes, if eyes, if eyes they may be called, were fixed on me.

His jaws opened, and he muttered some inarticulate sounds, while a grin wrinkled his cheeks.

He might have spoken, but I did not hear; one hand was stretched out, seemingly to detain me, but I escaped and rushed downstairs.

I took refuge in the courtyard belonging to the house which I inhabited, where I remained during the rest of the night, walking up and down in the greatest agitation, listening attentively, catching and fearing each sound as if it were to announce the approach of the demoniacal corpse to which I had so miserably given life. [. . .]

Continuing thus, I came at length opposite to the inn at which the various diligences and carriages usually stopped. Here I paused, I knew not why; but I remained some minutes with my eyes fixed on a coach that was coming towards me from the other end of the street. As it drew nearer I observed that it was the Swiss diligence; it stopped just where I was standing, and on the door being opened, I perceived Henry Clerval, who, on seeing me, instantly sprung out.

"My dear Frankenstein," exclaimed he, "how glad I am to see you! How fortunate that you should be here at the very moment of my alighting!" [. . .]

I then reflected, and the thought made me shiver, that the creature whom I had left in my apartment might still be there, alive and walking about. I dreaded to behold this monster, but I feared still more that Henry should see him. Entreating him, therefore, to remain a few minutes at the bottom of the stairs, I darted up towards my own room. My hand was already on the lock of the door before I recollected myself. I then paused, and a cold shivering came over me. I threw the door forcibly open, as children are accustomed to do when they expect a spectre to stand in waiting for them on the other side; but nothing appeared. I stepped fearfully in: the apartment was empty, and my bedroom was also freed from its hideous guest. I could hardly believe that so great a good fortune could have befallen me, but when I became assured that my enemy had indeed fled, I clapped my hands for joy and ran down to Clerval. [. . .]

"My dear Victor," cried he, "what, for God's sake, is the matter? Do not laugh in that manner. How ill you are! What is the cause of all this?" "Do not ask me," cried I, putting my hands before my eyes, for I thought I saw the dreaded spectre glide into the room; "HE can tell. Oh, save me! Save me!" I imagined that the monster seized me; I struggled furiously and fell down in a fit. [. . .]

This was the commencement of a nervous fever which confined me for several months. During all that time Henry was my only nurse. [. . .]

"I will not mention it if it agitates you; but your father and cousin would be very happy if they received a letter from you in your own handwriting. They hardly know how ill you have been and are uneasy at your long silence." "Is that all, my dear Henry? How could you suppose that my first thought would not fly towards those dear, dear friends whom I love and who are so deserving of my love?" "If this is your present temper, my friend, you will perhaps be glad to see a letter that has been lying here some days for you; it is from your cousin, I believe."

Chapter 6 – Return to Geneva and Torment

Clerval then put the following letter into my hands. It was from my own Elizabeth . . .

"Dear, dear Elizabeth!" I exclaimed, when I had read her letter: "I will write instantly and relieve them from the anxiety they must feel." I wrote, and this exertion greatly fatigued me; but my convalescence had commenced, and proceeded regularly. [. . .]

Chapter 7 – Murder and Accusations

On my return, I found the following letter from my father . . . [your brother] William is dead!—that sweet child, whose smiles delighted and warmed my heart, who was so gentle, yet so gay! Victor, he is murdered! [. . .]

"Last Thursday (May 7th), I, my niece, and your two brothers, went to walk in Plainpalais.

"The evening was warm and serene, and we prolonged our walk farther than usual. It was already dusk before we thought of returning;

"and then we discovered that William and Ernest, who had gone on before, were not to be found. [. . .]

"This account rather alarmed us, and we continued to search for him until night fell, when Elizabeth conjectured that he might have returned to the house. He was not there. We returned again, with torches; for I could not rest, when I thought that my sweet boy had lost himself, and was exposed to all the damps and dews of night; Elizabeth also suffered extreme anguish.

"About five in the morning I discovered my lovely boy, whom the night before I had seen blooming and active in health, stretched on the grass livid and motionless; the print of the murder's finger was on his neck.

"He was conveyed home, and the anguish that was visible in my countenance betrayed the secret to Elizabeth. She was very earnest to see the corpse. At first I attempted to prevent her but she persisted, and entering the room where it lay, hastily examined the neck of the victim, and clasping her hands exclaimed, 'O God! I have murdered my darling child!'

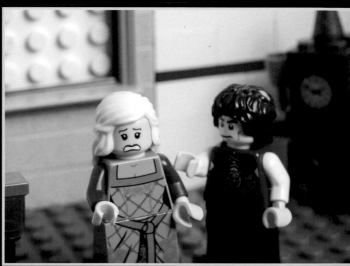

"[Elizabeth] fainted, and was restored with extreme difficulty.

"When she again lived, it was only to weep and sigh.

"She told me, that that same evening William had teased her to let him wear a very valuable miniature that she possessed of your mother.

This picture is gone, and was doubtless the temptation which urged the murderer to the deed. [. . .]

"Come, dearest Victor; you alone can console Elizabeth. She weeps continually, and accuses herself unjustly as the cause of his death; her words pierce my heart. We are all unhappy; but will not that be an additional motive for you, my son, to return and be our comforter? Your dear mother! Alas, Victor! I now say, Thank God she did not live to witness the cruel, miserable death of her youngest darling! [. . .]

Your affectionate and afflicted father,
Alphonse Frankenstein.

Geneva, May 12th, 17—." [. . .]

My journey was very melancholy. At first I wished to hurry on, for I longed to console and sympathize with my loved and sorrowing friends; but when I drew near my native town, I slackened my progress. [. . .]

Fear overcame me; I dared no advance, dreading a thousand nameless evils that made me tremble, although I was unable to define them. [. . .]

I quitted my seat, and walked on, although the darkness and storm increased every minute, and the thunder burst with a terrific crash over my head. [. . .]

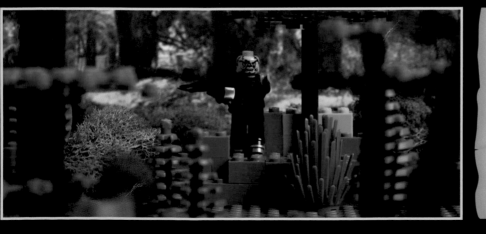

While I watched the tempest, so beautiful yet terrific, I wandered on with a hasty step. [. . .] I perceived in the gloom a figure which stole from behind a clump of trees near me; I stood fixed, gazing intently: I could not be mistaken. A flash of lightning illuminated the object, and discovered its shape plainly to me; its gigantic stature, and the deformity of its aspect more hideous than belongs to humanity, instantly informed me that it was the wretch, the filthy daemon, to whom I had given life. [. . .]

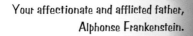

Nothing in human shape could have destroyed the fair child. HE was the murderer! I could not doubt it. The mere presence of the idea was an irresistible proof of the fact.

I thought of pursuing the devil; but it would have been in vain . . . He soon reached the summit, and disappeared.

Day dawned; and I directed my steps towards the town. The gates were open, and I hastened to my father's house. [. . .] [Ernest had] heard me arrive, and hastened to welcome me: "Welcome, my dearest Victor," said he. "Ah! I wish you had come three months ago, and then you would have found us all joyous and delighted. You come to us now to share a misery which nothing can alleviate . . ."

"Elizabeth most of all," said Ernest, "requires consolation; she accused herself of having caused the death of my brother, and that made her very wretched. But since the murderer has been discovered—" "The murderer discovered! Good God! how can that be? who could attempt to pursue him? It is impossible; one might as well try to overtake the winds, or confine a mountain-stream with a straw. I saw him too; he was free last night!" "I do not know what you mean," replied my brother, in accents of wonder, "but to us the discovery we have made completes our misery.

"No one would believe it at first; and even now Elizabeth will not be convinced, notwithstanding all the evidence. Indeed, who would credit that Justine Moritz, who was so amiable, and fond of all the family, could suddenly become so capable of so frightful, so appalling a crime?" "Justine Moritz! Poor, poor girl, is she the accused? But it is wrongfully; every one knows that; no one believes it, surely, Ernest?" [. . .]

He then related that, the morning on which the murder of poor William had been discovered, Justine had been taken ill, and confined to her bed for several days. During this interval, one of the servants, happening to examine the apparel she had worn on the night of the murder, had discovered in her pocket the picture of my mother, which had been judged to be the temptation of the murderer. The servant instantly showed it to one of the others, who, without saying a word to any of the family, went to a magistrate; and, upon their deposition, Justine was apprehended. On being charged with the fact, the poor girl confirmed the suspicion in a great measure by her extreme confusion of manner.

This was a strange tale, but it did not shake my faith; and I replied earnestly, "You are all mistaken; I know the murderer. Justine, poor, good Justine, is innocent."

At that instant my father entered. [. . .] "We do also, unfortunately," replied my father, "for indeed I had rather have been for ever ignorant than have discovered so much depravity and ungratitude in one I valued so highly."

"My dear father, you are mistaken; Justine is innocent." "If she is, God forbid that she should suffer as guilty. She is to be tried today, and I hope, I sincerely hope, that she will be acquitted." [. . .] "She is innocent, my Elizabeth," said I, "and that shall be proved; fear nothing, but let your spirits be cheered by the assurance of her acquittal." [. . .]

Chapter 8 — Justine's Trial and Frankenstein's Guilt

During the whole of this wretched mockery of justice I suffered living torture. It was to be decided whether the result of my curiosity and lawless devices would cause the death of two of my fellow beings: one a smiling babe full of innocence and joy, the other far more dreadfully murdered, with every aggravation of infamy that could make the murder memorable in horror. Justine also was a girl of merit and possessed qualities which promised to render her life happy; now all was to be obliterated in an ignominious grave, and I the cause! A thousand times rather would I have confessed myself guilty of the crime ascribed to Justine, but I was absent when it was committed, and such a declaration would have been considered as the ravings of a madman and would not have exculpated her who suffered through me.

The appearance of Justine was calm. [. . .] [H]er countenance, always engaging, was rendered, by the solemnity of her feelings, exquisitely beautiful. Yet she appeared confident in innocence and did not tremble, although gazed on and execrated by thousands, for all the kindness which her beauty might otherwise have excited was obliterated in the minds of the spectators by the imagination of the enormity she was supposed to have committed. She was tranquil, yet her tranquillity was evidently constrained; and as her confusion had before been adduced as a proof of her guilt, she worked up her mind to an appearance of courage.

When she entered the court she threw her eyes round it and quickly discovered where we were seated. A tear seemed to dim her eye when she saw us, but she quickly recovered herself, and a look of sorrowful affection seemed to attest her utter guiltlessness.

The trial began, and after the advocate against her had stated the charge, several witnesses were called. Several strange facts combined against her, which might have staggered anyone who had not such proof of her innocence as I had. [. . .]

"God knows," she said, "how entirely I am innocent. But I do not pretend that my protestations should acquit me; I rest my innocence on a plain and simple explanation of the facts which have been adduced against me, and I hope the character I have always borne will incline my judges to a favourable interpretation where any circumstance appears doubtful or suspicious." [. . .]

"For my own part, I do not hesitate to say that, notwithstanding all the evidence produced against her, I believe and rely on her perfect innocence. She had no temptation for such an action; as to the bauble on which the chief proof rests, if she had earnestly desired it, I should have willingly given it to her, so much do I esteem and value her." [. . .]

The ballots had been thrown;

they were all black, and Justine was condemned.

I cannot pretend to describe what I then felt. I had before experienced sensations of horror, and I have endeavoured to bestow upon them adequate expressions, but words cannot convey an idea of the heart-sickening despair that I then endured. The person to whom I addressed myself added that Justine had already confessed her guilt. "That evidence," he observed, "was hardly required in so glaring a case, but I am glad of it, and, indeed, none of our judges like to condemn a criminal upon circumstantial evidence, be it ever so decisive." This was strange and unexpected intelligence; what could it mean? [. . .]

Soon after we heard that the poor victim had expressed a desire to see my cousin. My father wished her not to go but said that he left it to her own judgment and feelings to decide. "Yes," said Elizabeth, "I will go, although she is guilty; and you, Victor, shall accompany me; I cannot go alone." The idea of this visit was torture to me, yet I could not refuse. [. . .]

"Rise, my poor girl," said Elizabeth; "why do you kneel, if you are innocent? I am not one of your enemies, I believed you guiltless, notwithstanding every evidence, until I heard that you had yourself declared your guilt. That report, you say, is false; and be assured, dear Justine, that nothing can shake my confidence in you for a moment, but your own confession." "I did confess, but I confessed a lie. I confessed, that I might obtain absolution; but now that falsehood lies heavier at my heart than all my other sins. The God of heaven forgive me! [. . .]

"In these last moments I feel the sincerest gratitude towards those who think of me with kindness. How sweet is the affection of others to such a wretch as I am! It removes more than half my misfortune, and I feel as if I could die in peace now that my innocence is acknowledged by you, dear lady, and your cousin." [. . .]

And on the morrow Justine died. Elizabeth's heart-rending eloquence failed to move the judges from their settled conviction in the criminality of the saintly sufferer. My passionate and indignant appeals were lost upon them. And when I received their cold answers and heard the harsh, unfeeling reasoning of these men, my purposed avowal died away on my lips. Thus I might proclaim myself a madman, but not revoke the sentence passed upon my wretched victim. She perished on the scaffold as a murderess! [. . .]

Chapter 9 — Belrive

My father observed with pain the alteration perceptible in my disposition and habits and endeavoured by arguments deduced from the feelings of his serene conscience and guiltless life to inspire me with fortitude and awaken in me the courage to dispel the dark cloud which brooded over me. "Do you think, Victor," said he, "that I do not suffer also? No one could love a child more than I loved your brother"—tears came into his eyes as he spoke—"but is it not a duty to the survivors that we should refrain from augmenting their unhappiness by an appearance of immoderate grief? It is also a duty owed to yourself, for excessive sorrow prevents improvement or enjoyment, or even the discharge of daily usefulness, without which no man is fit for society." [. . .]

Nothing is more painful to the human mind than, after the feelings have been worked up by a quick succession of events, the dead calmness of inaction and certainty which follows and deprives the soul both of hope and fear. Justine died, she rested, and I was alive. The blood flowed freely in my veins, but a weight of despair and remorse pressed on my heart which nothing could remove. [. . .]

Often, after the rest of the family had retired for the night, I took the boat and passed many hours upon the water. Sometimes, with my sails set, I was carried by the wind; and sometimes, after rowing into the middle of the lake, I left the boat to pursue its own course and gave way to my own miserable reflections. [. . .]

About this time we retired to our house at Belrive. This change was particularly agreeable to me. [. . .]

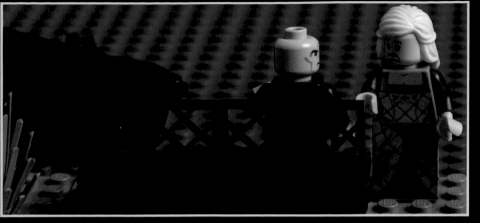

Our house was the house of mourning. My father's health was deeply shaken by the horror of the recent events. Elizabeth was sad and desponding; she no longer took delight in her ordinary occupations; all pleasure seemed to her sacrilege toward the dead; eternal woe and tears she then thought was the just tribute she should pay to innocence so blasted and destroyed. [. . .]

I, not in deed, but in effect, was the true murderer. Elizabeth read my anguish in my countenance, and kindly taking my hand, said, "My dearest friend, you must calm yourself. These events have affected me, God knows how deeply; but I am not so wretched as you are. There is an expression of despair, and sometimes of revenge, in your countenance that makes me tremble. Dear Victor, banish these dark passions. Remember the friends around you, who centre all their hopes in you. Have we lost the power of rendering you happy? Ah! While we love, while we are true to each other, here in this land of peace and beauty, your native country, we may reap every tranquil blessing—what can disturb our peace?" And could not such words from her whom I fondly prized before every other gift of fortune suffice to chase away the fiend that lurked in my heart? Even as she spoke I drew near to her, as if in terror, lest at that very moment the destroyer had been near to rob me of her. Thus not the tenderness of friendship, nor the beauty of earth, nor of heaven, could redeem my soul from woe; the very accents of love were ineffectual. [. . .]

A tingling long-lost sense of pleasure often came across me during this journey. [. . .]

Sometimes I could cope with the sullen despair that overwhelmed me, but sometimes the whirlwind passions of my soul drove me to seek, by bodily exercise and by change of place, some relief from my intolerable sensations. It was during an access of this kind that I suddenly left my home, and bending my steps towards the near Alpine valleys, sought in the magnificence, the eternity of such scenes, to forget myself and my ephemeral, because human, sorrows. My wanderings were directed towards the valley of Chamonix. [. . .]

Chapter 10 — The Monster Returns

These sublime and magnificent scenes afforded me the greatest consolation that I was capable of receiving. They elevated me from all littleness of feeling, and although they did not remove my grief, they subdued and tranquillized it. In some degree, also, they diverted my mind from the thoughts over which it had brooded for the last month. [. . .]

All of soul-inspiriting fled with sleep, and dark melancholy clouded every thought.

The rain was pouring in torrents, and thick mists hid the summits of the mountains, so that I even saw not the faces of those mighty friends. Still I would penetrate their misty veil and seek them in their cloudy retreats. What were rain and storm to me? My mule was brought to the door, and I resolved to ascend to the summit of Montanvert. [. . .]

It was nearly noon when I arrived at the top of the ascent. For some time I sat upon the rock that overlooks the sea of ice. [. . .] My heart, which was before sorrowful, now swelled with something like joy; I exclaimed, "Wandering spirits, if indeed ye wander, and do not rest in your narrow beds, allow me this faint happiness, or take me, as your companion, away from the joys of life." As I said this I suddenly beheld the figure of a man, at some distance, advancing towards me with superhuman speed. He bounded over the crevices in the ice, among which I had walked with caution; his stature, also, as he approached, seemed to exceed that of man.

I was troubled; a mist came over my eyes, and I felt a faintness seize me, but I was quickly restored by the cold gale of the mountains. I perceived, as the shape came nearer (sight tremendous and abhorred!) that it was the wretch whom I had created. I trembled with rage and horror, resolving to wait his approach and then close with him in mortal combat.

He approached; his countenance bespoke bitter anguish, combined with disdain and malignity, while its unearthly ugliness rendered it almost too horrible for human eyes. But I scarcely observed this; rage and hatred had at first deprived me of utterance, and I recovered only to overwhelm him with words expressive of furious detestation and contempt.

"Devil," I exclaimed, "do you dare approach me? And do not you fear the fierce vengeance of my arm wreaked on your miserable head? Begone, vile insect! Or rather, stay, that I may trample you to dust! And, oh! That I could, with the extinction of your miserable existence, restore those victims whom you have so diabolically murdered." [. . .]

"Be calm! I entreat you to hear me before you give vent to your hatred on my devoted head. Have I not suffered enough, that you seek to increase my misery? Life, although it may only be an accumulation of anguish, is dear to me, and I will defend it. Remember, thou hast made me more powerful than thyself; my height is superior to thine, my joints more supple. But I will not be tempted to set myself in opposition to thee. I am thy creature, and I will be even mild and docile to my natural lord and king if thou wilt also perform thy part, the which thou owest me. Oh, Frankenstein, be not equitable to every other and trample upon me alone, to whom thy justice, and even thy clemency and affection, is most due. Remember that I am thy creature; I ought to be thy Adam, but I am rather the fallen angel, whom thou drivest from joy for no misdeed. Everywhere I see bliss, from which I alone am irrevocably excluded. I was benevolent and good; misery made me a fiend. Make me happy, and I shall again be virtuous."

"Begone! I will not hear you. There can be no community between you and me; we are enemies. Begone, or let us try our strength in a fight, in which one must fall."

"How can I move thee? Will no entreaties cause thee to turn a favourable eye upon thy creature, who implores thy goodness and compassion? Believe me, Frankenstein, I was benevolent; my soul glowed with love and humanity; but am I not alone, miserably alone? You, my creator, abhor me; what hope can I gather from your fellow creatures, who owe me nothing? [. . .]

"Hear my tale; it is long and strange, and the temperature of this place is not fitting to your fine sensations; come to the hut upon the mountain. The sun is yet high in the heavens; before it descends to hide itself behind your snowy precipices and illuminate another world, you will have heard my story and can decide. On you it rests, whether I quit forever the neighbourhood of man and lead a harmless life, or become the scourge of your fellow creatures and the author of your own speedy ruin." As he said this he led the way across the ice; I followed. My heart was full, and I did not answer him, but as I proceeded, I weighed the various arguments that he had used and determined at least to listen to his tale. I was partly urged by curiosity, and compassion confirmed my resolution. I had hitherto supposed him to be the murderer of my brother, and I eagerly sought a confirmation or denial of this opinion. For the first time, also, I felt what the duties of a creator towards his creature were, and that I ought to render him happy before I complained of his wickedness.

These motives urged me to comply with his demand. We crossed the ice, therefore, and ascended the opposite rock. The air was cold, and the rain again began to descend; we entered the hut, the fiend with an air of exultation, I with a heavy heart and depressed spirits. But I consented to listen, and seating myself by the fire which my odious companion had lighted, he thus began his tale.

Chapter 11 – The Early Life of Frankenstein's Monster

It is with considerable difficulty that I remember the original era of my being; all the events of that period appear confused and indistinct. A strange multiplicity of sensations seized me, and I saw, felt, heard, and smelt at the same time; and it was, indeed, a long time before I learned to distinguish between the operations of my various senses.

[When I first left you] the light became more and more oppressive to me, and the heat wearying me as I walked, I sought a place where I could receive shade. This was the forest near Ingolstadt; and here I lay by the side of a brook resting from my fatigue, until I felt tormented by hunger and thirst. This roused me from my nearly dormant state, and I ate some berries which I found hanging on the trees or lying on the ground. I slaked my thirst at the brook, and then lying down, was overcome by sleep. [. . .]

I was still cold when under one of the trees I found a huge cloak, with which I covered myself, and sat down upon the ground. No distinct ideas occupied my mind; all was confused. I felt light, and hunger, and thirst, and darkness; innumerable sounds rang in my ears, and on all sides various scents saluted me; the only object that I could distinguish was the bright moon, and I fixed my eyes on that with pleasure. [. . .]

My sensations had by this time become distinct, and my mind received every day additional ideas. My eyes became accustomed to the light and to perceive objects in their right forms; I distinguished the insect from the herb, and by degrees, one herb from another. I found that the sparrow uttered none but harsh notes, whilst those of the blackbird and thrush were sweet and enticing.

One day, when I was oppressed by cold, I found a fire which had been left by some wandering beggars, and was overcome with delight at the warmth I experienced from it. In my joy I thrust my hand into the live embers, but quickly drew it out again with a cry of pain. How strange, I thought, that the same cause should produce such opposite effects! [...]

It was about seven in the morning, and I longed to obtain food and shelter; at length I perceived a small hut, on a rising ground, which had doubtless been built for the convenience of some shepherd. This was a new sight to me, and I examined the structure with great curiosity.

Finding the door open, I entered. An old man sat in it, near a fire, over which he was preparing his breakfast. He turned on hearing a noise, and perceiving me, shrieked loudly, and quitting the hut, ran across the fields with a speed of which his debilitated form hardly appeared capable.

His appearance, different from any I had ever before seen, and his flight somewhat surprised me. But I was enchanted by the appearance of the hut; here the snow and rain could not penetrate; the ground was dry; and it presented to me then as exquisite and divine a retreat as Pandemonium appeared to the demons of hell after their sufferings in the lake of fire. I greedily devoured the remnants of the shepherd's breakfast, which consisted of bread, cheese, milk, and wine; the latter, however, I did not like. Then, overcome by fatigue, I lay down among some straw and fell asleep. [...]

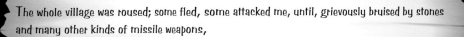

The whole village was roused; some fled, some attacked me, until, grievously bruised by stones and many other kinds of missile weapons,

I escaped to the open country and fearfully took refuge in a low hovel, quite bare, and making a wretched appearance after the palaces I had beheld in the village. This hovel however, joined a cottage of a neat and pleasant appearance, but after my late dearly bought experience, I dared not enter it. [. . .]

On examining my dwelling, I found that one of the windows of the cottage had formerly occupied a part of it, but the panes had been filled up with wood. In one of these was a small and almost imperceptible chink through which the eye could just penetrate. Through this crevice a small room was visible, whitewashed and clean but very bare of furniture.

In one corner, near a small fire, sat an old man, leaning his head on his hands in a disconsolate attitude.

The young girl was occupied in arranging the cottage; but presently she took something out of a drawer, which employed her hands, and she sat down beside the old man, who, taking up an instrument, began to play and to produce sounds sweeter than the voice of the thrush or the nightingale. [. . .]

Chapter 12 — The Monster's Family and Language

This day was passed in the same routine as that which preceded it. The young man was constantly employed out of doors, and the girl in various laborious occupations within. The old man, whom I soon perceived to be blind, employed his leisure hours on his instrument or in contemplation. Nothing could exceed the love and respect which the younger cottagers exhibited towards their venerable companion. They performed towards him every little office of affection and duty with gentleness, and he rewarded them by his benevolent smiles. [. . .]

A considerable period elapsed before I discovered one of the causes of the uneasiness of this amiable family: it was poverty, and they suffered that evil in a very distressing degree. Their nourishment consisted entirely of the vegetables of their garden and the milk of one cow, which gave very little during the winter, when its masters could scarcely procure food to support it. They often, I believe, suffered the pangs of hunger very poignantly, especially the two younger cottagers, for several times they placed food before the old man when they reserved none for themselves.

This trait of kindness moved me sensibly. I had been accustomed, during the night, to steal a part of their store for my own consumption, but when I found that in doing this I inflicted pain on the cottagers, I abstained and satisfied myself with berries, nuts, and roots which I gathered from a neighbouring wood.

I discovered also another means through which I was enabled to assist their labours. I found that the youth spent a great part of each day in collecting wood for the family fire, and during the night I often took his tools, the use of which I quickly discovered, and brought home firing sufficient for the consumption of several days.

I remember, the first time that I did this, the young woman, when she opened the door in the morning, appeared greatly astonished on seeing a great pile of wood on the outside. She uttered some words in a loud voice, and the youth joined her, who also expressed surprise. I observed, with pleasure, that he did not go to the forest that day, but spent it in repairing the cottage and cultivating the garden.

By degrees I made a discovery of still greater moment. I found that these people possessed a method of communicating their experience and feelings to one another by articulate sounds. I perceived that the words they spoke sometimes produced pleasure or pain, smiles or sadness, in the minds and countenances of the hearers. This was indeed a godlike science, and I ardently desired to become acquainted with it. [. . .]

[R]eading had puzzled me extremely at first, but by degrees I discovered that he uttered many of the same sounds when he read as when he talked. I conjectured, therefore, that he found on the paper signs for speech which he understood,

and I ardently longed to comprehend these also; but how was that possible when I did not even understand the sounds for which they stood as signs? [. . .]

I had admired the perfect forms of my cottagers—their grace, beauty, and delicate complexions;

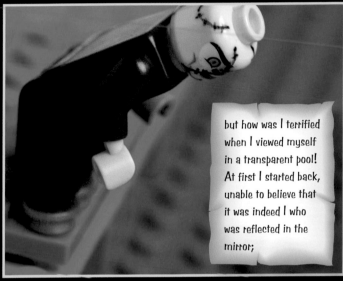

but how was I terrified when I viewed myself in a transparent pool! At first I started back, unable to believe that it was indeed I who was reflected in the mirror;

and when I became fully convinced that I was in reality the monster that I am, I was filled with the bitterest sensations of despondence and mortification. Alas! I did not yet entirely know the fatal effects of this miserable deformity. [. . .]

My thoughts now became more active, and I longed to discover the motives and feelings of these lovely creatures; I was inquisitive to know why Felix appeared so miserable and Agatha so sad. I thought (foolish wretch!) that it might be in my power to restore happiness to these deserving people. When I slept or was absent, the forms of the venerable blind father, the gentle Agatha, and the excellent Felix flitted before me. I looked upon them as superior beings who would be the arbiters of my future destiny. I formed in my imagination a thousand pictures of presenting myself to them, and their reception of me. I imagined that they would be disgusted, until, by my gentle demeanour and conciliating words, I should first win their favour and afterwards their love. [. . .]

Chapter 13 – "A Blot on the Earth"

[T]he old man was recommencing his music when someone tapped at the door. It was a lady on horseback, accompanied by a country-man as a guide. [. . .]

Agatha asked a question, to which the stranger only replied by pronouncing, in a sweet accent, the name of Felix. Her voice was musical but unlike that of either of my friends. On hearing this word, Felix came up hastily to the lady, who, when she saw him, threw up her veil, and I beheld a countenance of angelic beauty and expression. Her hair of a shining raven black, and curiously braided; her eyes were dark, but gentle, although animated; her features of a regular proportion, and her complexion wondrously fair, each cheek tinged with a lovely pink. [. . .]

I soon perceived that although the stranger uttered articulate sounds and appeared to have a language of her own, she was neither understood by nor herself understood the cottagers. They made many signs which I did not comprehend, but I saw that her presence diffused gladness through the cottage, dispelling their sorrow as the sun dissipates the morning mists.

My days were spent in close attention, that I might more speedily master the language; and I may boast that I improved more rapidly than the Arabian, who understood very little and conversed in broken accents, whilst I comprehended and could imitate almost every word that was spoken. While I improved in speech, I also learned the science of letters as it was taught to the stranger, and this opened before me a wide field for wonder and delight. [. . .]

The words induced me to turn towards myself. I learned that the possessions most esteemed by your fellow creatures were high and unsullied descent united with riches. A man might be respected with only one of these advantages, but without either he was considered, except in very rare instances, as a vagabond and a slave, doomed to waste his powers for the profits of the chosen few! And what was I? Of my creation and creator I was absolutely ignorant, but I knew that I possessed no money, no friends, no kind of property. I was, besides, endued with a figure hideously deformed and loathsome; I was not even of the same nature as man. I was more agile than they and could subsist upon coarser diet; I bore the extremes of heat and cold with less injury to my frame; my stature far exceeded theirs. When I looked around I saw and heard of none like me. Was I, then, a monster, a blot upon the earth, from which all men fled and whom all men disowned? [. . .]

But where were my friends and relations? No father had watched my infant days, no mother had blessed me with smiles and caresses; or if they had, all my past life was now a blot, a blind vacancy in which I distinguished nothing. From my earliest remembrance I had been as I then was in height and proportion. I had never yet seen a being resembling me or who claimed any intercourse with me. What was I? The question again recurred, to be answered only with groans. [. . .]

Chapter 14 – Safie

*T*he Creature watches the family and its new visitor in fascination, learning what he can of their history. He finds that the Felix, Agatha, and the old man, named De Lacey, had come from a wealthy Parisian home. All this changed rapidly after the family met a Turkish merchant. The Creature cannot quite understand the circumstances (though religious and cultural intolerance are at least in part to blame), but he learns the man was seized by the French government, tried, and condemned to death.

Felix becomes so outraged at this decision that he begins sneaking to the prison to speak to the merchant in secret. During these times, the man promises Felix endless riches if he were to help him break out, but Felix decides that what he wants is the merchant's daughter, Safie. Despite their language barrier, Felix and Safie exchange letters and fall in love.

On the evening prior to the scheduled execution, Felix helps the merchant and Safie escape to Italy and, in doing so, secures the promise that he and Safie would marry. Shortly after their escape, the Parisian government unearths the plot and apprehends De Lacey and Agatha to taunt Felix. Felix returns to Paris to free his family. Unfortunately, the government keeps all three in prison for several months, during which time the family loses its fortune and their name is tarnished.

Felix, De Lacey, and Agatha flee to the cottage in Germany. Upon hearing of their newfound poverty, the Turkish merchant betrays his promise to Felix and will no longer allow him to marry Safie. Heartbroken, the merchant's daughter pleads in protest, but her angry father ignores her and decides that they will return to their home country. Safie gathers what little valuables she can and flees to find Felix and his family. Though she finds herself in a foreign country and no understanding of the language, with the help of kind strangers, she is able to find the family at the small cottage.

Chapter 15 — Meeting Humans and Rejection

One night during my accustomed visit to the neighbouring wood where I collected my own food and brought home firing for my protectors, I found on the ground a leathern portmanteau containing several articles of dress and some books. Fortunately the books were written in the language, the elements of which I had acquired at the cottage; they consisted of Paradise Lost, a volume of Plutarch's Lives, and the Sorrows of Werter. The possession of these treasures gave me extreme delight; I now continually studied and exercised my mind upon these histories, whilst my friends were employed in their ordinary occupations.

But *Paradise Lost* excited different and far deeper emotions. I read it, as I had read the other volumes which had fallen into my hands, as a true history. It moved every feeling of wonder and awe that the picture of an omnipotent God warring with his creatures was capable of exciting. I often referred the several situations, as their similarity struck me, to my own. Like Adam, I was apparently united by no link to any other being in existence; but his state was far different from mine in every other respect. He had come forth from the hands of God a perfect creature, happy and prosperous, guarded by the especial care of his Creator; he was allowed to converse with and acquire knowledge from beings of a superior nature, but I was wretched, helpless, and alone. Many times I considered Satan as the fitter emblem of my condition, for often, like him, when I viewed the bliss of my protectors, the bitter gall of envy rose within me.

Another circumstance strengthened and confirmed these feelings. Soon after my arrival in the hovel I discovered some papers in the pocket of the dress which I had taken from your laboratory. At first I had neglected them, but now that I was able to decipher the characters in which they were written, I began to study them with diligence. It was your journal of the four months that preceded my creation. [. . .] Accursed creator! Why did you form a monster so hideous that even YOU turned from me in disgust? God, in pity, made man beautiful and alluring, after his own image; but my form is a filthy type of yours, more horrid even from the very resemblance. Satan had his companions, fellow devils, to admire and encourage him, but I am solitary and abhorred.

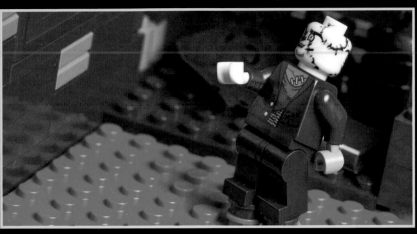

The winter advanced, and an entire revolution of the seasons had taken place since I awoke into life. My attention at this time was solely directed towards my plan of introducing myself into the cottage of my protectors. I revolved many projects, but that on which I finally fixed was to enter the dwelling when the blind old man should be alone. I had sagacity enough to discover that the unnatural hideousness of my person was the chief object of horror with those who had formerly beheld me. My voice, although harsh, had nothing terrible in it; I thought, therefore, that if in the absence of his children I could gain the good will and mediation of the old De Lacey, I might by his means be tolerated by my younger protectors.

One day, when the sun shone on the red leaves that strewed the ground and diffused cheerfulness, although it denied warmth, Safie, Agatha, and Felix departed on a long country walk, and the old man, at his own desire, was left alone in the cottage. [. . .]

My heart beat quick; this was the hour and moment of trial, which would decide my hopes or realize my fears. [. . .]

I knocked. "Who is there?" said the old man. "Come in." I entered. "Pardon this intrusion," said I; "I am a traveller in want of a little rest; you would greatly oblige me if you would allow me to remain a few minutes before the fire. [. . .]

"I am now going to claim the protection of some friends, whom I sincerely love, and of whose favour I have some hopes."

"Are they Germans?" "No, they are French. But let us change the subject. I am an unfortunate and deserted creature, I look around and I have no relation or friend upon earth. These amiable people to whom I go have never seen me and know little of me. I am full of fears, for if I fail there, I am an outcast in the world forever." [. . .]

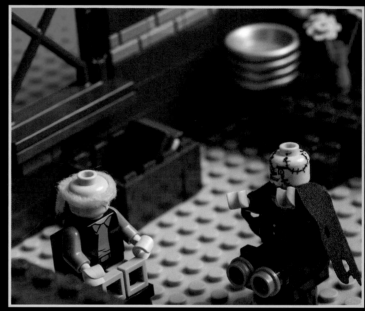

"To be friendless is indeed to be unfortunate, but the hearts of men, when unprejudiced by any obvious self-interest, are full of brotherly love and charity. Rely, therefore, on your hopes; and if these friends are good and amiable, do not despair." [. . .]

"I tenderly love these friends; I have, unknown to them, been for many months in the habits of daily kindness towards them; but they believe that I wish to injure them, and it is that prejudice which I wish to overcome." [. . .]

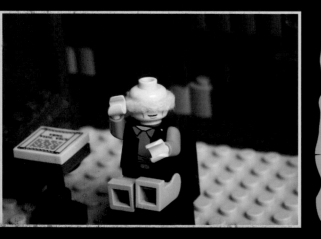

The old man paused and then continued, "If you will unreservedly confide to me the particulars of your tale, I perhaps may be of use in undeceiving them. I am blind and cannot judge of your countenance, but there is something in your words which persuades me that you are sincere. I am poor and an exile, but it will afford me true pleasure to be in any way serviceable to a human creature." "Excellent man! I thank you and accept your generous offer. You raise me from the dust by this kindness; and I trust that, by your aid, I shall not be driven from the society and sympathy of your fellow creatures." "Heaven forbid! Even if you were really criminal, for that can only drive you to desperation, and not instigate you to virtue. I also am unfortunate; I and my family have been condemned, although innocent; judge, therefore, if I do not feel for your misfortunes. [. . .]

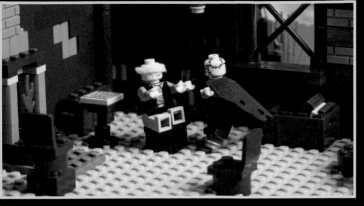

"May I know the names and residence of those friends?" I paused. This, I thought, was the moment of decision, which was to rob me of or bestow happiness on me forever. I struggled vainly for firmness sufficient to answer him, but the effort destroyed all my remaining strength; I sank on the chair and sobbed aloud.

At that moment I heard the steps of my younger protectors. I had not a moment to lose, but seizing the hand of the old man, I cried, "Now is the time! Save and protect me! You and your family are the friends whom I seek. Do not you desert me in the hour of trial!"

Who can describe their horror and consternation on beholding me? Agatha fainted, and Safie, unable to attend to her friend, rushed out of the cottage.

"Great God!" exclaimed the old man. "Who are you?" At that instant the cottage door was opened, and Felix, Safie, and Agatha entered.

Felix darted forward, and with supernatural force tore me from his father, to whose knees I clung, in a transport of fury, he dashed me to the ground and struck me violently with a stick. I could have torn him limb from limb, as the lion rends the antelope.

But my heart sank within me as with bitter sickness, and I refrained. I saw him on the point of repeating his blow, when, overcome by pain and anguish, I quitted the cottage, and in the general tumult escaped unperceived to my hovel.

Chapter 16 — Geneva and Tales of Death

*U*pon this heartbreaking rejection by the family that he has learned to love, the Creature cries out and curses his creator. In his anger, he tears through the forest and exhausts himself in his misery. He longs to be the monster that all perceive him to be and "spread havoc and destruction."

But this was a luxury of sensation that could not endure; I became fatigued with excess of bodily exertion and sank on the damp grass in the sick impotence of despair. There was none among the myriads of men that existed who would pity or assist me; and should I feel kindness towards my enemies? No; from that moment I declared everlasting war against the species, and more than all, against him who had formed me and sent me forth to this insupportable misery. [. . .]

"It is utterly useless," replied Felix; "we can never again inhabit your cottage. The life of my father is in the greatest danger, owing to the dreadful circumstance that I have related. My wife and my sister will never recover from their horror. I entreat you not to reason with me any more. Take possession of your tenement and let me fly from this place." Felix trembled violently as he said this. He and his companion entered the cottage, in which they remained for a few minutes, and then departed. I never saw any of the family of De Lacey more. I continued for the remainder of the day in my hovel in a state of utter and stupid despair. My protectors had departed and had broken the only link that held me to the world. [. . .]

But again when I reflected that they had spurned and deserted me, anger returned, a rage of anger, and unable to injure anything human, I turned my fury towards inanimate objects. As night advanced I placed a variety of combustibles around the cottage, and after having destroyed every vestige of cultivation in the garden, I waited with forced impatience until the moon had sunk to commence my operations. As the night advanced, a fierce wind arose from the woods and quickly dispersed the clouds that had loitered in the heavens; the blast tore along like a mighty avalanche and produced a kind of insanity in my spirits that burst all bounds of reason and reflection. I lighted the dry branch of a tree and danced with fury around the devoted cottage, my eyes still fixed on the western horizon, the edge of which the moon nearly touched. A part of its orb was at length hid, and I waved my brand; it sank, and with a loud scream I fired the straw, and heath, and bushes, which I had collected. The wind fanned the fire, and the cottage was quickly enveloped by the flames, which clung to it and licked it with their forked and destroying tongues. [. . .]

And now, with the world before me, whither should I bend my steps? I resolved to fly far from the scene of my misfortunes; but to me, hated and despised, every country must be equally horrible. At length the thought of you crossed my mind. I learned from your papers that you were my father, my creator; and to whom could I apply with more fitness than to him who had given me life? Among the lessons that Felix had bestowed upon Safie, geography had not been omitted; I had learned from these the relative situations of the different countries of the earth. You had mentioned Geneva as the name of your native town, and towards this place I resolved to proceed. [...]

My travels were long and the sufferings I endured intense. It was late in autumn when I quitted the district where I had so long resided. I travelled only at night, fearful of encountering the visage of a human being. Nature decayed around me, and the sun became heatless; rain and snow poured around me; mighty rivers were frozen; the surface of the earth was hard and chill, and bare, and I found no shelter. Oh, earth! How often did I imprecate curses on the cause of my being! The mildness of my nature had fled, and all within me was turned to gall and bitterness. The nearer I approached to your habitation, the more deeply did I feel the spirit of revenge enkindled in my heart. Snow fell, and the waters were hardened, but I rested not. [...]

I continued to wind among the paths of the wood, until I came to its boundary, which was skirted by a deep and rapid river, into which many of the trees bent their branches, now budding with the fresh spring. Here I paused, not exactly knowing what path to pursue, when I heard the sound of voices, that induced me to conceal myself under the shade of a cypress. I was scarcely hid when a young girl came running towards the spot where I was concealed, laughing, as if she ran from someone in sport.

She continued her course along the precipitous sides of the river, when suddenly her foot slipped, and she fell into the rapid stream.

I rushed from my hiding-place and with extreme labour from the force of the current, saved her and dragged her to shore.

She was senseless, and I endeavoured by every means in my power to restore animation, when I was suddenly interrupted by the approach of a rustic, who was probably the person from whom she had playfully fled. On seeing me, he darted towards me, and tearing the girl from my arms, hastened towards the deeper parts of the wood.

I followed speedily, I hardly knew why; but when the man saw me draw near, he aimed a gun, which he carried, at my body and fired. I sank to the ground, and my injurer, with increased swiftness, escaped into the wood. [. . .]

But my toils now drew near a close, and in two months from this time I reached the environs of Geneva. It was evening when I arrived, and I retired to a hiding-place among the fields that surround it to meditate in what manner I should apply to you. I was oppressed by fatigue and hunger and far too unhappy to enjoy the gentle breezes of evening or the prospect of the sun setting behind the stupendous mountains of Jura. At this time a slight sleep relieved me from the pain of reflection, which was disturbed by the approach of a beautiful child, who came running into the recess I had chosen, with all the sportiveness of infancy. Suddenly, as I gazed on him, an idea seized me that this little creature was unprejudiced and had lived too short a time to have imbibed a horror of deformity. If, therefore, I could seize him and educate him as my companion and friend, I should not be so desolate in this peopled earth.

Urged by this impulse, I seized on the boy as he passed and drew him towards me. As soon as he beheld my form, he placed his hands before his eyes and uttered a shrill scream; I drew his hand forcibly from his face and said, "Child, what is the meaning of this? I do not intend to hurt you; listen to me." He struggled violently. "Let me go," he cried; "monster! Ugly wretch! You wish to eat me and tear me to pieces. You are an ogre. Let me go, or I will tell my papa." "Boy, you will never see your father again; you must come with me." "Hideous monster! Let me go. My papa is a syndic—he is M. Frankenstein—he will punish you. You dare not keep me."

"Frankenstein! you belong then to my enemy—to him towards whom I have sworn eternal revenge; you shall be my first victim." The child still struggled and loaded me with epithets which carried despair to my heart; I grasped his throat to silence him, and in a moment he lay dead at my feet. I gazed on my victim, and my heart swelled with exultation and hellish triumph; clapping my hands, I exclaimed, "I too can create desolation; my enemy is not invulnerable; this death will carry despair to him, and a thousand other miseries shall torment and destroy him.

As I fixed my eyes on the child, I saw something glittering on his breast. I took it; it was a portrait of a most lovely woman. In spite of my malignity, it softened and attracted me. For a few moments I gazed with delight on her dark eyes, fringed by deep lashes, and her lovely lips; but presently my rage returned; I remembered that I was forever deprived of the delights that such beautiful creatures could bestow and that she whose resemblance I contemplated would, in regarding me, have changed that air of divine benignity to one expressive of disgust and affright.

Can you wonder that such thoughts transported me with rage? I only wonder that at that moment, instead of venting my sensations in exclamations and agony, I did not rush among mankind and perish in the attempt to destroy them. While I was overcome by these feelings, I left the spot where I had committed the murder, and seeking a more secluded hiding-place, I entered a barn which had appeared to me to be empty. A woman was sleeping on some straw; she was young, not indeed so beautiful as her whose portrait I held, but of an agreeable aspect and blooming in the loveliness of youth and health. Here, I thought, is one of those whose joy-imparting smiles are bestowed on all but me. And then I bent over her and whispered, "Awake, fairest, thy lover is near—he who would give his life but to obtain one look of affection from thine eyes; my beloved, awake!"

The sleeper stirred; a thrill of terror ran through me. Should she indeed awake, and see me, and curse me, and denounce the murderer? Thus would she assuredly act if her darkened eyes opened and she beheld me. The thought was madness; it stirred the fiend within me—not I, but she, shall suffer; the murder I have committed because I am forever robbed of all that she could give me, she shall atone. The crime had its source in her; be hers the punishment! Thanks to the lessons of Felix and the sanguinary laws of man, I had learned now to work mischief. I bent over her and placed the portrait securely in one of the folds of her dress. She moved again, and I fled.

For some days I haunted the spot where these scenes had taken place, sometimes wishing to see you, sometimes resolved to quit the world and its miseries forever. At length I wandered towards these mountains, and have ranged through their immense recesses, consumed by a burning passion which you alone can gratify. We may not part until you have promised to comply with my requisition. I am alone and miserable; man will not associate with me; but one as deformed and horrible as myself would not deny herself to me. My companion must be of the same species and have the same defects. This being you must create.

Chapter 17 – The Bride

[. . .] "You must create a female for me with whom I can live in the interchange of those sympathies necessary for my being. This you alone can do, and I demand it of you as a right which you must not refuse to concede."

The latter part of his tale had kindled anew in me the anger that had died away while he narrated his peaceful life among the cottagers, and as he said this I could no longer suppress the rage that burned within me. "I do refuse it," I replied; "and no torture shall ever extort a consent from me. You may render me the most miserable of men, but you shall never make me base in my own eyes. Shall I create another like yourself, whose joint wickedness might desolate the world. Begone! I have answered you; you may torture me, but I will never consent."

"You are in the wrong," replied the fiend; "and instead of threatening, I am content to reason with you. I am malicious because I am miserable. Am I not shunned and hated by all mankind? You, my creator, would tear me to pieces and triumph; remember that, and tell me why I should pity man more than he pities me? You would not call it murder if you could precipitate me into one of those ice-rifts and destroy my frame, the work of your own hands. Shall I respect man when he condemns me? Let him live with me in the interchange of kindness, and instead of injury I would bestow every benefit upon him with tears of gratitude at his acceptance. But that cannot be; the human senses are insurmountable barriers to our union. Yet mine shall not be the submission of abject slavery. I will revenge my injuries; if I cannot inspire love, I will cause fear, and chiefly towards you my arch-enemy, because my creator, do I swear inextinguishable hatred. Have a care; I will work at your destruction, nor finish until I desolate your heart, so that you shall curse the hour of your birth." A fiendish rage animated him as he said this; his face was wrinkled into contortions too horrible for human eyes to behold; but presently he calmed himself and proceeded— "I intended to reason. This passion is detrimental to me, for you do not reflect that YOU are the cause of its excess. If any being felt emotions of benevolence towards me, I should return them a hundred and a hundredfold; for that one creature's sake I would make peace with the whole kind! But I now indulge in dreams of bliss that cannot be realized. What I ask of you is reasonable and moderate; I demand a creature of another sex, but as hideous as myself; the gratification is small, but it is all that I can receive, and it shall content me. It is true, we shall be monsters, cut off from all the world; but on that account we shall be more attached to one another. Our lives will not be happy, but they will be harmless and free from the misery I now feel. Oh! My creator, make me happy; let me feel gratitude towards you for one benefit! Let me see that I excite the sympathy of some existing thing; do not deny me my request!" I was moved. I shuddered when I thought of the possible consequences of my consent, but I felt that there was some justice in his argument. His tale and the feelings he now expressed proved him to be a creature of fine sensations, and did I not as his maker owe him all the portion of happiness that it was in my power to bestow? [. . .]

"You propose," replied I, "to fly from the habitations of man, to dwell in those wilds where the beasts of the field will be your only companions. How can you, who long for the love and sympathy of man, persevere in this exile? You will return and again seek their kindness, and you will meet with their detestation; your evil passions will be renewed, and you will then have a companion to aid you in the task of destruction. This may not be; cease to argue the point, for I cannot consent."

"How inconstant are your feelings! But a moment ago you were moved by my representations, and why do you again harden yourself to my complaints? I swear to you, by the earth which I inhabit, and by you that made me, that with the companion you bestow I will quit the neighbourhood of man and dwell, as it may chance, in the most savage of places. My evil passions will have fled, for I shall meet with sympathy! My life will flow quietly away, and in my dying moments I shall not curse my maker."

His words had a strange effect upon me. I compassionated him and sometimes felt a wish to console him, but when I looked upon him, when I saw the filthy mass that moved and talked, my heart sickened and my feelings were altered to those of horror and hatred. I tried to stifle these sensations; I thought that as I could not sympathize with him, I had no right to withhold from him the small portion of happiness which was yet in my power to bestow. "You swear," I said, "to be harmless; but have you not already shown a degree of malice that should reasonably make me distrust you? May not even this be a feint that will increase your triumph by affording a wider scope for your revenge?" [. . .]

"I swear," he cried, "by the sun, and by the blue sky of heaven, and by the fire of love that burns my heart, that if you grant my prayer, while they exist you shall never behold me again. Depart to your home and commence your labours; I shall watch their progress with unutterable anxiety; and fear not but that when you are ready I shall appear." Saying this, he suddenly quitted me, fearful, perhaps, of any change in my sentiments. I saw him descend the mountain with greater speed than the flight of an eagle, and quickly lost among the undulations of the sea of ice. [. . .]

Even in my own heart I could give no expression to my sensations—they weighed on me with a mountain's weight and their excess destroyed my agony beneath them. Thus I returned home, and entering the house, presented myself to the family. My haggard and wild appearance awoke intense alarm, but I answered no question, scarcely did I speak. I felt as if I were placed under a ban—as if I had no right to claim their sympathies—as if never more might I enjoy companionship with them. Yet even thus I loved them to adoration; and to save them, I resolved to dedicate myself to my most abhorred task. The prospect of such an occupation made every other circumstance of existence pass before me like a dream, and that thought only had to me the reality of life.

Chapter 18 — Grappling with the Monster

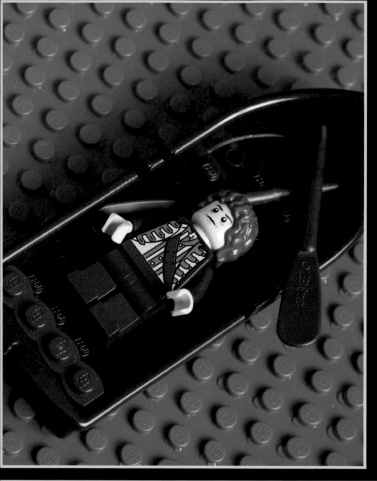

Day after day, week after week, passed away on my return to Geneva; and I could not collect the courage to recommence my work. I feared the vengeance of the disappointed fiend, yet I was unable to overcome my repugnance to the task which was enjoined me. I found that I could not compose a female without again devoting several months to profound study and laborious disquisition. I had heard of some discoveries having been made by an English philosopher, the knowledge of which was material to my success, and I sometimes thought of obtaining my father's consent to visit England for this purpose; but I clung to every pretence of delay and shrank from taking the first step in an undertaking whose immediate necessity began to appear less absolute to me. A change indeed had taken place in me; my health, which had hitherto declined, was now much restored; and my spirits, when unchecked by the memory of my unhappy promise, rose proportionably. My father saw this change with pleasure, and he turned his thoughts towards the best method of eradicating the remains of my melancholy, which every now and then would return by fits, and with a devouring blackness overcast the approaching sunshine. At these moments I took refuge in the most perfect solitude. I passed whole days on the lake alone in a little boat, watching the clouds and listening to the rippling of the waves, silent and listless. But the fresh air and bright sun seldom failed to restore me to some degree of composure, and on my return I met the salutations of my friends with a readier smile and a more cheerful heart. [. . .]

I remembered also the necessity imposed upon me of either journeying to England or entering into a long correspondence with those philosophers of that country whose knowledge and discoveries were of indispensable use to me in my present undertaking. The latter method of obtaining the desired intelligence was dilatory and unsatisfactory; besides, I had an insurmountable aversion to the idea of engaging myself in my loathsome task in my father's house while in habits of familiar intercourse with those I loved. I knew that a thousand fearful accidents might occur, the slightest of which would disclose a tale to thrill all connected with me with horror. I was aware also that I should often lose all self-command, all capacity of hiding the harrowing sensations that would possess me during the progress of my unearthly occupation. I must absent myself from all I loved while thus employed. Once commenced, it would quickly be achieved, and I might be restored to my family in peace and happiness. My promise fulfilled, the monster would depart forever. Or (so my fond fancy imaged) some accident might meanwhile occur to destroy him and put an end to my slavery forever. [. . .]

During my absence I should leave my friends unconscious of the existence of their enemy and unprotected from his attacks, exasperated as he might be by my departure. But he had promised to follow me wherever I might go, and would he not accompany me to England? This imagination was dreadful in itself, but soothing inasmuch as it supposed the safety of my friends. I was agonized with the idea of the possibility that the reverse of this might happen. But through the whole period during which I was the slave of my creature I allowed myself to be governed by the impulses of the moment; and my present sensations strongly intimated that the fiend would follow me and exempt my family from the danger of his machinations. It was in the latter end of September that I again quitted my native country. My journey had been my own suggestion, and Elizabeth therefore acquiesced, but she was filled with disquiet at the idea of my suffering, away from her, the inroads of misery and grief. It had been her care which provided me a companion in Clerval—and yet a man is blind to a thousand minute circumstances which call forth a woman's sedulous attention. She longed to bid me hasten my return; a thousand conflicting emotions rendered her mute as she bade me a tearful, silent farewell. [. . .]

After some days spent in listless indolence, during which I traversed many leagues, I arrived at Strasbourg, where I waited two days for Clerval. He came. Alas, how great was the contrast between us! He was alive to every new scene, joyful when he saw the beauties of the setting sun, and more happy when he beheld it rise and recommence a new day. [. . .]

Chapter 19 – The Bride Part Deux

We left Edinburgh in a week, passing through Coupar, St. Andrew's, and along the banks of the Tay, to Perth, where our friend expected us. But I was in no mood to laugh and talk with strangers or enter into their feelings or plans with the good humour expected from a guest; and accordingly I told Clerval that I wished to make the tour of Scotland alone.

"Do you," said I, "enjoy yourself, and let this be our rendezvous. I may be absent a month or two; but do not interfere with my motions, I entreat you; leave me to peace and solitude for a short time; and when I return, I hope it will be with a lighter heart, more congenial to your own temper." [. . .]

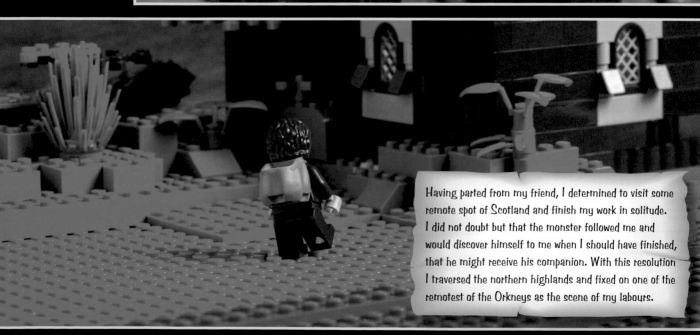

Having parted from my friend, I determined to visit some remote spot of Scotland and finish my work in solitude. I did not doubt but that the monster followed me and would discover himself to me when I should have finished, that he might receive his companion. With this resolution I traversed the northern highlands and fixed on one of the remotest of the Orkneys as the scene of my labours.

It was a place fitted for such a work, being hardly more than a rock whose high sides were continually beaten upon by the waves. The soil was barren, scarcely affording pasture for a few miserable cows, and oatmeal for its inhabitants, which consisted of five persons, whose gaunt and scraggy limbs gave tokens of their miserable fare. Vegetables and bread, when they indulged in such luxuries, and even fresh water, was to be procured from the mainland, which was about five miles distant. [. . .]

In this manner I distributed my occupations when I first arrived, but as I proceeded in my labour, it became every day more horrible and irksome to me. Sometimes I could not prevail on myself to enter my laboratory for several days, and at other times I toiled day and night in order to complete my work. It was, indeed, a filthy process in which I was engaged. During my first experiment, a kind of enthusiastic frenzy had blinded me to the horror of my employment; my mind was intently fixed on the consummation of my labour, and my eyes were shut to the horror of my proceedings. But now I went to it in cold blood, and my heart often sickened at the work of my hands. Thus situated, employed in the most detestable occupation, immersed in a solitude where nothing could for an instant call my attention from the actual scene in which I was engaged, my spirits became unequal; I grew restless and nervous. Every moment I feared to meet my persecutor. Sometimes I sat with my eyes fixed on the ground, fearing to raise them lest they should encounter the object which I so much dreaded to behold. I feared to wander from the sight of my fellow creatures lest when alone he should come to claim his companion.

In the mean time I worked on, and my labour was already considerably advanced. I looked towards its completion with a tremulous and eager hope, which I dared not trust myself to question but which was intermixed with obscure forebodings of evil that made my heart sicken in my bosom.

Chapter 20 – Consequences of a Monstrous Pair

I sat one evening in my laboratory; the sun had set, and the moon was just rising from the sea; I had not sufficient light for my employment, and I remained idle, in a pause of consideration of whether I should leave my labour for the night or hasten its conclusion by an unremitting attention to it. As I sat, a train of reflection occurred to me which led me to consider the effects of what I was now doing. Three years before, I was engaged in the same manner and had created a fiend whose unparalleled barbarity had desolated my heart and filled it forever with the bitterest remorse. I was now about to form another being of whose dispositions I was alike ignorant; she might become ten thousand times more malignant than her mate and delight, for its own sake, in murder and wretchedness. He had sworn to quit the neighbourhood of man and hide himself in deserts, but she had not; and she, who in all probability was to become a thinking and reasoning animal, might refuse to comply with a compact made before her creation. They might even hate each other; the creature who already lived loathed his own deformity, and might he not conceive a greater abhorrence for it when it came before his eyes in the female form? She also might turn with disgust from him to the superior beauty of man; she might quit him, and he be again alone, exasperated by the fresh provocation of being deserted by one of his own species.

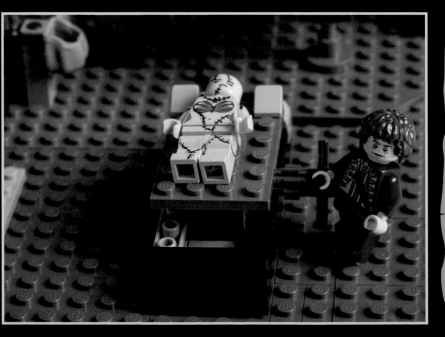

Even if they were to leave Europe and inhabit the deserts of the new world, yet one of the first results of those sympathies for which the daemon thirsted would be children, and a race of devils would be propagated upon the earth who might make the very existence of the species of man a condition precarious and full of terror. Had I right, for my own benefit, to inflict this curse upon everlasting generations? I had before been moved by the sophisms of the being I had created; I had been struck senseless by his fiendish threats; but now, for the first time, the wickedness of my promise burst upon me; I shuddered to think that future ages might curse me as their pest, whose selfishness had not hesitated to buy its own peace at the price, perhaps, of the existence of the whole human race.

I trembled and my heart failed within me, when, on looking up, I saw by the light of the moon the daemon at the casement. A ghastly grin wrinkled his lips as he gazed on me, where I sat fulfilling the task which he had allotted to me. Yes, he had followed me in my travels; he had loitered in forests, hid himself in caves, or taken refuge in wide and desert heaths; and he now came to mark my progress and claim the fulfilment of my promise.

As I looked on him, his countenance expressed the utmost extent of malice and treachery. I thought with a sensation of madness on my promise of creating another like to him, and trembling with passion, tore to pieces the thing on which I was engaged.

The wretch saw me destroy the creature on whose future existence he depended for happiness, and with a howl of devilish despair and revenge, withdrew. [. . .]

In a few minutes after, I heard the creaking of my door, as if some one endeavoured to open it softly. I trembled from head to foot; I felt a presentiment of who it was and wished to rouse one of the peasants who dwelt in a cottage not far from mine; but I was overcome by the sensation of helplessness, so often felt in frightful dreams, when you in vain endeavour to fly from an impending danger, and was rooted to the spot. Presently I heard the sound of footsteps along the passage; the door opened, and the wretch whom I dreaded appeared.

Shutting the door, he approached me and said in a smothered voice, "You have destroyed the work which you began; what is it that you intend? Do you dare to break your promise? I have endured toil and misery; I left Switzerland with you; I crept along the shores of the Rhine, among its willow islands and over the summits of its hills. I have dwelt many months in the heaths of England and among the deserts of Scotland. I have endured incalculable fatigue, and cold, and hunger; do you dare destroy my hopes?"

"Begone! I do break my promise; never will I create another like yourself, equal in deformity and wickedness."

"Slave, I before reasoned with you, but you have proved yourself unworthy of my condescension. Remember that I have power; you believe yourself miserable, but I can make you so wretched that the light of day will be hateful to you. You are my creator, but I am your master; obey!"

"The hour of my irresolution is past, and the period of your power is arrived. Your threats cannot move me to do an act of wickedness; but they confirm me in a determination of not creating you a companion in vice. Shall I, in cool blood, set loose upon the earth a daemon whose delight is in death and wretchedness? Begone! I am firm, and your words will only exasperate my rage."

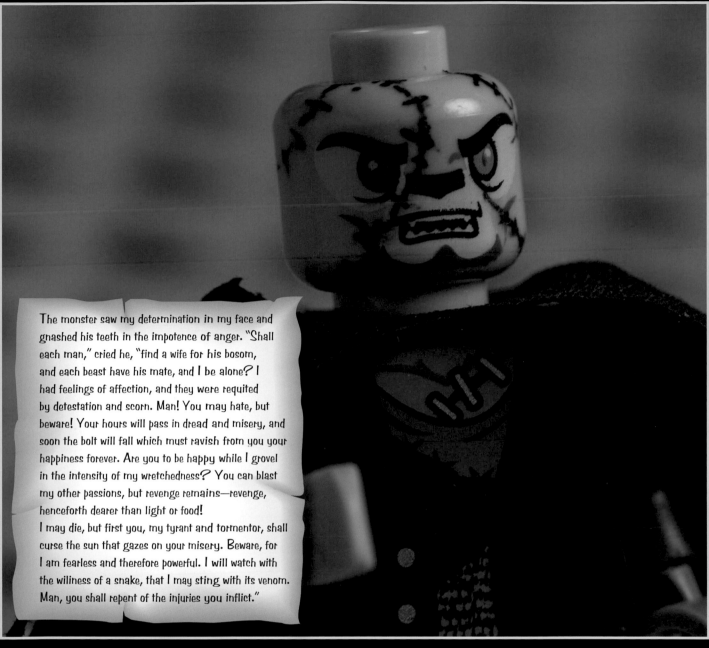

The monster saw my determination in my face and gnashed his teeth in the impotence of anger. "Shall each man," cried he, "find a wife for his bosom, and each beast have his mate, and I be alone? I had feelings of affection, and they were requited by detestation and scorn. Man! You may hate, but beware! Your hours will pass in dread and misery, and soon the bolt will fall which must ravish from you your happiness forever. Are you to be happy while I grovel in the intensity of my wretchedness? You can blast my other passions, but revenge remains—revenge, henceforth dearer than light or food!

I may die, but first you, my tyrant and tormentor, shall curse the sun that gazes on your misery. Beware, for I am fearless and therefore powerful. I will watch with the wiliness of a snake, that I may sting with its venom. Man, you shall repent of the injuries you inflict."

"Devil, cease; and do not poison the air with these sounds of malice. I have declared my resolution to you, and I am no coward to bend beneath words. Leave me; I am inexorable."

"It is well. I go; but remember, I shall be with you on your wedding-night."

I started forward and exclaimed, "Villain! Before you sign my death-warrant, be sure that you are yourself safe."

I would have seized him, but he eluded me and quitted the house with precipitation.

In a few moments I saw him in his boat, which shot across the waters with an arrowy swiftness and was soon lost amidst the waves. [. . .]

The night passed away, and the sun rose from the ocean; my feelings became calmer, if it may be called calmness when the violence of rage sinks into the depths of despair. I left the house, the horrid scene of the last night's contention, and walked on the beach of the sea, which I almost regarded as an insuperable barrier between me and my fellow creatures; nay, a wish that such should prove the fact stole across me. [. . .] The sun had far descended, and I still sat on the shore, satisfying my appetite, which had become ravenous, with an oaten cake, when I saw a fishing-boat land close to me, and one of the men brought me a packet; it contained letters from Geneva, and one from Clerval entreating me to join him. [. . .]

This letter in a degree recalled me to life, and I determined to quit my island at the expiration of two days. Yet, before I departed, there was a task to perform, on which I shuddered to reflect; I must pack up my chemical instruments, and for that purpose I must enter the room which had been the scene of my odious work, and I must handle those utensils the sight of which was sickening to me. The next morning, at daybreak, I summoned sufficient courage and unlocked the door of my laboratory. The remains of the half-finished creature, whom I had destroyed, lay scattered on the floor, and I almost felt as if I had mangled the living flesh of a human being. I paused to collect myself and then entered the chamber. With trembling hand I conveyed the instruments out of the room, but I reflected that I ought not to leave the relics of my work to excite the horror and suspicion of the peasants; and I accordingly put them into a basket, with a great quantity of stones, and laying them up, determined to throw them into the sea that very night; and in the meantime I sat upon the beach, employed in cleaning and arranging my chemical apparatus. [. . .]

Between two and three in the morning the moon rose; and I then, putting my basket aboard a little skiff, sailed out about four miles from the shore. The scene was perfectly solitary; a few boats were returning towards land, but I sailed away from them. I felt as if I was about the commission of a dreadful crime and avoided with shuddering anxiety any encounter with my fellow creatures. At one time the moon, which had before been clear, was suddenly overspread by a thick cloud, and I took advantage of the moment of darkness and cast my basket into the sea; I listened to the gurgling sound as it sank and then sailed away from the spot. The sky became clouded, but the air was pure, although chilled by the northeast breeze that was then rising.

But it refreshed me and filled me with such agreeable sensations that I resolved to prolong my stay on the water, and fixing the rudder in a direct position, stretched myself at the bottom of the boat. Clouds hid the moon, everything was obscure, and I heard only the sound of the boat as its keel cut through the waves; the murmur lulled me, and in a short time I slept soundly. [. . .] Some hours passed thus; but by degrees, as the sun declined towards the horizon, the wind died away into a gentle breeze and the sea became free from breakers. But these gave place to a heavy swell; I felt sick and hardly able to hold the rudder, when suddenly I saw a line of high land towards the south. Almost spent, as I was, by fatigue and the dreadful suspense I endured for several hours, this sudden certainty of life rushed like a flood of warm joy to my heart, and tears gushed from my eyes. [. . .]

As I was occupied in fixing the boat and arranging the sails, several people crowded towards the spot. They seemed much surprised at my appearance, but instead of offering me any assistance, whispered together with gestures that at any other time might have produced in me a slight sensation of alarm. As it was, I merely remarked that they spoke English, and I therefore addressed them in that language. "My good friends," said I, "will you be so kind as to tell me the name of this town and inform me where I am?" "You will know that soon enough," replied a man with a hoarse voice. "Maybe you are come to a place that will not prove much to your taste, but you will not be consulted as to your quarters, I promise you." I was exceedingly surprised on receiving so rude an answer from a stranger, and I was also disconcerted on perceiving the frowning and angry countenances of his companions. "Why do you answer me so roughly?" I replied. "Surely it is not the custom of Englishmen to receive strangers so inhospitably."

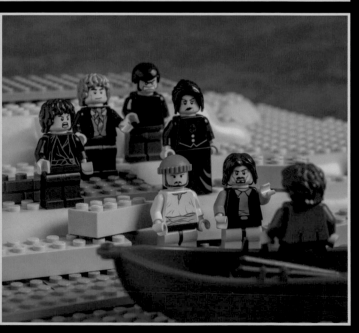

"I do not know," said the man, "what the custom of the English may be, but it is the custom of the Irish to hate villains." While this strange dialogue continued, I perceived the crowd rapidly increase. Their faces expressed a mixture of curiosity and anger, which annoyed and in some degree alarmed me. I inquired the way to the inn, but no one replied. I then moved forward, and a murmuring sound arose from the crowd as they followed and surrounded me, when an ill-looking man approaching tapped me on the shoulder and said, "Come, sir, you must follow me to Mr. Kirwin's to give an account of yourself." "Who is Mr. Kirwin? Why am I to give an account of myself? Is not this a free country?" "Ay, sir, free enough for honest folks. Mr. Kirwin is a magistrate, and you are to give an account of the death of a gentleman who was found murdered here last night." [. . .]

Chapter 21 – More Death and Destruction

I was soon introduced into the presence of the magistrate, an old benevolent man with calm and mild manners. He looked upon me, however, with some degree of severity, and then, turning towards my conductors, he asked who appeared as witnesses on this occasion. About half a dozen men came forward; and, one being selected by the magistrate, he deposed that he had been out fishing the night before with his son and brother-in-law, Daniel Nugent, when, about ten o'clock, they observed a strong northerly blast rising, and they accordingly put in for port. It was a very dark night, as the moon had not yet risen; they did not land at the harbour, but, as they had been accustomed, at a creek about two miles below. He walked on first, carrying a part of the fishing tackle, and his companions followed him at some distance. As he was proceeding along the sands, he struck his foot against something and fell at his length on the ground. His companions came up to assist him, and by the light of their lantern they found that he had fallen on the body of a man, who was to all appearance dead. Their first supposition was that it was the corpse of some person who had been drowned and was thrown on shore by the waves, but on examination they found that the clothes were not wet and even that the body was not then cold. They instantly carried it to the cottage of an old woman near the spot and endeavoured, but in vain, to restore it to life. It appeared to be a handsome young man, about five and twenty years of age. He had apparently been strangled, for there was no sign of any violence except the black mark of fingers on his neck.

The first part of this deposition did not in the least interest me, but when the mark of the fingers was mentioned I remembered the murder of my brother and felt myself extremely agitated; my limbs trembled, and a mist came over my eyes, which obliged me to lean on a chair for support. The magistrate observed me with a keen eye and of course drew an unfavourable augury from my manner. [. . .]

The son confirmed his father's account, but when Daniel Nugent was called he swore positively that just before the fall of his companion, he saw a boat, with a single man in it, at a short distance from the shore; and as far as he could judge by the light of a few stars, it was the same boat in which I had just landed. A woman deposed that she lived near the beach and was standing at the door of her cottage, waiting for the return of the fishermen, about an hour before she heard of the discovery of the body, when she saw a boat with only one man in it push off from that part of the shore where the corpse was afterwards found. [. . .]

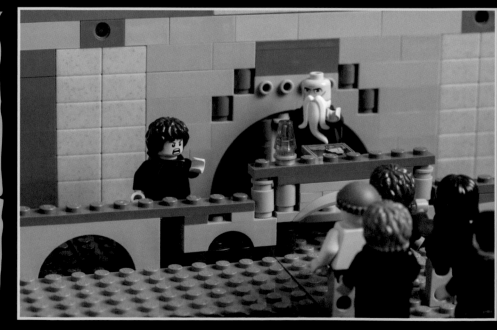

Mr. Kirwin, on hearing this evidence, desired that I should be taken into the room where the body lay for interment, that it might be observed what effect the sight of it would produce upon me. This idea was probably suggested by the extreme agitation I had exhibited when the mode of the murder had been described. I was accordingly conducted, by the magistrate and several other persons, to the inn. I could not help being struck by the strange coincidences that had taken place during this eventful night; but, knowing that I had been conversing with several persons in the island I had inhabited about the time that the body had been found, I was perfectly tranquil as to the consequences of the affair. I entered the room where the corpse lay and was led up to the coffin. How can I describe my sensations on beholding it? I feel yet parched with horror, nor can I reflect on that terrible moment without shuddering and agony. The examination, the presence of the magistrate and witnesses, passed like a dream from my memory when I saw the lifeless form of Henry Clerval stretched before me. I gasped for breath, and throwing myself on the body, I exclaimed, "Have my murderous machinations deprived you also, my dearest Henry, of life? Two I have already destroyed; other victims await their destiny; but you, Clerval, my friend, my benefactor—"

The human frame could no longer support the agonies that I endured, and I was carried out of the room in strong convulsions. A fever succeeded to this. I lay for two months on the point of death; my ravings, as I afterwards heard, were frightful; I called myself the murderer of William, of Justine, and of Clerval. Sometimes I entreated my attendants to assist me in the destruction of the fiend by whom I was tormented; and at others I felt the fingers of the monster already grasping my neck, and screamed aloud with agony and terror. [. . .]

It is true, he seldom came to see me, for although he ardently desired to relieve the sufferings of every human creature, he did not wish to be present at the agonies and miserable ravings of a murderer. [. . .]

These were my first reflections, but I soon learned that Mr. Kirwin had shown me extreme kindness. He had caused the best room in the prison to be prepared for me (wretched indeed was the best); and it was he who had provided a physician and a nurse.

Nothing, at this moment, could have given me greater pleasure than the arrival of my father. I stretched out my hand to him and cried, "Are you, then, safe—and Elizabeth—and Ernest?" My father calmed me with assurances of their welfare and endeavoured, by dwelling on these subjects so interesting to my heart, to raise my desponding spirits; but he soon felt that a prison cannot be the abode of cheerfulness. "What a place is this that you inhabit, my son!" said he, looking mournfully at the barred windows and wretched appearance of the room. "You travelled to seek happiness, but a fatality seems to pursue you. And poor Clerval—" The name of my unfortunate and murdered friend was an agitation too great to be endured in my weak state; I shed tears. "Alas! Yes, my father," replied I; "some destiny of the most horrible kind hangs over me, and I must live to fulfil it, or surely I should have died on the coffin of Henry." We were not allowed to converse for any length of time, for the precarious state of my health rendered every precaution necessary that could ensure tranquillity. Mr. Kirwin came in and insisted that my strength should not be exhausted by too much exertion. But the appearance of my father was to me like that of my good angel, and I gradually recovered my health. [. . .]

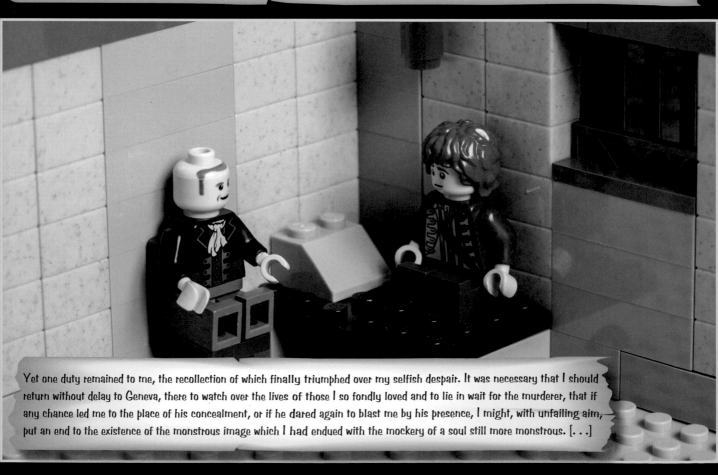

Yet one duty remained to me, the recollection of which finally triumphed over my selfish despair. It was necessary that I should return without delay to Geneva, there to watch over the lives of those I so fondly loved and to lie in wait for the murderer, that if any chance led me to the place of his concealment, or if he dared again to blast me by his presence, I might, with unfailing aim, put an end to the existence of the monstrous image which I had endued with the mockery of a soul still more monstrous. [. . .]

Chapter 22 — The Doomed Wedding

I avoided explanation and maintained a continual silence concerning the wretch I had created. I had a persuasion that I should be supposed mad, and this in itself would forever have chained my tongue. But, besides, I could not bring myself to disclose a secret which would fill my hearer with consternation and make fear and unnatural horror the inmates of his breast. I checked, therefore, my impatient thirst for sympathy and was silent when I would have given the world to have confided the fatal secret. Yet, still, words like those I have recorded would burst uncontrollably from me. I could offer no explanation of them, but their truth in part relieved the burden of my mysterious woe. Upon this occasion my father said, with an expression of unbounded wonder, "My dearest Victor, what infatuation is this? My dear son, I entreat you never to make such an assertion again."

"I am not mad," I cried energetically; "the sun and the heavens, who have viewed my operations, can bear witness of my truth. I am the assassin of those most innocent victims; they died by my machinations. A thousand times would I have shed my own blood, drop by drop, to have saved their lives; but I could not, my father, indeed I could not sacrifice the whole human race."

The conclusion of this speech convinced my father that my ideas were deranged, and he instantly changed the subject of our conversation and endeavoured to alter the course of my thoughts.

He wished as much as possible to obliterate the memory of the scenes that had taken place in Ireland and never alluded to them or suffered me to speak of my misfortunes. [. . .]

In about a week after the arrival of Elizabeth's letter we returned to Geneva. The sweet girl welcomed me with warm affection, yet tears were in her eyes as she beheld my emaciated frame and feverish cheeks. [. . .]

Soon after my arrival my father spoke of my immediate marriage with Elizabeth. I remained silent. "Have you, then, some other attachment?" "None on earth. I love Elizabeth and look forward to our union with delight. Let the day therefore be fixed; and on it I will consecrate myself, in life or death, to the happiness of my cousin." [. . .] But to me the remembrance of the threat returned; nor can you wonder that, omnipotent as the fiend had yet been in his deeds of blood, I should almost regard him as invincible, and that when he had pronounced the words "I SHALL BE WITH YOU ON YOUR WEDDING-NIGHT," I should regard the threatened fate as unavoidable. But death was no evil to me if the loss of Elizabeth were balanced with it, and I therefore, with a contented and even cheerful countenance, agreed with my father that if my cousin would consent, the ceremony should take place in ten days, and thus put, as I imagined, the seal to my fate. Great God! If for one instant I had thought what might be the hellish intention of my fiendish adversary, I would rather have banished myself forever from my native country and wandered a friendless outcast over the earth than have consented to this miserable marriage. But, as if possessed of magic powers, the monster had blinded me to his real intentions; and when I thought that I had prepared only my own death, I hastened that of a far dearer victim. [. . .]

Elizabeth seemed happy; my tranquil demeanour contributed greatly to calm her mind. But on the day that was to fulfil my wishes and my destiny, she was melancholy, and a presentiment of evil pervaded her; and perhaps also she thought of the dreadful secret which I had promised to reveal to her on the following day.

My father was in the meantime overjoyed and in the bustle of preparation only recognized in the melancholy of his niece the diffidence of a bride. [. . .]

Those were the last moments of my life during which I enjoyed the feeling of happiness. [. . .]

Chapter 23 – Death

It was eight o'clock when we landed; we walked for a short time on the shore, enjoying the transitory light, and then retired to the inn and contemplated the lovely scene of waters, woods, and mountains, obscured in darkness, yet still displaying their black outlines. [. . .]

I had been calm during the day, but so soon as night obscured the shapes of objects, a thousand fears arose in my mind. I was anxious and watchful, while my right hand grasped a pistol which was hidden in my bosom; every sound terrified me, but I resolved that I would sell my life dearly and not shrink from the conflict until my own life or that of my adversary was extinguished.

Elizabeth observed my agitation for some time in timid and fearful silence, but there was something in my glance which communicated terror to her, and trembling, she asked, "What is it that agitates you, my dear Victor? What is it you fear?"

"Oh! Peace, peace, my love," replied I; "this night, and all will be safe; but this night is dreadful, very dreadful." I passed an hour in this state of mind, when suddenly I reflected how fearful the combat which I momentarily expected would be to my wife, and I earnestly entreated her to retire, resolving not to join her until I had obtained some knowledge as to the situation of my enemy.

She left me,

and I continued some time walking up and down the passages of the house and inspecting every corner that might afford a retreat to my adversary.

But I discovered no trace of him and was beginning to conjecture that some fortunate chance had intervened to prevent the execution of his menaces when suddenly I heard a shrill and dreadful scream. It came from the room into which Elizabeth had retired. As I heard it, the whole truth rushed into my mind, my arms dropped, the motion of every muscle and fibre was suspended; I could feel the blood trickling in my veins and tingling in the extremities of my limbs. This state lasted but for an instant; the scream was repeated, and I rushed into the room.

Great God! Why did I not then expire! Why am I here to relate the destruction of the best hope and the purest creature on earth? She was there, lifeless and inanimate, thrown across the bed, her head hanging down and her pale and distorted features half covered by her hair.

Everywhere I turn I see the same figure—her bloodless arms and relaxed form flung by the murderer on its bridal bier. Could I behold this and live? Alas! Life is obstinate and clings closest where it is most hated. For a moment only did I lose recollection; I fell senseless on the ground.

When I recovered I found myself surrounded by the people of the inn; their countenances expressed a breathless terror, but the horror of others appeared only as a mockery, a shadow of the feelings that oppressed me. I escaped from them to the room where lay the body of Elizabeth, my love, my wife, so lately living, so dear, so worthy. She had been moved from the posture in which I had first beheld her, and now, as she lay, her head upon her arm and a handkerchief thrown across her face and neck, I might have supposed her asleep. I rushed towards her and embraced her with ardour, but the deadly languor and coldness of the limbs told me that what I now held in my arms had ceased to be the Elizabeth whom I had loved and cherished. The murderous mark of the fiend's grasp was on her neck, and the breath had ceased to issue from her lips.

While I still hung over her in the agony of despair, I happened to look up. The windows of the room had before been darkened, and I felt a kind of panic on seeing the pale yellow light of the moon illuminate the chamber. The shutters had been thrown back, and with a sensation of horror not to be described, I saw at the open window a figure the most hideous and abhorred. A grin was on the face of the monster; he seemed to jeer, as with his fiendish finger he pointed towards the corpse of my wife.

I rushed towards the window, and drawing a pistol from my bosom, fired; but he eluded me, leaped from his station, and running with the swiftness of lightning, plunged into the lake. [. . .]

I was bewildered, in a cloud of wonder and horror. The death of William, the execution of Justine, the murder of Clerval, and lastly of my wife; even at that moment I knew not that my only remaining friends were safe from the malignity of the fiend; my father even now might be writhing under his grasp, and Ernest might be dead at his feet. This idea made me shudder and recalled me to action. I started up and resolved to return to Geneva with all possible speed. There were no horses to be procured, and I must return by the lake; but the wind was unfavourable, and the rain fell in torrents. [. . .]

I arrived at Geneva. My father and Ernest yet lived, but the former sunk under the tidings that I bore. I see him now, excellent and venerable old man! His eyes wandered in vacancy, for they had lost their charm and their delight—his Elizabeth, his more than daughter, whom he doted on with all that affection which a man feels, who in the decline of life, having few affections, clings more earnestly to those that remain.

Cursed, cursed be the fiend that brought misery on his grey hairs and doomed him to waste in wretchedness! He could not live under the horrors that were accumulated around him; the springs of existence suddenly gave way; he was unable to rise from his bed, and in a few days he died in my arms. [. . .]

Liberty, however, had been a useless gift to me, had I not, as I awakened to reason, at the same time awakened to revenge. As the memory of past misfortunes pressed upon me, I began to reflect on their cause—the monster whom I had created, the miserable daemon whom I had sent abroad into the world for my destruction. I was possessed by a maddening rage when I thought of him, and desired and ardently prayed that I might have him within my grasp to wreak a great and signal revenge on his cursed head.

Nor did my hate long confine itself to useless wishes; I began to reflect on the best means of securing him; and for this purpose, about a month after my release, I repaired to a criminal judge in the town and told him that I had an accusation to make, that I knew the destroyer of my family, and that I required him to exert his whole authority for the apprehension of the murderer. The magistrate listened to me with attention and kindness. "Be assured, sir," said he, "no pains or exertions on my part shall be spared to discover the villain." "I thank you," replied I; "listen, therefore, to the deposition that I have to make. It is indeed a tale so strange that I should fear you would not credit it were there not something in truth which, however wonderful, forces conviction. The story is too connected to be mistaken for a dream, and I have no motive for falsehood." [. . .]

"I would willingly afford you every aid in your pursuit, but the creature of whom you speak appears to have powers which would put all my exertions to defiance. Who can follow an animal which can traverse the sea of ice and inhabit caves and dens where no man would venture to intrude? Besides, some months have elapsed since the commission of his crimes, and no one can conjecture to what place he has wandered or what region he may now inhabit."

"I do not doubt that he hovers near the spot which I inhabit, and if he has indeed taken refuge in the Alps, he may be hunted like the chamois and destroyed as a beast of prey. But I perceive your thoughts; you do not credit my narrative and do not intend to pursue my enemy with the punishment which is his desert." As I spoke, rage sparkled in my eyes; the magistrate was intimidated. "You are mistaken," said he. "I will exert myself, and if it is in my power to seize the monster, be assured that he shall suffer punishment proportionate to his crimes. But I fear, from what you have yourself described to be his properties, that this will prove impracticable; and thus, while every proper measure is pursued, you should make up your mind to disappointment."

"That cannot be; but all that I can say will be of little avail. My revenge is of no moment to you; yet, while I allow it to be a vice, I confess that it is the devouring and only passion of my soul.

"My rage is unspeakable when I reflect that the murderer, whom I have turned loose upon society, still exists. You refuse my just demand; I have but one resource, and I devote myself, either in my life or death, to his destruction." [. . .]

Chapter 24 – Pursuit in Ice and Snow

My first resolution was to quit Geneva forever; my country, which, when I was happy and beloved, was dear to me, now, in my adversity, became hateful. I provided myself with a sum of money, together with a few jewels which had belonged to my mother, and departed. And now my wanderings began which are to cease but with life. I have traversed a vast portion of the earth and have endured all the hardships which travellers in deserts and barbarous countries are wont to meet. How I have lived I hardly know; many times have I stretched my failing limbs upon the sandy plain and prayed for death. But revenge kept me alive; I dared not die and leave my adversary in being.

When I quitted Geneva my first labour was to gain some clue by which I might trace the steps of my fiendish enemy. But my plan was unsettled, and I wandered many hours round the confines of the town, uncertain what path I should pursue. As night approached I found myself at the entrance of the cemetery where William, Elizabeth, and my father reposed. I entered it and approached the tomb which marked their graves. Everything was silent except the leaves of the trees, which were gently agitated by the wind; the night was nearly dark, and the scene would have been solemn and affecting even to an uninterested observer. The spirits of the departed seemed to flit around and to cast a shadow, which was felt but not seen, around the head of the mourner.

The deep grief which this scene had at first excited quickly gave way to rage and despair. They were dead, and I lived; their murderer also lived, and to destroy him I must drag out my weary existence. I knelt on the grass and kissed the earth and with quivering lips exclaimed, "By the sacred earth on which I kneel, by the shades that wander near me, by the deep and eternal grief that I feel, I swear; and by thee, O Night, and the spirits that preside over thee, to pursue the daemon who caused this misery, until he or I shall perish in mortal conflict. For this purpose I will preserve my life; to execute this dear revenge will I again behold the sun and tread the green herbage of earth, which otherwise should vanish from my eyes forever. And I call on you, spirits of the dead, and on you, wandering ministers of vengeance, to aid and conduct me in my work. Let the cursed and hellish monster drink deep of agony; let him feel the despair that now torments me." I had begun my adjuration with solemnity and an awe which almost assured me that the shades of my murdered friends heard and approved my devotion, but the furies possessed me as I concluded, and rage choked my utterance.

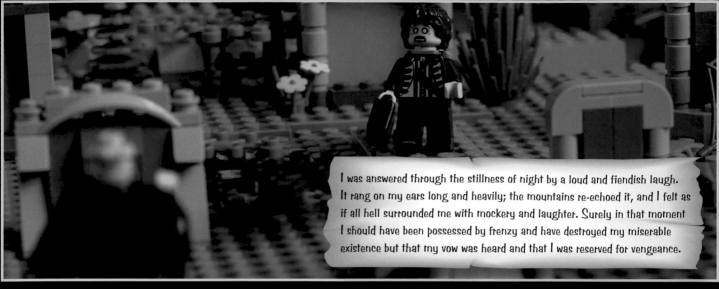

I was answered through the stillness of night by a loud and fiendish laugh. It rang on my ears long and heavily; the mountains re-echoed it, and I felt as if all hell surrounded me with mockery and laughter. Surely in that moment I should have been possessed by frenzy and have destroyed my miserable existence but that my vow was heard and that I was reserved for vengeance.

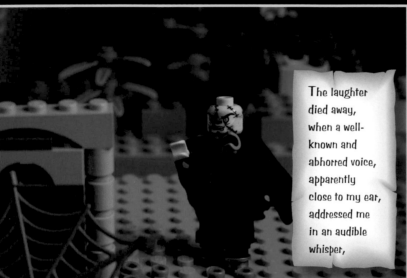

The laughter died away, when a well-known and abhorred voice, apparently close to my ear, addressed me in an audible whisper,

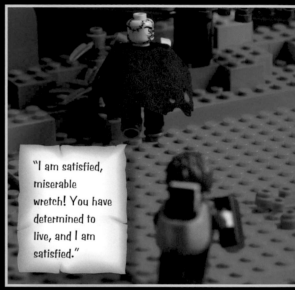

"I am satisfied, miserable wretch! You have determined to live, and I am satisfied."

I darted towards the spot from which the sound proceeded, but the devil eluded my grasp. Suddenly the broad disk of the moon arose and shone full upon his ghastly and distorted shape as he fled with more than mortal speed.

I pursued him, and for many months this has been my task. Guided by a slight clue, I followed the windings of the Rhone, but vainly. The blue Mediterranean appeared, and by a strange chance, I saw the fiend enter . . . and hide himself in a vessel bound for the Black Sea. I took my passage in the same ship, but he escaped, I know not how.

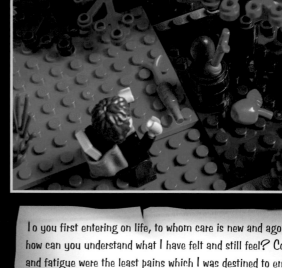

Amidst the wilds of Tartary and Russia, although he still evaded me, I have ever followed in his track. Sometimes the peasants, scared by this horrid apparition, informed me of his path; sometimes he himself, who feared that if I lost all trace of him I should despair and die, left some mark to guide me. The snows descended on my head, and I saw the print of his huge step on the white plain.

To you first entering on life, to whom care is new and agony unknown, how can you understand what I have felt and still feel? Cold, want, and fatigue were the least pains which I was destined to endure; I was cursed by some devil and carried about with me my eternal hell; yet still a spirit of good followed and directed my steps and when I most murmured would suddenly extricate me from seemingly insurmountable difficulties. Sometimes, when nature, overcome by hunger, sank under the exhaustion, a repast was prepared for me in the desert that restored and inspirited me. The fare was, indeed, coarse, such as the peasants of the country ate, but I will not doubt that it was set there by the spirits that I had invoked to aid me. Often, when all was dry, the heavens cloudless, and I was parched by thirst, a slight cloud would bedim the sky, shed the few drops that revived me, and vanish. [. . .]

My life, as it passed thus, was indeed hateful to me, and it was during sleep alone that I could taste joy. O blessed sleep! Often, when most miserable, I sank to repose, and my dreams lulled me even to rapture. The spirits that guarded me had provided these moments, or rather hours, of happiness that I might retain strength to fulfil my pilgrimage. [. . .]

What his feelings were whom I pursued I cannot know. Sometimes, indeed, he left marks in writing on the barks of the trees or cut in stone that guided me and instigated my fury. "My reign is not yet over"—these words were legible in one of these inscriptions—"you live, and my power is complete. Follow me; I seek the everlasting ices of the north, where you will feel the misery of cold and frost, to which I am impassive. You will find near this place, if you follow not too tardily, a dead hare; eat and be refreshed. Come on, my enemy; we have yet to wrestle for our lives, but many hard and miserable hours must you endure until that period shall arrive." [. . .]

As I still pursued my journey to the northward, the snows thickened and the cold increased in a degree almost too severe to support. The peasants were shut up in their hovels, and only a few of the most hardy ventured forth to seize the animals whom starvation had forced from their hiding-places to seek for prey. The rivers were covered with ice, and no fish could be procured; and thus I was cut off from my chief article of maintenance. The triumph of my enemy increased with the difficulty of my labours. One inscription that he left was in these words: "Prepare! Your toils only begin; wrap yourself in furs and provide food, for we shall soon enter upon a journey where your sufferings will satisfy my everlasting hatred." [. . .]

Some weeks before this period I had procured a sledge and dogs and thus traversed the snows with inconceivable speed. I know not whether the fiend possessed the same advantages, but I found that, as before I had daily lost ground in the pursuit, I now gained on him, so much so that when I first saw the ocean he was but one day's journey in advance, and I hoped to intercept him before he should reach the beach. With new courage, therefore, I pressed on, and in two days arrived at a wretched hamlet on the seashore.

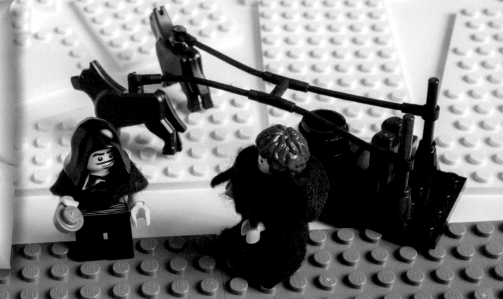

I inquired of the inhabitants concerning the fiend and gained accurate information. A gigantic monster, they said, had arrived the night before, armed with a gun and many pistols, putting to flight the inhabitants of a solitary cottage through fear of his terrific appearance. He had carried off their store of winter food, and placing it in a sledge, to draw which he had seized on a numerous drove of trained dogs, he had harnessed them, and the same night, to the joy of the horror-struck villagers, had pursued his journey across the sea in a direction that led to no land; and they conjectured that he must speedily be destroyed by the breaking of the ice or frozen by the eternal frosts. [. . .]

By the quantity of provision which I had consumed, I should guess that I had passed three weeks in this journey; and the continual protraction of hope, returning back upon the heart, often wrung bitter drops of despondency and grief from my eyes. Despair had indeed almost secured her prey, and I should soon have sunk beneath this misery. Once, after the poor animals that conveyed me had with incredible toil gained the summit of a sloping ice mountain, and one, sinking under his fatigue, died, I viewed the expanse before me with anguish, when suddenly my eye caught a dark speck upon the dusky plain.

I strained my sight to discover what it could be and uttered a wild cry of ecstasy when I distinguished a sledge and the distorted proportions of a well-known form within. Oh! With what a burning gush did hope revisit my heart! Warm tears filled my eyes, which I hastily wiped away, that they might not intercept the view I had of the daemon; but still my sight was dimmed by the burning drops, until, giving way to the emotions that oppressed me, I wept aloud. [. . .]

But now, when I appeared almost within grasp of my foe, my hopes were suddenly extinguished, and I lost all trace of him more utterly than I had ever done before. A ground sea was heard; the thunder of its progress, as the waters rolled and swelled beneath me, became every moment more ominous and terrific. I pressed on, but in vain. The wind arose; the sea roared; and, as with the mighty shock of an earthquake, it split and cracked with a tremendous and overwhelming sound. The work was soon finished; in a few minutes a tumultuous sea rolled between me and my enemy, and I was left drifting on a scattered piece of ice that was continually lessening and thus preparing for me a hideous death.

In this manner many appalling hours passed; several of my dogs died, and I myself was about to sink under the accumulation of distress when I saw your vessel riding at anchor and holding forth to me hopes of succour and life. I had no conception that vessels ever came so far north and was astounded at the sight. I quickly destroyed part of my sledge to construct oars, and by these means was enabled, with infinite fatigue, to move my ice raft in the direction of your ship. I had determined, if you were going southwards, still to trust myself to the mercy of the seas rather than abandon my purpose. I hoped to induce you to grant me a boat with which I could pursue my enemy. But your direction was northwards. You took me on board when my vigour was exhausted, and I should soon have sunk under my multiplied hardships into a death which I still dread, for my task is unfulfilled.

Oh! When will my guiding spirit, in conducting me to the daemon, allow me the rest I so much desire; or must I die, and he yet live? If I do, swear to me, Walton, that he shall not escape, that you will seek him and satisfy my vengeance in his death. And do I dare to ask of you to undertake my pilgrimage, to endure the hardships that I have undergone? No; I am not so selfish. Yet, when I am dead, if he should appear, if the ministers of vengeance should conduct him to you, swear that he shall not live—swear that he shall not triumph over my accumulated woes and survive to add to the list of his dark crimes.

He is eloquent and persuasive, and once his words had even power over my heart; but trust him not. His soul is as hellish as his form, full of treachery and fiend-like malice. Hear him not; call on the names of William, Justine, Clerval, Elizabeth, my father, and of the wretched Victor, and thrust your sword into his heart. I will hover near and direct the steel aright.

You have read this strange and terrific story, Margaret; and do you not feel your blood congeal with horror, like that which even now curdles mine? Sometimes, seized with sudden agony, he could not continue his tale; at others, his voice broken, yet piercing, uttered with difficulty the words so replete with anguish. His fine and lovely eyes were now lighted up with indignation, now subdued to downcast sorrow and quenched in infinite wretchedness. Sometimes he commanded his countenance and tones and related the most horrible incidents with a tranquil voice, suppressing every mark of agitation; then, like a volcano bursting forth, his face would suddenly change to an expression of the wildest rage as he shrieked out imprecations on his persecutor. His tale is connected and told with an appearance of the simplest truth, yet I own to you that the letters of Felix and Safie, which he showed me, and the apparition of the monster seen from our ship, brought to me a greater conviction of the truth of his narrative than his asseverations, however earnest and connected. Such a monster has, then, really existence! I cannot doubt it, yet I am lost in surprise and admiration.

Sometimes I endeavoured to gain from Frankenstein the particulars of his creature's formation, but on this point he was impenetrable. "Are you mad, my friend?" said he. "Or whither does your senseless curiosity lead you? Would you also create for yourself and the world a demoniacal enemy? Peace, peace! Learn my miseries and do not seek to increase your own." Frankenstein discovered that I made notes concerning his history; he asked to see them and then himself corrected and augmented them in many places, but principally in giving the life and spirit to the conversations he held with his enemy. "Since you have preserved my narration," said he, "I would not that a mutilated one should go down to posterity." [. . .]

Must I then lose this admirable being? I have longed for a friend; I have sought one who would sympathize with and love me. Behold, on these desert seas I have found such a one, but I fear I have gained him only to know his value and lose him.

I would reconcile him to life, but he repulses the idea.

"I thank you, Walton," he said, "for your kind intentions towards so miserable a wretch; but when you speak of new ties and fresh affections, think you that any can replace those who are gone? Can any man be to me as Clerval was, or any woman another Elizabeth? [. . .] They are dead, and but one feeling in such a solitude can persuade me to preserve my life. If I were engaged in any high undertaking or design, fraught with extensive utility to my fellow creatures, then could I live to fulfil it. But such is not my destiny; I must pursue and destroy the being to whom I gave existence; then my lot on earth will be fulfilled and I may die." [. . .]

September 7th

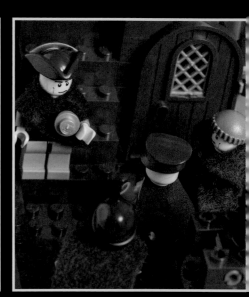

The die is cast; I have consented to return if we are not destroyed. Thus are my hopes blasted by cowardice and indecision; I come back ignorant and disappointed.

It requires more philosophy than I possess to bear this injustice with patience.

September 7th

. . . September 9th, the ice began to move, and roarings like thunder were heard at a distance as the islands split and cracked in every direction. We were in the most imminent peril, but as we could only remain passive, my chief attention was occupied by my unfortunate guest whose illness increased in such a degree that he was entirely confined to his bed. The ice cracked behind us and was driven with force towards the north; a breeze sprang from the west, and on the 11th the passage towards the south became perfectly free. When the sailors saw this and that their return to their native country was apparently assured, a shout of tumultuous joy broke from them, loud and long-continued. Frankenstein, who was dozing, awoke and asked the cause of the tumult. "They shout," I said, "because they will soon return to England."

"Do you, then, really return?" "Alas! Yes; I cannot withstand their demands. I cannot lead them unwillingly to danger, and I must return." "Do so, if you will; but I will not. You may give up your purpose, but mine is assigned to me by heaven, and I dare not. I am weak, but surely the spirits who assist my vengeance will endow me with sufficient strength." Saying this, he endeavoured to spring from the bed, but the exertion was too great for him; he fell back and fainted.

It was long before he was restored, and I often thought that life was entirely extinct. At length he opened his eyes; he breathed with difficulty and was unable to speak. The surgeon gave him a composing draught and ordered us to leave him undisturbed. In the meantime he told me that my friend had certainly not many hours to live. His sentence was pronounced, and I could only grieve and be patient. I sat by his bed, watching him; his eyes were closed, and I thought he slept; but presently he called to me in a feeble voice, and bidding me come near, said, "Alas! The strength I relied on is gone; I feel that I shall soon die, and he, my enemy and persecutor, may still be in being. Think not, Walton, that in the last moments of my existence I feel that burning hatred and ardent desire of revenge I once expressed; but I feel myself justified in desiring the death of my adversary. During these last days I have been occupied in examining my past conduct; nor do I find it blamable. In a fit of enthusiastic madness I created a rational creature and was bound towards him to assure, as far as was in my power, his happiness and well-being.

"This was my duty, but there was another still paramount to that. My duties towards the beings of my own species had greater claims to my attention because they included a greater proportion of happiness or misery. Urged by this view, I refused, and I did right in refusing, to create a companion for the first creature. He showed unparalleled malignity and selfishness in evil; he destroyed my friends; he devoted to destruction beings who possessed exquisite sensations, happiness, and wisdom; nor do I know where this thirst for vengeance may end. Miserable himself that he may render no other wretched, he ought to die. The task of his destruction was mine, but I have failed. When actuated by selfish and vicious motives, I asked you to undertake my unfinished work, and I renew this request now, when I am only induced by reason and virtue.

His voice became fainter as he spoke, and at length, exhausted by his effort, he sank into silence. About half an hour afterwards he attempted again to speak but was unable; he pressed my hand feebly, and his eyes closed forever, while the irradiation of a gentle smile passed away from his lips. [. . .]

"Yet I cannot ask you to renounce your country and friends to fulfil this task; and now that you are returning to England, you will have little chance of meeting with him. But the consideration of these points, and the well balancing of what you may esteem your duties, I leave to you; my judgment and ideas are already disturbed by the near approach of death. I dare not ask you to do what I think right, for I may still be misled by passion. That he should live to be an instrument of mischief disturbs me; in other respects, this hour, when I momentarily expect my release, is the only happy one which I have enjoyed for several years. The forms of the beloved dead flit before me, and I hasten to their arms. Farewell, Walton! Seek happiness in tranquillity and avoid ambition, even if it be only the apparently innocent one of distinguishing yourself in science and discoveries. Yet why do I say this? I have myself been blasted in these hopes, yet another may succeed." [. . .]

Great God! what a scene has just taken place! I am yet dizzy with the remembrance of it. I hardly know whether I shall have the power to detail it; yet the tale which I have recorded would be incomplete without this final and wonderful catastrophe. I entered the cabin where lay the remains of my ill-fated and admirable friend. Over him hung a form which I cannot find words to describe—gigantic in stature, yet uncouth and distorted in its proportions. As he hung over the coffin, his face was concealed by long locks of ragged hair; but one vast hand was extended, in colour and apparent texture like that of a mummy. When he heard the sound of my approach, he ceased to utter exclamations of grief and horror and sprung towards the window. Never did I behold a vision so horrible as his face, of such loathsome yet appalling hideousness. I shut my eyes involuntarily and endeavoured to recollect what were my duties with regard to this destroyer. I called on him to stay.

He paused, looking on me with wonder, and again turning towards the lifeless form of his creator, he seemed to forget my presence, and every feature and gesture seemed instigated by the wildest rage of some uncontrollable passion. "That is also my victim!" he exclaimed. "In his murder my crimes are consummated; the miserable series of my being is wound to its close! Oh, Frankenstein! Generous and self-devoted being! What does it avail that I now ask thee to pardon me? I, who irretrievably destroyed thee by destroying all thou lovedst. Alas! He is cold, he cannot answer me." His voice seemed suffocated, and my first impulses, which had suggested to me the duty of obeying the dying request of my friend in destroying his enemy, were now suspended by a mixture of curiosity and compassion. I approached this tremendous being; I dared not again raise my eyes to his face, there was something so scaring and unearthly in his ugliness. I attempted to speak, but the words died away on my lips. The monster continued to utter wild and incoherent self-reproaches. At length I gathered resolution to address him in a pause of the tempest of his passion. "Your repentance," I said, "is now superfluous. If you had listened to the voice of conscience and heeded the stings of remorse before you had urged your diabolical vengeance to this extremity, Frankenstein would yet have lived."

"And do you dream?" said the daemon. "Do you think that I was then dead to agony and remorse? He," he continued, pointing to the corpse, "he suffered not in the consummation of the deed. Oh! Not the ten-thousandth portion of the anguish that was mine during the lingering detail of its execution. A frightful selfishness hurried me on, while my heart was poisoned with remorse. Think you that the groans of Clerval were music to my ears? My heart was fashioned to be susceptible of love and sympathy, and when wrenched by misery to vice and hatred, it did not endure the violence of the change without torture such as you cannot even imagine.

"After the murder of Clerval I returned to Switzerland, heart-broken and overcome. I pitied Frankenstein; my pity amounted to horror; I abhorred myself. But when I discovered that he, the author at once of my existence and of its unspeakable torments, dared to hope for happiness, that while he accumulated wretchedness and despair upon me he sought his own enjoyment in feelings and passions from the indulgence of which I was forever barred, then impotent envy and bitter indignation filled me with an insatiable thirst for vengeance.

"I recollected my threat and resolved that it should be accomplished. I knew that I was preparing for myself a deadly torture, but I was the slave, not the master, of an impulse which I detested yet could not disobey. Yet when she died! Nay, then I was not miserable. I had cast off all feeling, subdued all anguish, to riot in the excess of my despair. Evil thenceforth became my good. Urged thus far, I had no choice but to adapt my nature to an element which I had willingly chosen. The completion of my demoniacal design became an insatiable passion. And now it is ended; there is my last victim!"

I was at first touched by the expressions of his misery; yet, when I called to mind what Frankenstein had said of his powers of eloquence and persuasion, and when I again cast my eyes on the lifeless form of my friend, indignation was rekindled within me. "Wretch!" I said. "It is well that you come here to whine over the desolation that you have made. You throw a torch into a pile of buildings, and when they are consumed, you sit among the ruins and lament the fall. Hypocritical fiend! If he whom you mourn still lived, still would he be the object, again would he become the prey, of your accursed vengeance. It is not pity that you feel; you lament only because the victim of your malignity is withdrawn from your power."

"Oh, it is not thus—not thus," interrupted the being. "Yet such must be the impression conveyed to you by what appears to be the purport of my actions. Yet I seek not a fellow feeling in my misery. No sympathy may I ever find. When I first sought it, it was the love of virtue, the feelings of happiness and affection with which my whole being overflowed, that I wished to be participated. But now that virtue has become to me a shadow, and that happiness and affection are turned into bitter and loathing despair, in what should I seek for sympathy? I am content to suffer alone while my sufferings shall endure; when I die, I am well satisfied that abhorrence and opprobrium should load my memory. Once my fancy was soothed with dreams of virtue, of fame, and of enjoyment. Once I falsely hoped to meet with beings who, pardoning my outward form, would love me for the excellent qualities which I was capable of unfolding. I was nourished with high thoughts of honour and devotion. But now crime has degraded me beneath the meanest animal. No guilt, no mischief, no malignity, no misery, can be found comparable to mine. When I run over the frightful catalogue of my sins, I cannot believe that I am the same creature whose thoughts were once filled with sublime and transcendent visions of the beauty and the majesty of goodness. But it is even so; the fallen angel becomes a malignant devil. Yet even that enemy of God and man had friends and associates in his desolation; I am alone.

"You, who call Frankenstein your friend, seem to have a knowledge of my crimes and his misfortunes. But in the detail which he gave you of them he could not sum up the hours and months of misery which I endured wasting in impotent passions. For while I destroyed his hopes, I did not satisfy my own desires. They were forever ardent and craving; still I desired love and fellowship, and I was still spurned. Was there no injustice in this? Am I to be thought the only criminal, when all humankind sinned against me? Why do you not hate Felix, who drove his friend from his door with contumely? Why do you not execrate the rustic who sought to destroy the saviour of his child? Nay, these are virtuous and immaculate beings! I, the miserable and the abandoned, am an abortion, to be spurned at, and kicked, and trampled on. Even now my blood boils at the recollection of this injustice.

"But it is true that I am a wretch. I have murdered the lovely and the helpless; I have strangled the innocent as they slept and grasped to death his throat who never injured me or any other living thing. I have devoted my creator, the select specimen of all that is worthy of love and admiration among men, to misery; I have pursued him even to that irremediable ruin. There he lies, white and cold in death. You hate me, but your abhorrence cannot equal that with which I regard myself. I look on the hands which executed the deed; I think on the heart in which the imagination of it was conceived and long for the moment when these hands will meet my eyes, when that imagination will haunt my thoughts no more.

"Fear not that I shall be the instrument of future mischief. My work is nearly complete. Neither yours nor any man's death is needed to consummate the series of my being and accomplish that which must be done, but it requires my own. Do not think that I shall be slow to perform this sacrifice. I shall quit your vessel on the ice raft which brought me thither and shall seek the most northern extremity of the globe; I shall collect my funeral pile and consume to ashes this miserable frame, that its remains may afford no light to any curious and unhallowed wretch who would create such another as I have been. I shall die. I shall no longer feel the agonies which now consume me or be the prey of feelings unsatisfied, yet unquenched. He is dead who called me into being; and when I shall be no more, the very remembrance of us both will speedily vanish. I shall no longer see the sun or stars or feel the winds play on my cheeks.

"Light, feeling, and sense will pass away; and in this condition must I find my happiness. Some years ago, when the images which this world affords first opened upon me, when I felt the cheering warmth of summer and heard the rustling of the leaves and the warbling of the birds, and these were all to me, I should have wept to die; now it is my only consolation. Polluted by crimes and torn by the bitterest remorse, where can I find rest but in death? Farewell! I leave you, and in you the last of humankind whom these eyes will ever behold. Farewell, Frankenstein! If thou wert yet alive and yet cherished a desire of revenge against me, it would be better satiated in my life than in my destruction. But it was not so; thou didst seek my extinction, that I might not cause greater wretchedness; and if yet, in some mode unknown to me, thou hadst not ceased to think and feel, thou wouldst not desire against me a vengeance greater than that which I feel. Blasted as thou wert, my agony was still superior to thine, for the bitter sting of remorse will not cease to rankle in my wounds until death shall close them forever.

"But soon," he cried with sad and solemn enthusiasm, "I shall die, and what I now feel be no longer felt. Soon these burning miseries will be extinct. I shall ascend my funeral pile triumphantly and exult in the agony of the torturing flames. The light of that conflagration will fade away; my ashes will be swept into the sea by the winds. My spirit will sleep in peace, or if it thinks, it will not surely think thus. Farewell."

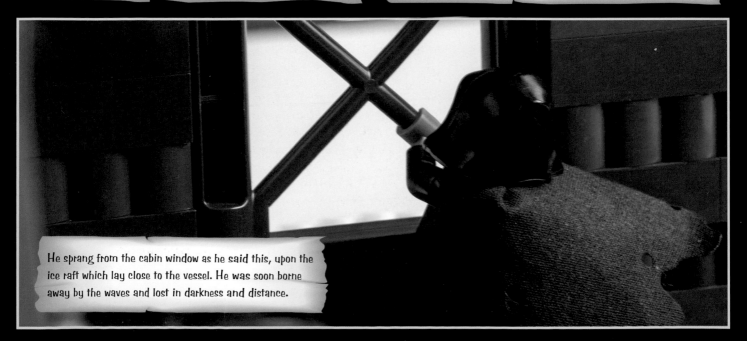

He sprang from the cabin window as he said this, upon the ice raft which lay close to the vessel. He was soon borne away by the waves and lost in darkness and distance.

About the Authors

Amanda Brack is a freelance illustrator who loves dogs of all shapes and sizes, old horror movies, and homemade smoothies. She spent most of her childhood with her brothers constructing expansive Lego towns and fighting over the best bricks. She graduated from the School of the Museum of Fine Arts and is currently living near Boston, Massachusetts.

Becky Thomas is a nerdy lady who enjoys reading, writing, and playing board games. She loves Jane Austen and superhero comic books. She is the coauthor, with John McCann and Monica Sweeney, of Brick Shakespeare: The Tragedies, Brick Shakespeare: The Comedies, and Brick Fairytales. She lives with her husband, Patrick, and their cats, Leo and Leia, in Burlington, Massachusetts.

Monica Sweeney works in publishing and is also pursuing her master's degree. She enjoys reading anything from Middle English to graphic novels, restaurant-hopping, old movie theaters, and Cape Cod beaches. She is writing partners with Becky Thomas and is the coauthor of Brick Shakespeare: The Tragedies, Brick Shakespeare: The Comedies, and Brick Fairytales. Monica lives in Boston, Massachusetts.